Let's Send Him to America

Peter Desberg

ISBN-13: 978-1-960583-98-7 print edition
ISBN-13: 978-1-960583-99-4 e-book edition

Waterside Productions
2055 Oxford Ave
Cardiff, CA 92007
www.waterside.com

Table of Contents

Chapter 1

It was no surprise to have my breathing ritual interrupted by a nighttime knock. "Healer" is another word for "sleep deprived." At this time of night, the intensity of a knock is usually soft because the knocker is struggling to balance his level of need with the guilt of such a late night imposition.

This was not that kind of knock. Three intense thuds. I opened the door to find a group of armed soldiers. "Boy, wake your father up and bring him here ... now."

"I live alone. Who are you looking for?"

"A healer named Lo Wan."

"That's me."

The soldiers shrugged. "You have to come with us. Quickly gather whatever tools, medicines and instruments you need. Can't keep the Chancellor waiting."

They're pulling me out as I'm buttoning my shirt. They haven't even closed the door to the carriage and those huge horses are already running. Racing through the city I can see the Chancellor's castle lit up in the distance. The main gate is opening without us having to slow down. Massive gardens, now it's turning into a forest. I can see lights from the castle in the distance. Who lives like this?

The soldiers are shoving me through corridors. Magnificent paintings and scrolls. I'm deposited into a small room. There are only two chairs. I guess I'm supposed to sit in this one. The other chair looks like a throne. I'd get a neck ache having a long conversation with this Chancellor ... his chair is raised so high.

Every inch of this room is carved jade. The jade ceiling is inlaid with gold. I reach out and touch the only object in the room, a finely carved ivory tusk. This must have taken years to create. Look at the fine details in the carving.

As I'm taking this in, the Chancellor bursts into the room and sits down. His Viceroy and an enormous guard flank him.

"Who's this kid?"

The Viceroy said, "This is Lo Wan … the healer you sent your soldiers to find."

How old are you?

"I'm nineteen my Lord.

The Chancellor turns to his Viceroy, "Why is he dressed like a peasant?" The Viceroy whispers something back to the Chancellor.

"My daughter's gravely ill. She's my greatest treasure. You must cure her. I'll pay anything."

"My Lord, I'd be honored to help, but surely you have access to the greatest physicians in China. With all due respect, shouldn't they be the ones you consult?"

"I've already had the greatest so-called physicians here and they've proven worthless. I sent people out to scour the city to find the most proficient healer and they came back with you. I don't know how or why, but I trust them so you're my final hope. When you save her, you may ask for any reward. She's my life. If you have to move heaven and earth, she must survive. You'll begin immediately."

I'm whisked to a large room with nurses applying cold compresses to a young girl's forehead and body. The nurses and physicians all stare at me. The Viceroy announces that I'm now in charge of the recovery. Everyone in the room has unanswered questions staring at a shabbily dressed boy who probably shouldn't even be allowed in the room.

I rush to the bed and feel her forehead. She's burning up. When I hold her wrist there are fading vital signs. I raised my voice a little calling out for a list of herbs. Without waiting for a response, I begin inserting a series of slim needles into key meridians to redirect her chi. As I look up I notice sticks of incense burning everywhere. I yell to extinguish them immediately. Nurses run to remove them. When the herbs arrive I yell out orders, "Boil these, pulverize the green ones and make these into a paste." I hurry to apply them all. As everyone sees my decisive actions, they follow my orders without question. I'm not nearly as sure of myself as they seem to be.

I minister to her for three days and go without sleep the entire time. The nurses and physicians rotate in shifts and are well rested. I know the Chancellor is one of the most powerful men in China, but all I see is a loving father terrified over the possibility of losing his precious daughter. I try every remedy I know. Perhaps if I had been called sooner... but in the end, I'm unable to save her. I'm holding her hand as she expires.

I feel dreadful about the young girl's passing and ask to see the Chancellor immediately to explain what happened and provide comfort during his hour of need. His Viceroy enters and insists I get a good night's sleep and see the Chancellor first thing the following morning so I'll be fresher to provide my essential soothing and support. He says I've gone too long without sleep. I agree and am given a cup of soothing herbal tea as they guide me to a room in the lavish guest quarters. I climb into a large feather down bed with silk sheets and embroidered quilts. A servant extinguishes the lights.

I feel like there's an immense weight on my chest and everything's spinning and tilting. I'm gagging and I'm going to throw up again. I've got to keep my head still. I don't feel better after throwing up. Opening my yes makes everything worse. I feel like I've got to hold onto the sides of the bed. It's like I'm spinning on multiple axes. Moving hurts. Everything seems to be moving at a third its speed. My head feels like it's stuffed with rancid tofu and my tongue's made of wet, dirty wool.

I can't seem to hold any continuous thoughts. Was I drugged? Moving hurts. I pull my pant leg up to see why. I got it up a couple of inches. I raise my head a little and see dried blood, scrapes and bruises. Drugged... beaten.

I'm very thirsty. I try to say "water," but no sound comes out.

Day 2 and the haze is lifting a little. I take a personal inventory. Brutal beating, no permanent damage. No broken bones. Where the hell am I? The only sound is moaning. I look around and see a honeycomb of beds. Triple rows of beds stacked one on top of the other everywhere there's wall space. It's the same in the center of the room. It looks like people loaded onto warehouse shelves.

I look next to my bed and there's a glass of water. I force myself to drink it slowly. It helps, but it's gone too soon. Where'd it come from? I try to say "more," but no sound comes out. The only light comes from two tiny windows. It looks like they're round.

I think this is my third day. The room's not spinning as much. I'm going to try to crawl to the round windows. I'm on my hands and knees. I use my hands to pull myself up and see. Looking out all I can see is water…I'm on a ship. I ask a man near the window. "Where we going?"

"America."

As I crawl back to bed, I hear a crinkling sound in my jacket. I push hand in pocket and remove a piece of paper. After a few attempts I see that it's a blurry note from Chancellor written in elegant calligraphy:

"You ruined my life… so in return, I'm ruining yours. Your devastation was done very quickly… mine will last very, very much longer."

It's day four. I try to walk a few steps. I hear another crinkling sound. This paper is sewn into my jacket lining.

"I will keep track of you wherever you go, and if I discover that you have a child, I will wait long enough for you to develop a strong attachment to it. Then I will have it killed as you are forced to watch. I have very long arms. I wish you a pleasant voyage."

The man's a lunatic.

Staying in bed waiting for more chemicals to leave my body. In the corner of the room I see a barrel of water. I crawl over and try to force down as much water as possible to flush the toxins out of my system and work to redirect my Chi flow through affected meridians to heal my bruises. The water's warm and filthy. My current goal is to feel like a human who's very, very sick.

I need sleep. I'm going to see if I can use my breathing ritual to help. I close my eyes but I can tell the hand under my pillow is not mine. There are papers being wedged under my pillow. There…got him. This man is very soft. I feel no resistance. I'm only using a simple joint lock with one hand, almost no pressure and he's submitting. I snatched the papers from his hand. I can feel him shake. I begin reading while still holding onto his wrist. I feel no power coming back from this little man.

My name is printed on a steamship ticket along with papers indicating I'm from Kwangtung and bound for San Francisco. I'll be working for the Sam Ping Mining Company who advanced the money for this trip. I owe them five years of servitude to pay back the fare, a place to stay, food and all the interest that has and will accrue on their loan.

All this time I'm still gripping the man's wrist. I see a plump, moist man in his late thirties. His Spleen Meridian isn't receiving a sufficient supply of Chi and this is the primary cause of his weakness. His shaking coupled with his Earth sign suggests he's probably an honest man. His dominant Yin traits make it clear why he's terrified and couldn't loosen my hold.

I don't make it a point to diagnose every person's Chi flow. It's just something I do. Some people are good observers. There are witnesses who can tell a constable that the man who grabbed his money belt had hair parted down the middle, but needed a haircut, was just over five feet tall and his black tunic was clean but worn…especially at the elbows They're prepared to go on unless stopped. Others asked for the same description say, "He was sort of average." I'm not sure if my analytic ability is an asset, but I've learned to accept it, and sometimes it's proven useful.

"Where did you get these papers? Who told you to give them to me? Why did you agree to do it?"

"They told me you wouldn't wake up for days and all I had to do is slip them under your pillow. Please stop hurting me."

What's happened to me? A drugging isn't a reason to be injuring this little man who can't fight back. I release his hand. "I'm sorry for hurting you, but I need to know who sent you?"

"A well dressed official, and a few soldiers. They were the ones who brought you on the ship. I was waiting to board and this official said if I helped him he'd pay me three pieces of silver. He warned that if I didn't, they'd hear about it and somebody would kill me when we arrived in San Francisco. You weren't supposed to know anything. You were supposed to be sleeping because you were drugged. I delivered the papers. I'd like to leave now ... please."

"Not quite yet. Do you have any connections aboard this ship? Are you supposed to contact anyone once we get to San Francisco? Are you supposed to tell them what you did?"

"No. My job is done. I didn't look at the papers. I wasn't asked to do it, I was ordered and paid and now it's done. I'd like to go now please."

I've seen enough frightened men to know this one is telling the truth. His balance is off and his Yin dominates his Yang. As I'm about to let him creep out of the room, I ask, "Is there a place on the ship where I can wash my clothes?"

"I'll take you there if you let me leave after."

I wash the only clothes I have and put them back on still wet, but now clean, and return to my bed to reflect on what I'd done to this small man. He's weak and I hurt him. The worst thing I can accuse him of is surprising me. I'll try to blame my actions on being drugged and disoriented ... but I know that won't work.

I lie down and begin my breathing ritual again. The dream I descend into helps soothe my agitated state.

I was seven-years old and limped into the compound. "What happened son?"

"I tripped and banged my leg on a fallen tree. It really hurts, but I want to show you something that'll make you proud. I've been practicing

what you taught me and I'm going to heal the injury myself." I began massaging the ligaments in my thigh and within a minute I stood and pranced around. "Look father, I used acupressure to cure my own injury."

Father gestured for me to come to him. As soon as I arrived by my father's side, he gently held onto my hips and turned me sideways. Then he punched me in the thigh... hard.

I began crying and limped away from father and sat down. "Why did you hit me?"

"Stand up. Walk from here to the bushes and back again. As you walk, notice how you're limping. The Rectus Femoris muscle is contracting and the biceps Femoris muscle is spasaming. I see by the grimace on your face that you're really in pain now. You weren't hurt before when you told me you were. I punched you to teach you a lesson about lying to your father. More importantly, I wanted to help you recognize what pain in that area looked and felt like."

Helping me onto the ground, my father began rubbing my leg with his fingers and occasionally using his elbows and knuckles. Within a few minutes, he had me stand.

"How did you do that father? My pain is gone."

As my father started walking back into the house, he turned and smiled, "Real acupressure."

"Father, I'm confused. You punched me in the leg and hurt me. Am I supposed to be angry or grateful?"

"Did you walk away from the punch hurt or smarter?"

"Father... Thank you for punching me."

Two years later, when I was nine I was in a state of panic. "Father, Pao can't run. He's hurt his rear paw. Look... he's crying."

"Calm yourself. Lay him here on the ground. Go into the house and bring the needles in the green wrapping. The short ones."

My father rubbed two points on my dog's neck and he stopped whimpering. Then father sank two needles into his head and my dog suddenly stopped moving."

"Father, you killed Pao!"

He laughed, "No, I just put him to sleep so he wouldn't feel any more pain." Then he placed a series of needles from Pao's head down

7

through his paw. "Let's place him on the ground gently and leave him for 10 minutes."

We came back and father removed the needles, saving the two in his head for last. The dog sat and snuffled around for a minute, then began shuffling around the grass without any evident pain.

"Father, how did you heal him so quickly?"

"First I manipulated two acupressure points to relax him. Then I inserted two acupuncture needles to put him to sleep so he wouldn't feel much pain. Then I added some needles at the Three Yin Intersection Point on his inner leg. As I did this I also applied deep pressure behind his tibia, massaging with a circular motion for a few seconds."

"I want to be learn how to do that father."

"You'll have to pay more attention to tracing the body's Chi flow along the fourteen energy pathways. It's in the book you're supposed to be studying. You're going to have to learn all 365 acupuncture points mapped along the 14 major channel lines. There's one channel for each of the 12 inner organs, one channel along the spine and another along the middle of the abdomen."

"I'll study harder. Until today, they were just words and pictures in a book."

"Tonight we'll begin your actual healing lessons. You're nine now. It's time."

———————————

Today... going to try to talk to some of the men on the ship. I'll have to hear the 'how old are you sonny?' jibes, but there are a few things I need to find out about this voyage.

I walk over to the three men sitting on a bed talking. They're in their late twenties, dressed in worn work clothes. They look like they're from small villages.

"Hey, you're alive. They way they dumped you on your bed, we weren't sure you were gonna' make it. You must've really pissed somebody off to be tossed down like that. A few of us placed bets to see if you'd make it or not."

"Who won?"

"We're not sure. We need to see if you make it until Saturday."

"Who bet on Saturday?"

"I did, but not by choice. It was the only day left. I believed you'd be dead by now. How'd you end up here?"

"Not sure. I drank a glass of tea and the next thing I knew I woke up here.

"You're not the only one here who got shanghaied, but you're probably the youngest. How old are you? It's another bet we made."

"Nineteen."

"Sh_t, I had sixteen."

"When did we leave port?"

"Four days ago. For the first three days we took turns bringing you water and soup to keep you going. Glad to see you alive friend."

"Thank you. I owe you my life."

"It just meant carrying a cup. You don't owe us anything. We went through your pockets and you didn't have any money or we would've taken it. You had nothing except a piece of paper. We thought it might be important so we left it in your pocket."

"Well thanks anyway. Why are you going to America?"

"I'm going to California to dig for gold. These two are bragging about getting high paying jobs and sending money home to their families. One of them pulled out a crumpled circular posted in his village. "Do you know how to read? He wants the others to hear it.

> Americans are all rich people. They want the Chinaman to come and make him very welcome. There you will have big pay, large house and clothing of the finest quality. You can send money home to your family. We guarantee safe delivery. There are no soldiers or mandarins to fear. Many Chinaman are there already so you will not feel like you are in a strange country. China God is there and you will be lucky.

The man with the circular says he can't read it, but an elder in his village read it to him and it sounded so good that he's here. He folds up the circular and puts it back in his pocket. He wants the others to know what it says. I manage to get back to my bed and collapse.

Even these short walks are tiring me out. Time for my nightly breathing ritual. Seems to help my disposition.

I was ten-years-old walking home through the forest carrying a basket of berries. Two older, larger boys blocked my path and demanded my basket. When I refused, they punched me several times, and one of them tripped me. They kicked me several more times, laughed and walked away with my fruit basket. I laid on the ground grumbling. I knew I could have easily won a fight against these two boys but chose not to engage with them.

I returned home and told my father what happened. "I'm very proud of you not fighting back. Tonight I'm going to show you how to prevent a beating while avoiding a fight."

My father showed me a series of evasive movements that made me appear clumsy while enabling me to avoid getting hit. It was easy for me since I've been learning to fall as a regular part of my martial training. Then my father showed me how I could actually cause pain to my opponents while still appearing to be awkward. No one would ever suspect that I could fight; yet they would walk away not just losing, but nursing a series of bruises.

A few weeks later, at dusk, I was walking home with a basket of apples when the same two boys who stole my berries came walking up the path with a third friend. One of them gave me a broad smile. "I see you've picked some apples for us. Thank you."

"Please, these are for my family. It took me hours to pick them. Just let me go home in peace."

"You aren't a very fast learner are you? What's your name?"

"My name's Lo Wan and I just want to go home with my apples, but I'd be happy to give each of you one to take with you."

All three laughed as the first boy said, "Thank you. First, I'll take the apple you offered me and then I'll have the rest." When he lunged forward to grab the basket, I wasn't there. The boy ended up on the ground. The other two boys laughed at him, helped him up and they surrounded me.

As they moved in quickly, I appeared to trip and two of the boys banged their heads together. Then the third boy tripped over the other two. After several more clumsy attempts, all three boys were on the ground moaning. One boy had dislocated his elbow in the process and was now crying. I walked over and began massaging the boy's arm. Then I suddenly grabbed and twisted his elbow. The boy howled in pain, and all of a sudden he jumped up and yelled, "The pain's gone. My arm's better. You fixed it just like that. How did you do that?"

"It's called acupressure. Now you can hold that apple I promised you."

I smiled as I handed father the basket of apples as my way of saying "Thank you."

Day five. Force myself to drink a lot of water to flush out remaining toxins. The water's so polluted it's like 'out with the bad, in with a different bad.' My head's beginning to clear but my body still aches with every movement. I've gotta' force myself to begin some light stretches and exercises. Not good at passivity. There's not enough space for any of my full routines. I've found a few remote areas I can sneak into, the rest of the time I get up in the middle of the night to practice. One great thing is the ship's constant motion. It's helpful for practicing my stability. I've gotten pretty good at looking like I'm losing my balance when someone happens to see me.

As I was beginning my nighttime breathing ritual, I heard a faint noise. I noticed a slight movement to my left. Someone was approaching me in the semi-dark room. As the man got closer, I saw a raised arm holding a wooden club.

The Chancellor insisted his Viceroy provide an update on the little healer.

"I sent a telegram to the Ping Mining Company with instructions concerning how to treat him. It said if he ever has a pleasant day, someone isn't doing his job. I let them know we want a telegram every week with an update. His misery will earn them bonuses."

It was essential for the Viceroy to have the Chancellor see him as effective. Any mention of the young healer brought out the Chancellor's venom and reminded the Viceroy of how the Chancellor punished his uncle. Disappointment brought out the absolute worst in him. An involuntary shiver is a powerful memory trigger.

The Viceroy's uncle was in charge of training the castle army in hand-to-hand combat. The Viceroy assisted him in getting that job.

A year ago, the Chancellor was excited when the Emperor's brother decided to spend a few days as his guest. After a banquet they were drinking wine late into the night and the wine spurred their competitive spirit. The Prince was getting drunk and as he fell into the Chancellor's shoulder he smiled up at him. "I'd wager my best fighter can defeat any champion you have here."

The next day, a huge crowd had been gathered in the expansive gardens surrounding the castle. The Chancellor's champion, a large, well-muscled man in his mid-twenties walked out to the cheers of the crowd. He bent over touching his palms to the floor without any warm up, and then threw a few practice kicks at boards that were held over his head. He shattered each one with speed and power. The Chancellor sat back and smiled.

The Prince walked out next to a wiry man who was in his late forties. He was a full head shorter than the Chancellor's champion and made no attempt to stretch or warm up. He bowed to the larger man and smiled.

The Castle champion walked up to the Prince, "Your man looks like a nice enough fellow. I have no wish to hurt him."

The Prince smiled back. "I'll remind you of these words after the competition."

The Chancellor asked the Prince if he still intended to go through with this competition at the risk of having his man hurt.

The Prince laughed, "Let's make this a bit more interesting with a small side wager. If your man wins, you may have your choice of any of my concubines. If I win, I'll select one of yours."

The Chancellor called his champion over, covered his mouth and whispered, "You may kill him during the fight if the opportunity presents himself." Then he nodded to the Prince and accepted his wager.

The Prince's fighter held his elbows close to his ribs and kept his hands relaxed. He didn't clench them into fists. The fight began with the Chancellor's man throwing a punch as a feint to see how the smaller man would react. The smaller man barely moved and remained just out of reach. The Chancellor's man interpreted this lack of a reaction as an insult. The smaller man seemed to be saying he didn't take him seriously. His facial expression registered his anger as he rushed in with a furious attack. First a strong kick, followed by a punch with devastating intention.

The smaller man moved slightly to the side to avoid the kick, then he grabbed the big man's arm using his own energy against him, redirecting him to the ground. He landed on top of the big man with his knee driving deep into the larger man's solar plexus. The Chancellor's champion couldn't catch his breath. The Prince's man moved around and placed the bigger man into a chokehold submitting him easily.

The Chancellor yelled, "You may kill him if you'd like."

The smaller man looked up at the Chancellor, "He's done nothing to me. I bear him no ill will. It wasn't his wish to fight me." The Prince rose and asked his fighter to accompany him as they walked toward where the Chancellor's concubines were seated. He yelled, "Since you won the competition, I'd be honored if you help me choose one of these beautiful young girls. I'll even give you the first turn with her tonight." He smiled at the Chancellor as he made the remark."

They agreed upon a stunning young concubine who was the Chancellor's favorite. In truth, as they walked by each of the girls, they looked at the Chancellor's face. He made it clear which one he didn't want them to select, so they chose her.

The Chancellor had the Viceroy's Uncle exiled to the Island of Macau and mandated that he perform physical labor in the fields until he died.

The Viceroy learned to remain in the Chancellor's good graces regardless of his demands. From the Chancellor's perspective, he didn't care whether others followed his orders out of respect or fear ... as long as he got what he wanted.

I see the man crawling from the shadows with a raised club. As he reaches my bed the club comes crashing down on the spot where my body was. While rolling and flailing in panic I strike a pressure point in this attacker's arm that ends up immobilizing it.

"I can't move my arm. What did you do?" He looks more closely at me. "Damn, what are you ... fifteen? They didn't say I was going to bash a kid."

"I'm nineteen, and I'd like to know who told you to hit me? How much are they paying you? Are there any more of you on the ship?"

The man expressed his answer by switching the club to his other hand to take another swing at me. I move back and when he finishes his swing, I grab the club from his hand and poke his injured shoulder with it. He tries to keep his voice down, while the pain registers on his face.

The man's Chi flow to the Small Intestine meridian needs to be increased substantially. His Fire element dominates his strong Yang energy flow. This feeds his impulsivity and leads to an over-estimation of his strength. He relies on his size to intimidate.

He tries to jump on top of me keeping his bad shoulder away. I move aside and smack his shoulder again using his club, harder this time. He winces and swings with his other arm. I grab his wrist and twist it.

"You're very playful." Twisting his arm I ask, "Now who told you to hit me?"

He makes a show of scrunching up his lips to show his refusal to talk. I apply more pressure and he holds up his other hand to stop me and begins spewing out a rush of words. I tell him to slow down. "I was paid to wait until you were asleep and hit your body a few times, but never your head. Then, I was supposed to wait a few days and do it again. I'm supposed to inflict enough pain to make moving difficult. The plan is to make your trip unpleasant. You're supposed to get off the ship aching."

"Who paid you?"

"Never saw him before. He picked me cause I'm big. 'You look like a thug. You have any experience beating people up?'"

"I smiled, he hired me, and gave me four silver coins. 'When we arrive in San Francisco, find a man named Ho Lim. He'll give you another five silver coins if he looked injured enough.'"

"Did he hire any more men like you?"

"Don't know. He picked me out, told me what to do, paid me and left."

"This is a problem. I'm a healer, but I don't heal people who try to hurt me."

"A healer? Tell you what. I'll give you one of my silver coins if you fix my arm."

I hit his shoulder with his club. "That's for trying to hit a kid."

"But you're not a kid."

"But you thought I was."

Then I hit him again. "And that's for saying my treatment is only worth one silver coin. Take your silver coin and rub it on your shoulder to heal it. Now get out of here."

"I'm sorry ... please help me."

"OK, I'll fix your arm for six silver pieces."

"I don't have six, will you please do it for the four silver pieces I have ... I'm begging you."

"What else of value do you have?"

He reaches into his pocket, pulls out a small knife and hands it to me.

Here's my final offer. First, apologize for attacking me, and promise never to do it again. Then, give me your knife and your club, and of course, get your four pieces of silver."

"Yes, yes. I'm sorry for attacking you. Here's my club. You've already got my knife. I'll be back here in a few minutes."

This man deserves all the pain he's got. I hope it teaches him a lesson. But what lesson will he actually learn if he sees that I get to profit from his silver? It'll undo the point of the lesson. I'd hate to think of how disappointed my father would be if he were watching this. But he didn't teach me to heal souls.

The man runs back and prepares to hand me his silver coins. "Wait, a minute, you're just a kid. How do I know you can fix my arm?"

I use his club to smack his shoulder again. "You're right. I'm just a kid. Go away."

He bows his head to the floor. "I'm sorry … I'm not thinking clearly. Help me … please."

"There's a reason why you've been given your size and strength. You should use them to help protect weaker people. Promise you'll never use your size to hurt people again."

"Yes … yes."

I push my thumb along a meridian that controls his bicep and elbow while tugging hard on his forearm. A shock of horror flashes across his face, then he shakes his arm and says, "How'd you do that? It's like a new arm."

"Remember, your treatment wasn't just physical. It was designed to teach you not to bully people smaller than you."

"Yeh … sure … thank you." The man hurries away.

I know there was no personal enlightenment for this man. I wish father was here to tell me what to do. I feel like I failed. I was only trained to heal bodies. Even though I was tired, it took a long time to get to sleep.

Chapter 2

I wake up hearing a man's voice saying strange words followed by a group who tries to repeat them. This man seems to know a lot of English words and is teaching them to anyone who wants to learn. I sit at the edge of the group and join in. The differences I hear between teacher and students make me laugh, until I realize my own mispronunciations only add to the jumbled chorus.

After it's over I introduce myself. The man is in his mid-fifties, and keeps himself in excellent shape. He's well groomed which really makes him stand out here. It's like he's on the wrong ship. I later find out he's quartered in the ship's only stateroom. His Chi flow is functioning ideally. He's a Fire sign, evidenced by his display of enthusiasm and commitment. He radiates balance. I thank him and comment on the variations in pronunciation I heard from the models he presented.

"Chinese all read the same writing but no two provinces speak the same dialect. So what you notice isn't surprising. And we're not travelling with a lot of scholars. I doubt if there are five men on this ship who're literate."

"You're offering these men a wonderful gift. Why do you do it?"

"You're all going to America for lots of different reasons. Some are accurate most aren't, but you'll find no welcome there. The better you can communicate, the better you can adapt... but it'll still be terrible."

"Where'd you learn English? And do you just know a collection of words or are you fluent? Have you been to America? And..."

He raises his hand to stop me. "You're a curious young man. You're also very young to be on this ship. How old are you?"

I'm nineteen years old, but as you've noticed, I look younger."

"I can tell by your questions you're probably one of the five readers on this ship, but are all your conversations just a series of questions? I find it difficult to have a conversation with you. Is this the way you speak to your friends?"

"I've never had friends and I don't have conversations. I didn't go to school. All my time was spent with my family. I'm a healer, raised by my father and brother. They were my teachers. I've never had the time or the opportunity to make friends. The only talking I ever do is when I'm trying to help people. In that setting my 'conversations' consist of a series of diagnostic questions so I can find out what's wrong with them, then telling them what to do to get better. At home I either asked my brother and father for their help when I didn't know what to do, or I reported the results my daily work.

You're an unusual fellow. How'd you get here?"

"That question will take a long time to answer. With all due respect sir, how did you come to learn their language?"

"I've been living in California for over twenty years. I'm returning from visiting my family in china. I like to go back every five years or so. I speak English fluently and have only a slight accent. I have to speak well because I'm on the Board of Directors of the Six Companies."

"What are the Six Companies?"

"Another difficult question. I suggest we get to know one another better so conversation may move more fluidly between us. My name is Tu Chan."

"I'm Lo Wan. It's my pleasure to meet you sir."

"Well Lo Wan, for the time being, let's see what passes for food this morning to give us the strength to find out what passes for food tomorrow morning."

"In answer to your question, I was placed on this ship without my consent, but I didn't commit any crimes in my homeland."

"Whoever placed you on this ship wasn't doing you any favors. In America they'll treat you like an outcast. They brought us over to build their railroads and work their mines. Now, their mines are played out and the railroads are built, but we're still in their country and they don't want us there. They already hate you even though they've never met you. You don't speak their language. In their eyes, you want to make money in America and send it back to China. You'll work for less money than they do so you'll be taking their jobs. When we arrive in San Francisco you'll probably need the Six Companies so I might as well tell you a little about what we do."

"A description of the Six Companies will depend on who you ask. *We* like to think we're a benevolent association. Our Board members are wealthy merchants who use political power to deal with the government on immigration and work issues. We help Chinese who come from and return to China. The day before I left San Francisco a family came in for help. Within a half hour I was able to send a man to a healer, provide food for the family and send the grandfather's remains back to China for burial."

"The people who *hate* the Six Companies think we're greedy and dishonest. Some call us the largest Tong in Chinatown."

"What's a Tong?"

"Where'd you live in China?"

"A number of small villages."

"Were these villages ever troubled by bandits?"

"Constantly.

"Tongs are large groups of organized bandits who fight with each other for domination of Chinatown in San Francisco. We try to keep the peace between the Tongs, the people of Chinatown and the police. The Tongs control the flow of opium, and run the dens where opium smokers go. They also run prostitution and gambling. People are terrified of them and the police avoid contact with them whenever they can. I recognized one Tong member aboard this ship. I'll point him out when we see him."

"I feel like a student listening to you talk and I love being a student. I'm so happy I met you. You'll see me sitting in the group learning Enrish at your feet every morning you're willing to teach us."

"Thank you Lo Wan. You've provided the first stimulating talk I've had on this trip."

The following morning, you could hear me saying, "Herro, how a you?" just like the other students sitting at their instructor's feet. While Tu Chan's class size is shrinking a little every day, I can always be found sitting in the front asking questions and trying to increase the length of each lesson. After, we take our now customary stroll around the ship's deck. As we're walking, I notice a man whose clothes were more stylish than most of the other passengers. He's talking to a nervous man at the railing. The man reaches into his pocket and gives the well-dressed fellow a small copper coin. The man smiles and bows his head.

Tu Chan nods. "What do you think we just witnessed?"

"We just saw a man who can sleep comfortably tonight knowing he saved himself from a beating. I don't think you'll have to point out the Tong member. Do they generally carry weapons?"

"If we were in Chinatown, he'd surely have a hatchet and knife. Some even carry pistols now. I suspect this one carries a small knife he conceals. I'm sure before you leave this ship, Doy Low will make your acquaintance."

I stretched out on my mattress and began my breathing ritual. Once again I fall into a dream state that is as close to relaxation as I can hope for.

"Father, if I'm learning to be a great fighter, why do I need to learn so much about healing? It's boring compared to fighting."

"You're not being raised to be a great fighter. You're being raised to be a great healer. Fighting is always a last resort. And if you hurt someone,

you should know how to heal him afterwards. I'm training you to be a 'Twin Dragon.' Hit and heal, clobber and cure... eh... smack and sew up." My poor father ran out of alliterations so he was forced to stop.

"Let me share one of life's great ironies. In learning to heal, you're learning to identify the greatest vulnerabilities in a man's body. It's the essence of being a Twin Dragon."

"But father, shouldn't I be proud to be a good fighter instead of keeping it a secret?"

"Would you be proud to hurt or cripple or even kill someone with your fighting skills?"

Lo Wan looked down and shook his head.

"But that's what can happen in a fight. Your best-kept secret should always be that you're a skilled fighter." I want you to promise that you'll never use your fighting skills unless it's a matter of life-or-death. Not vanity, not anger and certainly not pride.'"

"I promise."

"I know it doesn't make sense, but once people know you can fight, they'll be curious to find out just how good you are. To know if you're tougher than they are."

"If people know I'm a good fighter, won't it make them scared so they'll want to avoid fighting with me?"

"Let's not waste time arguing. We'll conduct an experiment. The Wei family lives in the next village. Tomorrow, I planned to bring them some herbs. I want you to deliver them instead. They have a son named Sam Yee who's a year older than you. Get into a conversation with him and just happen to mention that you're a good fighter and let's see what happens."

The next night I arrive home filthy and my tunic is torn. "I tried your experiment father. I said, 'Sam Yee, your family has a very well run farm. You're lucky being trained to farm. You'll always be able to have a good life with skills like that. I know a little about farming, but my father insists that I learn to be a good fighter instead."

"Really, show me what he's teaching you."

"Oh, I don't like to demonstrate my fighting skills because it's too dangerous."

"I don't believe you're a good fighter. I'm bigger than you and stronger than you. If we got into a fight, I'd hurt you and you'd run home crying to your father."

"You're right Sam Yee. You are bigger and stronger. I'm sure you'd win in a fight, and I don't like to fight, and I certainly don't like getting hurt. If I said something that made you angry, I apologize."

"No . . . If you couldn't fight, you wouldn't have mentioned it. Stand up and fight me."

"Sorry, but I have to go home."

"Sam Yee stepped into my path and shoved my shoulder. I tried to back down in every way I could think of. I apologized. I agreed that Sam Yee was a better fighter. I begged him not to hurt me. Everything I said seemed to make him more determined to want to fight with me."

"Sam Yee tried to punch me and I used the evasive techniques you taught me. After what seemed like an eternity, even though it was just a few minutes, Sam Yee was finally exhausted and I ran home with his curses ringing in my ears."

I'm holding onto the railing while standing on the deck as Doy Low walks up behind me. "I'm a bit short of money my young friend. Do you have a copper coin or two to spare?"

"Sorry friend, but all the money I have is here in my hand." I open my hand revealing its emptiness.

"Perhaps you can ask around and one of your friends can give you something for me."

"I have as many friends on this ship as I have coins. I'm sorry, but I'm afraid I can't help you."

The Tong member has a large Chi blockage in his Kidney meridian. Like many Water signs, he shows a great deal of determination and seems to have an agile mind, but underneath his resolve to show strength, his excessive Yin lets fear and recklessness seep into his actions. I think he would collapse under pressure like a fallen persimmon encountering a foot not paying attention to the road where he is walking.

"You're just a kid and don't seem to understand who you're talking to. Let me explain what the word 'insurance' means. If you give me a coin or two, you'll arrive in San Francisco healthy and safe."

"I'm sure that's just how I'll arrive if I give you a coin or not. I walk around the deck every day for exercise. I'm young and have no diseases."

"You don't seem very smart. Let me be more direct. If you give me some money, I won't have to hurt you. Notice I'm a lot bigger than you."

"You don't have to hurt me whether I give you money or not. Our sizes shouldn't matter."

"You can't be this stupid boy. Let me give you a small sample of what getting hurt feels like." Doy Low pulls his fist back and throws a punch at me. As the punch arrives, I trip and fall to the floor and the Tong man's punch lands on the metal structure behind me.

"Are you alright? I slipped and saw that you hurt your hand trying to catch me. Thanks for trying to help."

Doy Low curses as he walks away nursing his hand. Tu Chan saw the episode and approaches me laughing. "Lucky you stumbled just in time to avoid being hit. That was very fortunate, but I don't think you made a friend today."

I went back to my bed and began my breathing ritual.

I love my brother Li Wing but he has a serious flaw. He's too perfect. Studying isn't work for him. It's entertainment. Martial arts are just a series of games. By the age of twelve he's a gifted healer. And he doesn't limit healing to people. If he finds a bird with a broken wing or a squirrel with a bad leg, Li Wing finds a way to mend it. He's the worst possible role model for me. "Perfect" is difficult to compete with.

I walk into our room and throw my clothes into a corner and dress for bed. "Li Wing, how am I supposed to measure up to you?"

"You're only nine years old, you shouldn't. I'm a quarter of a lifetime older than you. You're already better than I was at everything when I was your age."

"That's exactly what a perfect brother would say."

Every day I sit with a smaller number of men than the day before learning English. After each meeting, I pester Tu Chan to teach me a little more. I can't carry on much of a conversation in English, but I'm learning useful phrases, and developing a sizable vocabulary. I'm even beginning to catch on to English sentence structure. I find myself walking around the ship practicing this new language. I'm so absorbed I almost miss Doy Low approaching me. "Have you managed to find a coin or two for me?"

"Sorry, I thought I made it clear. I don't have any money, and I don't know anyone who does."

"That's it. It's time you learned a lesson." Doy Low aimed a kick at my head. As the kick arrives, I trip and stumble into Doy Low's planted foot causing him to fall. I try to catch him, but miss and Doy Low is on his back having banged his head on the deck railing on his way down.

"Are you alright? I saw you start to fall and tried to catch you, but I was too clumsy. Your head's bleeding." I tore a piece of his shirt to stem the bleeding.

Doy Low grabs the piece of his shirt out of my hand. "Fool. You've just ruined an expensive shirt. You'll have to pay for it."

"You sound delirious. You should sit down till your thinking clears. Your head hit the deck pretty hard. Let me to see if I can find some medical help?"

"Leave me alone … fool."

The next morning, Tu Chan is giving a conjugation lesson to the four men who are still his students. From there we enjoy another conversation. Since Tu Chan is teaching me English and providing me with essential survival skills for America, I reciprocate by showing him some exercises and stretches. I also help him get rid of a few aches and pains with acupressure, but first, I make him promise not to reveal that I have healing skills. I never mention my martial arts skills.

As I begin my nighttime breathing exercises I begin to laugh to myself. It seems whenever I begin them they're often intruded on and rarely are those interruptions salubrious.

I notice Doy Low's shadow before I see the man himself. I also notice the glint of a small metal object. Doy Low is down on his hands and knees and crawling slowly toward my bed ... very slowly. I notice the Tong man move his knife gradually until it is just inches away from my throat.

Chapter 3

In the mountains outside Sacramento a messenger is having a meeting with the manager of the Sam Ping Mining Company. "You're getting a laborer direct from China named Lo Wan. A powerful Chancellor from China is going to pay you to make this man's time here miserable. He wants him demoralized, but alive. Give him the most unpleasant jobs. If he makes any mistakes, discipline him. He can be hurt, but not maimed. The key is suffering stretched out as long as possible. Any questions?"

"Yes, what's so special about this guy?"

"That's none of your business. Any other questions?"

"No."

"I understand that was your official message to us, but now, since no one is around to hear us, who is this Chancellor?"

"He's someone you don't want to make angry. He doesn't hold a grudge; he wraps it around your neck and strangles you with it ... slowly. You have a choice of making him angry, or making a huge amount of money by doing exactly what he wants. Seems like an easy decision."

When Doy Low gets close, he thrusts his knife into the pillow where my throat was and begins moaning because his wrist is causing him a lot of pain. As he tries to scream he feels a jolt in his neck and no sound comes out. I hold on to his wrist with a painful joint lock and scoop up his small knife. I nudge him toward the small adjacent storeroom so we can talk, or at least so I can. This is only the second time I've ever disabled a man's speech. It's terrifying for both of us. I take a long, slow breath to calm myself. This man just tried to kill me and now his fate is in my hands. I still think of myself as a boy, but I can't reveal that here. What would my perfect brother do?

I begin with a smile hoping his fear will keep him from noticing what's beneath it. "Doy Low, esteemed Tong member. You bragged you were a smart man. You attacked me twice and both times it was you who walked away in pain. Although I pretended that both times were accidents, I thought you were intelligent enough to figure out they weren't, but you decided to bet your life they were. I re-arranged your body to prevent you from speaking. Use your head to indicate if you think what you did tonight was a smart idea."

The frightened Tong member shook his head vigorously from side-to-side. "If I release you, I know you'll make more attempts on my life. So ... I guess I have to figure out the best way to kill you so I can get a good night's sleep. If our situations were reversed, you've already shown what you would do. You made that very clear with this pretty little knife. By the way, thank you. It's a lovely gift. I'll treasure it."

The combination of the pain in his wrist, the fear of his imminent demise added to his sudden inability to speak leaves him with only two forms of emotional release. One is his flood of tears and the other is considerably more odiferous.

"Your body seems to understand the position you're in even if you don't. 'Would you prefer a slow painful death as punishment for the three times you attacked me or would you prefer that I be merciful and just break both your arms and throw you overboard for a quick death ... unless the sharks get to you first?'"

"Don't bother answering, I have a confession to make. I don't like killing. I'm going to give you back your voice if you promise you won't raise it. Show me with your head if you agree."

Doy Low bobs his head up-and-down.

Using two fingers and a little pressure, I restore his speech. "If I let you live, how do I know you won't make another attempt on my life?"

"I swear on the lives of my mother, father and grandfather."

"Seeing several examples of your compassion, I can picture you hating all three of them. You make your promise sound very sincere, but from what I've heard, Tong promises are only binding if they're made to other members of his Tong."

In this dimly lit little room I'm trying to make sense of my situation. If this man was willing to kill me over such a petty dispute, surely he's killed before, and will again. I'm ready to release this murderer based on his promise that he won't try to kill me again. I know I can't change his morality. I know how to heal bodies, but I don't have the slightest idea how to heal a man's spirit. Is it my responsibility to even try? What if he's a truly evil man and I let him live, and he goes on to injure someone else? Will it be my fault, his or both?

When I was five my father said, "Son, turn sideways." Without warning he punched me in the leg then made me walk around to experience three things: the pain of the lie I told him, an opportunity to learn more about physiology and to teach me a lesson … all with one punch. I smiled and looked up. Thank you father.

"Stand up." As soon as Doy Low stood, I released his wrist and I hit him on the right side of his left knee. To his credit he winced hard, but didn't scream. "Try to walk." He groaned as he found he could walk, but with a painful limp caused by what I did to his left knee.

As he stood there in shock I walked over to his right side and used my middle knuckle to center a punch at his right shoulder then asked him to move his arm around. Doy Low found he could use his right arm, but each movement caused him considerable pain. "I'm leaving you with these two reminders of this unpleasant evening. Break your word to me and you'll regret it for the short time you have left to live."

"I want you to promise not to attack me or anyone on this ship for the duration of our voyage. And, I want you to acknowledge that I let you keep your life. You'll show me you mean this promise by coming to me every day and giving me a smile and a head nod. No one will be aware of what you're doing except the two of us. If you fulfill this promise, just before we reach San Francisco, I'll release you from the pain in your knee and arm. I thank you for making me feel good about myself for not killing you.

"I promise..."

"You may leave now. Thanks again for this lovely little knife."

I began another round of my breathing ritual, but I found it difficult to fall asleep until I had a pleasing thought. "Thank you again father."

All in all, I came aboard this ship with pain and nausea and now I have four silver pieces, a club and two knives. I guess that's a form of progress. Will my lesson reform this criminal? I doubt it, but I feel better trying. I think five weeks of daily pain stands a chance of being a good morality teacher, but I'm not optimistic by nature.

———————

"Since we were going to arrive in San Francisco soon, I go to Tu Chan to ask a favor. "I told you I didn't choose to come on this ship. I moved to Peking about six months ago and began working as a healer. A quirk of fate led me to the Chancellor's castle where he begged me to save his dying daughter's life. Many of the best physicians in China had already tried without success. For three days and nights I did everything I could, but in the end I couldn't save her."

"Next morning I awoke to find myself drugged and beaten on this ship with a note promising a slow and dreadful revenge. This passage to America was his first step in that revenge. These papers were shoved under my pillow while I was passed out. What can I expect from my new life in California?"

"According to this contract, you owe the next five years of your life to the Sam Ping Mining Company. You'll be working in one of their mines until you pay off your debt to them. I'm afraid you'll be forced to perform backbreaking labor for the duration of this contract. It appears to be legal which means if you try to escape they can punish you severely or have you sent to prison. I know too much about these kinds of arrangements and frankly I don't envy your new life."

"The only useful advice I can offer is, do what they say and don't cause problems. If you do, they'll break you down. You can't win against them. I wish there was some way for me to intervene, but my hands are tied. We'll be docking in San Francisco tomorrow. You'll wait on the dock for your name to be called, be placed in a wagon and transported to the mine. I'd be pleased if you'd accept this small parting gift."

Tu Chan hands me his English-Chinese dictionary. He leaves his Six Companies business card in the dictionary as a bookmark. I hand him my four silver pieces, the two knives and the club and ask him to hold on to them for me. Sometimes I am an optimist.

The next morning as we can see San Francisco in the distance, Doy Low approaches me. "I've kept my word. Will you keep yours?"

I gesture to the small, adjacent room where I jam my middle knuckle hard into the Tong member's shoulder then his knee. Both times Doy Low shudders from the pain, but then smiles as he realizes he's been released from his agony.

"I hope you've learned something from both the pain and your release from it. You are in an excellent position to be a model for other people. I hope you remember the lesson of generosity of spirit you learned from this experience."

Doy Low smiles at me and gives me a small bow. "I wonder if the fates will ever have our paths cross again?"

As I walk off the gangplank I hear several men calling out names from different wagons. When I hear my name I walk toward an open wagon. Unlike the other wagons packed with Chinese men, mine's empty. There are two large White guards on the wagon seat. I tried using some of the English I was learning. "Herro, I Lo Wan. Happy meet you."

"Hey Tom, is there some mistake? We were supposed to pick up some special troublemaking chink, the one we're supposed to keep miserable. Sh_t, this one's just a kid. Should we let him sit up here with us, or roll around in the wagon?"

"What do you think?"

"Let's be polite and introduce him to American splinters."

We leave as soon as I climb on. There are no seats. I move into a corner in the back and try to find a place to hold on. If they want me to be comfortable, there's ample room on the bench they're sitting on ... so their goal is my discomfort.

Neither speaks to me during the entire ride to the mine. The only stops we make are to relieve ourselves, on their schedule, and all communication is performed in pantomime with the aid of the guards prodding me with their axe handles. From time-to-time, they pass a canteen back-and-forth, but do not offer me any of their water.

Not wanting to disappoint these men, occasionally when we go around a sharp curve, I let go of the side of the wagon and roll around. To complete my gift, I make noises that indicate I'm banging into the sides of the wagon and in pain. I moan to put a ribbon on my gift.

As the wagon climbs higher, the vegetation grows sparser. At dusk, the wagon climbs a steep, winding road and stops in front of a cabin surrounded by twelve decrepit shacks and a few outhouses. They don't appear to be built with comfort in mind. Over to the side is a larger building where they store tools and food. On the other side of that building is a kennel housing large, snarling dogs.

I'm shoved into the last shack. A large Chinese man yells, "You begin working when the sun comes up and finish when the sun sets. You came too late for the evening meal. Sleep while you can." I look around the shack. There are no beds. "Find a place on the floor to stretch out, but not the place next to the window.

That's my spot." There's no source of light and no conversation. Everyone goes to sleep. I begin my nighttime breathing ritual. As I try to sleep, I think of my new home and find the poetic side of myself able to describe my new surroundings accurately with a single word ... bleak.

In the morning we're all given a bowl of gruel. Everyone is eating as fast as possible. A large white guard walks over and pokes one of the other new men and me and motions for us to follow. We're each given a pick and pushed into a mineshaft. The guard gestures and the other man starts digging at the spot he's pointing to. He points at another place for me to dig and walks out without ever saying a word.

"Mine name's Loo Toy."

"Lo Wan. Pleased to meet you. How long's your contract?"

"Four years, yours?"

"Five years, and I confess to already hating it here."

"Shhh. You're obviously young and inexperienced, but don't let anyone hear you talking like that. Someone'll tell one of the guards to curry favor with them. These guards don't strike me as having much of a sense of humor."

There is no Chi blockage in any of Loo Toy's meridians. Being a Metal sign, he demonstrates ambition and a sense of righteousness. He seems to take good care of himself. I'm fortunate to be partnered with this fellow.

"What'd you do to get yourself here?"

"Apparently, I made the wrong person angry."

"Who was he?"

"A Chancellor in China."

"When you make enemies, you aim high."

"He was the one who exiled me here. By having me work at the mine, he can orchestrate my misery and keep track of me for the next five years to make sure my life remains horrible. How'd you get here?"

"I thought my situation was bad, but I can't match your story ... but mine's bad enough. I was panning for gold when two

Irish guys tried to rob me. I was fighting them off when I was arrested and taken to court. I thought I'd be able to explain what happened and get everything back."

"Judge," I pointed at the two men, "The two man ... "

"Quiet Chinaman. This is America. You don't get to talk here. Your kind doesn't have any rights in our courts."

"Please Judge, I try defend what is my ... "

"Say another word and I'll send you to jail for an extra year. You Chinese all lie and you don't believe in God or the Bible so you can't be sworn in ... so you have no rights here."

"I was about to be sent to jail for striking two white men who robbed me when an agent from this mining company paid my fine. I was grateful until I found out I owed the company four years of my life."

The guard comes back and finds us talking. He's angry. There's a blockage of his Chi meridian in the Small Intestine. His Fire sign and his behavior show confusion from being emotionally overwhelmed. This man is unstable, and not too bright.

The guard backhands Loo Toy across the face and swings his axe handle at me. I slip and fall causing me to duck under his club. At least that's what it looks like to the guard. My foot causes him to stumble and bang his head against the mine wall. It results in a gash in his cheek. "You hurt sir?" The guard was leaking blood all over his shirt. He shoves me down and storms out.

I rushed to Loo Toy, "Are you alright?"

"He hits like a girl. Did you hurt yourself when you tripped?"

"No, I was lucky. We'd better get back to work. I hope this doesn't cause the guards to be angry at us."

"I don't think they will. We're both strong and work hard. We're what they want here and we didn't start the trouble." Loo Toy was wrong. The next day, the same guard comes back and brings an even larger guard with him. They're both carrying ax handles. They are the two guards who brought me here in the wagon.

"These the two Chinks you're talkin' 'bout who ain't workin'?"

"Yup. The little one's the special guy from China they told us about."

"C'mere Chink." The man gestures for me to come toward him. As soon as they push me outside, they each swing their axe handles at me. I panic, trip and fall down. They can't stop their swings so each axe handle ends up smashing into the other's rib cage. I offer to help but they push me away and leave cursing.

After my first two weeks at the mine, I find myself going to sleep with a smile. "Their gruel is an improvement over the ship's food and the water is clean. All the exercising I'm getting is helping me get back into shape. My bruises are healing and I'm working with a pleasant enough fellow. This is as good a place as any to begin creating my plan for getting back to China."

During my nighttime breathing ritual I feel a hand on my thigh. A whispered voice says, "I'm going to have my way with you now, it'll only take a few minutes and you can go back to sleep. You might even like it."

"No thank you. Please remove your hand."

"I've done this to everyone here except you and the other new guy. You're smaller and prettier so I'm starting with you."

"No, I'd rather not if it's OK with you."

"No, it's not OK with me. Know why I do it to everyone whenever I want? Cause they want to continue walking and using their arms. If they refuse, they know I break limbs. Be quiet about it no matter how good I make you feel. Heh heh."

I grab his wrist and twist it while also grabbing one of his fingers. "Is this the finger you'd like me to break first?"

Although I couldn't see the man crying in the dark, it seems like I can hear the tears in his whisper. "Please let me go. I was just joking. I wasn't going to do anything to you."

"Maybe I should just break one of the smaller fingers. It'll be a *little* joke between us. You might even enjoy it."

"No please. I promise never to come near you again."

"And what about Loo Toy?"

"If you want, I'll leave him alone too."

"Do I have your promise?"

"Yes … anything. Just let go of my wrist and leave my fingers as they were."

I use an open hand to deliver a sharp slap to the man's genital area. "There, now you got to use that thing you were going to pleasure me with. Crawl away from me quietly unless you want to make me angry."

The man moans and slinks away to the far corner of the room. The next day the supervisors bring the big man in and ask how his sexual encounter with me went. "He squealed like a baby pig and cried the whole time." The big man knew when you get an assignment from the mining company you better not fail.

Working in the mines settles into a routine. Every day's the same. Eat gruel, work, eat more gruel, sleep … until one morning something changed. The cook got an assistant. A fifteen-year-old girl introduced as Mei Sam. When someone new enters the camp, there's never an introduction. This time is different.

"Everybody listen carefully. This is Mei Sam. She's fifteen years old. She'll be working here until the week before she turns sixteen. Then she'll become a Singsong girl. She's *not* to be touched. She's an extremely valuable property of this mining company. If anyone lays so much as a finger on her, he'll pray for a speedy death. You'll only hear this announcement once."

Loo toy pulls me aside. "Since you're new to America, you may not have noticed there are very few Chinese females in America. There's even a law now that makes it illegal for them to be admitted into the country. We're called the "Bachelor Society." That's because they only brought men here for work. The few Chinese girls who found their way here usually work as whores. This one will become a Singsong girl. That means a more expensive whore. She's a valuable piece of property because she's so young and pretty. Her virginity will bring a high price."

While no one dares touch Mei Sam, the men eventually begin to whistle at her and soon after, they begin making lewd remarks. One morning a man stops in front of her and grabs his crotch.

"Want to see what one looks like? You're going to find out soon enough." A bunch of men laugh. Soon almost every man begins to make a sport of taunting her. The poor young girl looks terrified.

"Why doesn't she just run away?"

"They'd catch her right away. See the big dogs in those cages? They're 'bloodhounds.' The guards'll take a piece of her clothing, let the dogs sniff it and within a few minutes, they'd track her down. She'd be brought back and punished."

In the late afternoon, one of the two guards comes into the mine and motions Loo Toy to follow him. A few minutes later, he stumbled back into the mineshaft, his face dripping blood. He's holding on to his side. The two guards beat him for no reason.

One of the guards gestures for me to follow him outside where the other guard is waiting. Their axe handles are on the ground. Looks like they think it'll be more fun to use their bare hands.

"Ah, two real American men against one scrawny Chink." One of the men pushes me into the other's arms. That man punches me, but I start falling before he makes full contact to minimize the effect of the blow. It provides the illusion that I'm being hit without the pain that normally accompanies it. Then the other man grabs my shirt, pulls me up and shoves me into his partner's arms where that man takes his turn punching me. Again I'm able to blunt the blow, and fall, rolling over to make the man believe he'd knocked me down and really hurt me. I add a moan for his benefit.

The first man runs over and delivers a haymaker at my head just as I stumble. This causes his punch to land on his partner's jaw and knocks him down. He gets up furious that his partner hit him and the two begin to fight with each other. I crawl away leaving the two fighting and hurry back to the mine. I help Loo Toy with his wounds. The two guards don't return.

Back to the routine, each day the same as the previous one. This continues until one of the miners takes the bold step of finally exposing himself to the girl. She turns away and begins to cry. That night she slips out of the camp. In the middle of the night the cook clangs his chow triangle, the dogs bark and every man is roused and told there will be a reward given to the man who brings her back. But, she's not to be harmed, disfigured or molested in any way.

Loo Toy and I join the search. After about a mile and a half we come to a fork in the road. Loo Toy goes left and indicates I should go right.

As we're moving down the mountain, the vegetation is beginning to grow thicker. I have excellent night vision having spent most of my life in small, dark villages where I became a good tracker. I catch up to the girl about a half-mile down the road. I put my index finger to my lips then rip off her dress. I brought my long shirt and tell her to put it on. She asks me to turn around. Then we run through the forest to find a place to hide and figure out what to do. Unfortunately, we run into a clearing, face-to-face with the two men who wielded the axe handles in the mine. Loo Toy has already found them and paid the price. He is lying on the ground holding his ribs and moaning.

They hurt my friend badly enough that I can't take him with us. There's no reason why they should've done this. We don't have much time, but I have the opportunity to make the world a little better by educating these two.

I run up to them, "I find girl. I get reward?"

The two smile as they approach me. Each is carrying his favorite weapon, but this time they don't spring at me. They stalk me as if they plan to savor the pain they'll give me. As the closer one swings his axe handle I jump to one side staying close and stomp on his instep. The man yells, drops his axe handle and begins hopping around as if that will rid him of the pain of a shattered bone in his foot.

The other man pulls back on his axe handle, which is unfortunate for him because it gives me enough time to push my fingertips into his throat and he falls down holding it, making a gurgling sound trying to breathe.

His partner picks up his weapon and is limping toward me. The sight of him following me dragging his painful leg is sadly funny. He swings the handle and I duck and angle to his side. I hit him in a spot behind his neck that knocks him out. The location where I hit him guarantees he'll stay unconscious for at least four or five hours and he'll be limping for several weeks. I go back and give the other man the same courtesy strike to his neck. They won't remember much of what happened to them. I'd like to do more, but we have to move on. Then I get an idea.

I take off each unconscious man's clothes. I toss them around to make it difficult for them to collect them later.

I run back to help Loo Toy up, but he's hurt too badly. His leg and a few ribs are broken. "Just leave me here, I'll be alright. Those two will have a hard enough time explaining why they hurt a man who was trying to help them search for the girl. Take her and get as far away from here as you can. This is your chance to get out from under your Chancellor's grip. Away from the mine, he'll have no way to keep track of you ... and you'll have a pretty companion." He smiled.

"I'll tell them I never saw you because I was unconscious, but mention that I thought I heard the men say they were going to ravage the girl. I'll say I can't be sure because of how badly they beat me, but it's what I thought I heard. Good luck my friend."

I used some acupressure to reduce Loo Toy's pain then we ran off.

As we're running, I occasionally rip off a bit of Mei Sam's dress and tie the cloth around a rock and heave it in new a direction each time to confuse the dogs. We run until we come to a deep canyon. I tie a heavier rock to what remains of her dress and throw it as far into the canyon as I can. That should distract the bloodhounds for hours. As we run, we came across a shallow brook and jog in it to further conceal our scent.

Running alongside this girl, I assess her. There is no Chi meridian blockage. She's clearly a Fire sign who radiates both strength and softness. I don't assess her any farther. Running was more important, although I did notice how she looked in my shirt from the back.

Mei Sam doesn't say a word, she doesn't ask a question. She just runs next to me. I'm happy she doesn't tire and doesn't complain. By morning we no longer hear the dogs. We hear no men yelling.

"How were you able to fight those two men off earlier?"

"I have good night vision. They didn't."

She shrugs her shoulders and says she's hungry, bends down to eat some berries. I run over and slap them out of her hands.

"Hey, that hurt. I'm hungry damn it. I wanted those berries."

"If you eat those now, you'll die a horrible death within the hour. They're poisonous."

We walk a bit farther where I find some blackberries. I gather a bunch and give them to her. For the first time, I see her smile. "My name is Mei Sam. What should I call you?"

"A wanted man ... but my name is Lo Wan."

"Aren't you too young to be working in a mine? I can't believe I got rescued by a kid who's younger than me."

"I'm nineteen, and we have to figure where we're going. Do you know anyone anywhere near here? Do you have any friends or relatives?"

"No. I was brought here from Sacramento and we're a long way from there. Besides, I only have one cousin there, and if I was to meet up with him I'd try to kill him. He's the one who sold me to become a Singsong girl. There was one old man who was always nice to me. He sold herbs and sweets. Perhaps if we could get to him, he might be able to help us.

On our second night under the stars as we prepared to go to sleep she looked over at me, "Is this the night you plan to rape me?"

"Oh no. I always wait until the third night for that. I rolled over and began my breathing ritual."

"Don't you think I'm pretty?"

"I think you're beautiful, but I've never been with ... eh, I don't know much about being with girls. My mother died when

I was seven years old. My father and older brother raised me. I've spent my whole life learning and training. I never had time for girls. If I wanted to rape you I'm not sure I'd know how to go about doing it, but rest assured that the thought has never occurred to me."

"But you do think I'm pretty?"

I re-started my breathing ritual until I fell asleep.

When I was fourteen a new family moved into our village. My father often asked me to deliver herbs there. They had a fourteen-year-old daughter who was very pretty. All the boys in the village chased after her. She seemed to enjoy embarrassing me by flirting with me. She quickly identified my naiveté and would flirt with me shamelessly enjoying every blush and every drop of perspiration she caused. I was too embarrassed to mention it to my father or brother. Whenever my father told me he had to make a delivery there, part of me groaned in frustration, but not the other part.

Being around Mei Sam brings back all of those feelings. Fortunately, at nighttime my breathing routine helped me get past my body chemistry and physiology before they betrayed me and I'm able to get some sleep. During the day we avoid roads and use as much natural cover as we can find. When we stop at the end of the day, I ask her to start a cooking fire while I go off hunting and gathering more wood.

I hear Mei Sam scream and run back to our camp to find two men holding her down while a third is pulling down his pants about to climb on top of her. At the edge of the clearing I yell, "You bad man, go now soon yes."

The men begin laughing. The large man who is pulling his pants down begins pulling them back up. "Boys, you just keep her here for me."

"He must be her kid brother."

I look at this man approaching me and detect blocked Chi in his Bladder meridian. He demonstrates no brightness or mental agility common in many sharing the Water sign. He shows the type of determination that triumphs with weak competition, but against any real strength, he wilts like a melon left by the side of the road.

He picks up a large stick and walks toward me. The next thing he notices is that he's using the stick as a cane because his left knee is shattered. The other two men jump up. One grabs a knife from his belt and the other bends down and picks up a large rock. One is knocked unconscious by the large rock he remembers carrying a few seconds ago while the other is struggling to pull out his knife which is now embedded deep into his thigh.

"I kill now, yes?"

All three fall to their knees, assume a prayerful position and shake their heads "no." Although my English is far from adequate I understand fear, tears and begging. Those are universals.

"Tell girl sorry."

"We're sorry, miss."

"You come back?"

They shake their heads as if they're choreographed. They resume their prayerful pose. "You go now?"

The three men shake their heads and I let them limp away as the two with leg injuries help the one with the head injury. "Never seen nothing like that. Hell no, not coming back here for more of that. Guy was like an army."

"I hope their injuries are serious enough to make them question their path through life. I wish I had more than pain to rehabilitate them."

I'm holding the new addition to my new knife collection. Mei Sam runs over and grabs me tightly. Her body is shaking and her tears are flowing. She can't stop thanking me for saving her. "How did you do all that so quickly?"

"I don't know. I just got mad and I guess I reacted. It was instinct."

As we're ready to go to sleep she leans over. "Everybody wants to rape me except you."

"I think you'll rape me before I rape you."

She throws a handful of small stones at me. I think I fell asleep long before she did.

By the end of the next day we approach Sacramento. "Who do you want to see here?"

"I want to visit the kind old shopkeeper I told you about and two close girlfriends, but I definitely don't want to see my cousin."

"We agree on part of your plan and not about the other parts. We'll definitely see the old shopkeeper, but we disagree from there. I think it would be foolish to see your two friends because they might accidentally give us away. You know how young girls love to talk."

Mei Sam punches me in the arm. "It's sad but you're right about avoiding my friends."

"It's essential that we see your cousin."

"No! I hate him for selling me."

"I'm sure the people from the mine who bought you will come to see him first as they search for you. We don't know what he might tell them. We need to convince him he should tell them absolutely nothing. I know you don't trust him, but I'll trust him a lot more after we have a talk with him."

On the way to see her cousin, two men are walking up the street toward us. One of the men lowers his shoulder and bumps into me. "Hey Chinks, you're in our way. Walk on the other side of the street ... now."

I bow, take Mei Sam's hand, and drag her across the street as I say in a low voice, "If a dog was walking toward them on the street, they wouldn't have made it cross over, but insisted that we do. We don't have the rights of a dog here. They don't know us ... even a little. Why are they consumed with so much hate for us?"

"If they're so terrible, why did you let them bully you? I've seen you fight. You could have smashed their heads in."

"For what purpose? Would it have made them hate us less? You shouldn't fight unless there's no other way. It was easier for us to walk across the street. See, we didn't get hurt. Neither did the two men. Everybody wins. Fighting for pride is stupid." Mei Sam looks disappointed.

We walk to a tiny shack on the edge of the city. A dim candle is the only light source. The cabin has a small bed, a broken table with two old chairs. The place is filthy. Mei Sam walks in while I wait outside the door. I want to observe how he reacts to seeing her.

"What the Hell are you doing here? I sold you. If you escaped this is the first place they'll come looking for you. That could put me in danger. I can't have 'em think I had anything to do with you escaping. I'm taking you back right now." He grabs Mei Sam by the arm and starts dragging her out the door. I'm in my slouching stance making myself look as small as possible. When he opens the door he almost bumps into me. "Who the hell is this kid? Out of my way boy."

A quick glance at Mei Sam's cousin makes it clear his Chi is blocked in his Colon meridian. I was willing to wager that constipation is his constant visitor. He shows none of the ambition associated with his Metal sign.

"I was curious to see how you'd react when you saw your cousin. What kind of man sells a member of his own family into a life of prostitution? A young girl who's just lost both parents?"

"Listen kid, I don't know who the hell you think you are, but get out of my way before I get mad."

I step in front of him and he takes a step back and grabs a small knife from a shelf next to the door. "I'm gonna' cut the ears off your little boy friend here and take you back to the mine." He tries to slice me with his knife. I grab a chair and use it to push him down to the floor and grab the knife out of his hand. Sitting on the chair with him underneath it, I close the knife and toss it to Mei Sam. Another addition to my new knife collection.

After my successful experience with the Tong member aboard the ship, I decide to use a wrist joint lock again. As I begin twisting his hand, her cousin is convulsing in pain. With tears streaming down his face he begs me to stop. I keep my hold as I'm sitting on the chair that's pinning him down on the floor.

I twist his wrist a bit more. "You're a very rude man. How much did the mining company pay you for your cousin?"

"Twelve pieces of gold."

"Where did you hide them?"

"Sir, I'm very sorry. I spent two of the pieces already. There are only ten pieces left. They're under a loose board there ... under the table. Please stop hurting me."

I ask Mei Sam to pry the board loose and she holds the ten gold pieces in her hand. I ask him, "What do *you* think we should do with this gold? Do you think your cousin should keep it to help make up for the pain you caused her?"

"Perhaps I could keep just one coin and give her the other nine?"

I twist his wrist a little more. "No, wait, she should have them all."

Mei Sam smiles and puts them in her pocket.

"That's very generous of you. Now, I agree with you that the men you sold her to will come here looking for her. Your job is to be stunned when they tell you she's escaped. You'll tell them you have no idea of her whereabouts regardless of what they say or do to you. Do you agree?"

He shakes his head up and down.

"I'm afraid that's not good enough. Have you ever been beaten up?"

Her cousin tries to inch away so I twist his wrist a little harder. He stops. "Yes, a few times."

"When you got a bad beating, how long did the effects of that beating last?"

"I limped around and was in pain for about a week. By then most of the pain was gone."

"I'm going to ask you to think like a man of science. If the number 1 represents a punch that you can barely feel and a 10 represents so much pain that you would prefer to die than to remain in that state, how much pain were you in from that bad beating?"

"A lot."

"You act like you didn't understand me … I want you to give me a number from 1 to 10."

"I guess number 7 or maybe an 8 would represent a really brutal beating."

"I'm about to help you experience *serious* pain for four seconds. Then I'll make it stop."

Before the poor man could react, I pulled the chair off him, placed my hand over his mouth to silence him, then used my middle knuckle to jab a place on his chest and he jumps. His eyes open very wide and he almost passes out. After the four seconds I touch another point and the pain stops. He falls to the floor, but never takes his eyes off me. He continues to shake and releases his bladder. He's sobbing.

"Using our 1-to-10 scale of pain, I'd say that was a 14. I can make it go much higher." I get down on one knee and grab her cousin by his ears, pulling him to within six inches of my face. As I squeeze his ears I shake them just a little. "Listen to me *very* carefully. If I find out that you said even a single word about having seen Mei Sam or me, or that you have any idea of our whereabouts, I'll come back and inflict that pain again, but I won't make it stop. Instead, I'll make it much worse. Do you understand me?"

Mei Sam's cousin is crying and feebly nodding his head up-and-down.

I want you to think about something. If you had been nice to Mei Sam, none of this pain would have happened to you. I'm going to check back here in a few months. If I hear that you've become a better person, I'll take you out to fine restaurant for dinner. If I find out that you are still a nasty, miserable person doing terrible things … take my word for it, you will not like the results. This is not a suggestion … it's a warning.

As we're walking out I silently thanked my father for teaching me so much about the workings of the body. As a healer, I suppose I should feel guilty for using my skills to inflict pain, but I know I'm trying to use it for a greater good. But I still feel feeble about trying to get this man to become a better person. Leaving him with a threat hanging over his head is an embarrassingly impoverished idea. That just shows the scarcity of the arrows in my quiver. I think my mother would have had a better way to deal with this awful man's soul. She had such good insights into people. I only have skills with their muscles, tendons and bones.

When we were out of her cousin's shack, Mei Sam grabs my arm and spins me around, "Just who the hell are you? How did you learn to do what you just did to my cousin?"

"Give me a moment to think."

Until three days ago, I was formulating a plan to get back to China. All it would require is finding a way to escape from the Sam Ping Mining Company, move from the Chinatown in one city to the Chinatown in another until I accumulated enough money with my healing skills to afford a ticket home, then ask Tu Chan to help me book passage under a new identity. Admittedly, the plan had one or two rough spots, but I was early in the planning phase when a needy fifteen-year-old girl was dumped in my lap.

If I abandon her here in Sacramento, in the care of the nice man we're about to visit, she'll surely end up being caught, brought back to the mine for punishment and end up as a prostitute. I despise her cousin for what he did to her but I would be no better than him, consigning her to that fate. Her rotten cousin sold this 15 year-old girl into a life of prostitution right after her parents had been killed in a riot. I have an image of my face on his body.

Just a few short months ago she was growing up within a secure family and now she's totally alone in the world. I stop walking and grab her shoulders. "Mei Sam, I have no idea where I'm going, or what I'm gong to do next. I've only been in America for a short time and I never planned for any of this. My only goal has been to figure out a way to get myself back to China, but right now I'm terrified about what'll happen to you if I abandon you here. Would you like to continue travelling with me until you can figure out what you're going to do?"

She begins to cry and hugs me. "Thank you. I don't know you very well, but from what I've seen, you're very weird, but a good person and I feel safe when I'm with you. And wherever you go seems better than becoming a prostitute ... which seems to be the only other alternative I have. Now let's get back to who the hell are you?"

"It's a complicated story. For now let's go see the one person who was nice to you."

When father was teaching me to fall properly as part of my martial arts training, he showed me that keeping my body relaxed makes the fall less painful. Traveling with this girl will delay my return to China and reunite with my family. If I let this delay upset me, every part of my life will become more painful. I will have to flow with these changes and accept them as part of a new path and relax into it.

"The Viceroy walks into the Jade Room. I just received word that Lo Wan has escaped from the mine with a young girl."

The Chancellor slams his hand down on the table. "Fools. They had one simple job to do and failed. Find a way to punish the owners of the mining company, make sure the mine owners are financially ruined."

The Viceroy was pacing. "What should we do about the young healer?"

"Before you ruin the mining company, make sure they notify the authorities that he escaped and owes the company years of salary. We might as well have the American authorities helping us. Meanwhile, assemble a team of skilled men to travel to America to track him down. I knew I would have to do everything myself."

Chapter 4

We walk to the shopkeeper's store. "I'm looking forward to meeting someone who showed you some kindness."

The shop is closed and the lights are off. Mei Sam walks around to the back and knocks gently. A lamp is lit and a plump old Chinese man with a full gray beard motions us to walk around to the front. She grabs my arm and pulls me in close and whispers, "Stand up straight, don't slouch, and talk on the low side of your voice."

When the old man recognizes Mei Sam he beams and hugs her. She introduces me as her rescuer.

The old man shows no signs of Chi blockage and his Wood sign radiates the benevolence associated with this type of element. This is the first time I feel like I can relax since finding myself in America.

The inside of the old man's store looks like a Chinese New Year parade began marching through his store and decided to stay. There are hundreds of small boxes containing herbs and candies … all of them in brightly colored boxes and trays. It's the happiest place I've ever stepped into. I can't stop smiling. The old man reaches into a barrel and offers Mei Sam a sweet. Then he goes back and gets one for me.

When we sit, he says, "I heard what your pig of a cousin did to you. I'll never forgive him for such a greedy, mean-hearted act." The old man locks the front door and we go in the back to talk. Mei Sam fills him in on what's happened.

He shows me around the store and I'm happy the man sells sweets, but he's also an herbalist. I feel at home with the familiar smells and sights.

"Venerable sir, pardon me for being so forward but I notice that when you walk, your right hip dips low to one side and produces a noticeable limp. It appears to cause you pain."

"Lo Wan, stop that. You're embarrassing me. Be polite. He's my friend."

"Do you by any chance have a set of acupuncture needles?"

"An old healer traded some to me for some herbs months ago. I have no use for them. Acupuncture is a skill I never learned."

"Would you be kind enough to bring them to me along with some alcohol."

He hands me the needles. "Please lay down and remove your trousers."

Without hesitation, the man follows my request. Mei Sam averts her eyes and blushes.

I rub the old man down with alcohol and I place the first needle into the old man's hip."

"Stop that. You're hurting my friend." She's embarrassed when we both laugh at her reaction.

I spend the next four minutes placing needles into his hip and leg. I even place two needles into his head. It's difficult for Mei Sam to watch. After I place them, I find a few pieces of cotton, wrap a small piece around several of the needles and light the cotton on each one. That's enough to cause Mei Sam to leave the room in tears. I leave the needles burning for two minutes and then extinguished them. I twist a few of the other needles. Then I tell the old man to relax and I'll return in ten minutes. I leave the room and join Mei Sam in the other room. "If you hurt my friend, I'll never forgive you. And I really want to know, just who the hell are you?"

"I'm a healer. What you saw in the other room is a procedure called acupuncture. It's been used throughout China for centuries. It took me years of dedicated study to learn. My father's a healer and taught me. My brother's also a healer. My mother also practiced the healing arts. It's very rare to find women healers, but my mother was very special."

"Whenever there was a complicated birthing in our village, my mother was there to help. You know better than me that females don't receive the same level of respect and care men do. My mother made it her mission to treat women who needed her help. She was very compassionate. Not a day goes by that her memory doesn't inspire me. She died from a rare disease she caught from someone she was trying to help. She'll always be my spiritual mentor."

After ten minutes, I go back and remove the needles. I ask the old man to turn on to his other side and begin doing an acupressure treatment for balancing the two sides. Then I call Mei Sam in ... after the old man has replaced his pants. "Please walk across the room."

After taking a few tentative steps, he begins to walk more freely. Then he begins to hop up-and-down and then skips a few steps. Then he walks over and embraces me. "Look at the miraculous gift you've me in return for a piece of candy." The old man quickly gathers up the needles, washes them off with alcohol and runs back inside the store. After a minute he hands me the pack of needles, after carefully gift-wrapping them. "Please accept this meager gift. You've given me back my youth." The old man has tears in his eyes. Mei Sam is staring at me.

The old man asks us to sit at the table while he prepares some food. He's an excellent cook and it was the first real meal either of us has eaten in a long time. Then we begin talking about the fact that we can't stay in Sacramento because it's the first place the men from the mining company will scour looking for Mei Sam. We ask the old man if he has any advice.

"My old friend Li Ting lives in Stockton. It's about fifty miles from here so it'll be quite a trek, but no one will think to look for you there. And certainly, no one will know you in Stockton. You'll both be safe there. My friend is an herbalist, although he's much older than you, I don't think his skills are as sophisticated as yours, but never mention I said that."

"I'll write a letter introducing you telling him you would like to apprentice with him. He's a very proud man so I would suggest that you begin your relationship with this little ruse in mind. Soon the two of you will balance things out. He has a very big heart." With that the old man took out paper and pen and wrote the letter. He says he'll post it in tomorrow morning's mail. "I told him you'd arrive in about three days. It'll take at least that long to walk to Stockton. Here's his address. The two of you will spend the night as guests here in my home and leave at first light."

The old man lights a candle and shows the two of us into his room and he spends the night on two chairs pushed together in his shop. Although we insist the old man sleep in his own bed, he insists that we take it.

For the first time Mei Sam and I have the opportunity to wash before going to sleep. We climb under the thick blanket. The large bed takes up almost the entire room and we each move to our own end of the bed and try to go to sleep. Mei Sam turns toward me and says, "You smell really nice."

"Move a little closer so I can smell you. She moves way closer than smelling range and for the first time we hold each other. We didn't release each other when the sniffing ended.

"Would it be considered a rape if I were to kiss you?"

"I won't know until you do it."

We spend a long time kissing each other. We are afraid our breathing will awaken the old man. Then our hands begin to explore. It is all happening very slowly, as if someone is given a small, rare delicacy and is eating it little-by-little to make it last as long as possible. We touch each other over our bedclothes everywhere it's possible to touch. Then our hands stray under our bedclothes. Her hand strays down to my thigh and I gasp. She quickly withdraws her hand thinking she has done something wrong until I touch her thigh and she understands what my gasp means. She quickly replaces her hand so I won't remove mine.

Innocence produces its own magic and throughout the night we explore each other's bodies until we stumble across the concept of release. If this was a wedding night, it would not have been technically considered "consummated," but it was the best night that either of us have ever had. We will remember it throughout our lives.

In the morning the three of us share a pleasant morning meal. There are thanks and good wishes all around and we leave just before the sun comes up.

I'm surprised by how quiet Mei Sam is. We leave Sacramento and continue avoiding major roads on our way to the new city. "We have an important decision to make. We have two choices in how we present ourselves to Li Ting. Would you prefer being introduced as my sister or my wife?"

"We don't look alike in any way. I don't think anyone would believe we were born into the same family."

"So that settles it. We'll pretend to be husband and wife. After spending last night with you, I hardly feel like it's pretending." She walks over and kisses me on the cheek. "But there's much more I want to talk to you about. I have so much on my mind."

I remember all the warnings I'd heard about how females only focus on wanting to get married and have a family. I think, "Here comes *the talk*."

"I want to become your student. I want to learn about herbs. I also want to know how to defend myself. Will you teach me?"

I wonder if she can hear my sigh of relief? "Let's start right now. See that plant growing under this tree. It's called Ginseng. It increases mental and physical energy. Pick a few samples and we'll keep them in our bundle. And tonight, I'll give you your first lesson in self defense."

"How long until I can give you a sound beating?"

"That could take weeks."

"She's a girl. Stop trying to make her into a boy. You'll only be creating a life of pain for her."

Mei Sam was born on her parents' farm. It wasn't really their farm. A white farmer gave them food and a place to live and four dollars a month in pay in exchange for the crops they grew. He was a nice man and her parents were hard workers. Both sides felt it was a fair deal.

By the time she was five, her greatest pleasure was to go out into the fields with her father and help him. "Mei Sam, see all of those weeds in the radish patch. Can you pull them out?" She rushed in and attacked the weeds ferociously. A few times the weeds were so big that she had to use all her weight to pull them out. When they gave way she'd fall backwards. She and her father would both laugh.

Every night after Mei Sam was asleep her mother cornered her father. "She acts more like a boy than a girl. She idolizes you so much she resists every attempt I make to raise her as a girl."

"Mei Sam, take this needle and thread. Your hands are big enough to sew."

"I don't want to sew, I'm a farmer!" Mei Sam resisted "girl" tasks and begged to spend more time with her father until her mother put her foot down.

She pulled her father into their bedroom and pleaded. Through her tears she said, "Please, if you keep her in the fields all day with you she'll never grow up to be anyone's wife. I know you wanted a boy. So did I, but she's who we got. If we were in China now I'd begin binding her feet so she could marry into a rich family. She's a very pretty little girl. I just want her to have a better life by making a good marriage for her. This'll never happen if she keeps pretending to be a boy."

Her father reluctantly agreed and Mei Sam spent every day in the house with her mother. She learned to cook, clean and sew. Their compromise was that on Sundays, she could go out in the fields with her father.

"Eew, what's that stuff you're spreading on the onions? It smells awful."

"It's fertilizer. It makes the plants grow faster and stronger. It's like food for them."

"Why do you water some plants more than the other ones?"

"Some have larger roots and require more water."

"I want to know about every plant so that I may grow up to be a good farmer like you."

Four weeks before her fifteenth birthday her parents went to Sacramento to visit friends. There was an anti-Chinese rally that day. It suddenly turned violent and both her parents were killed. No one was arrested even though the riot left twelve Chinese dead. Her cousin, who lived in Sacramento, took her in. No one thought that was a good idea.

As we walk along the trail, I show her three more plants used in different types of healing. "And that's the end of our herb lesson for today."

"No. I can learn more. That's only four plants. Don't you think I'm smart enough to learn more?"

"If I didn't think you were smart enough, I would have stopped at the second plant. Four plants doesn't sound like much now, but after another day that'll be eight plants. Soon they'll all start to look alike unless you spend enough time learning the intricacies of each. Don't be impatient. Learn as much as you can about each of these four. Learn them by sight, by feel, by smell and by taste. Be able to differentiate them with your eyes closed. You'll have to differentiate hundreds of plants, how to prepare each one, know its uses and its dangers. There are no shortcuts. A mistake can be fatal. It takes a lifetime of discipline. I sound like my father when I talk like this."

"I hope I meet him some day. He sounds like an incredible man."

Mei Sam's comment sinks my mood. I wonder if I'll ever see my father again. So much has happened to me in such a short time that my mind always seems to be engaged in how to survive, but during quiet moments, I recognize the emptiness of being without my family. To improve my mood, I walk up to Mei Sam and throw a punch at her face. She screams, jumps back and turns her head away. Barely a second later, she swings one of her arms as if she's shooing a fly.

"Excellent. You did exactly what an untrained person would do if attacked. I noticed that you barely tried to hit me back."

"I couldn't. You were too far away."

"True, but it didn't help that your eyes were closed. Not a good way to defend yourself."

"Take a good look at how I'm holding my arm. Now I'm going to swing my arm across my body from right-to-left. Try it."

She repeats my movement. "Good. Now very slowly, punch me in the face and I'll repeat this motion. It's called an Outside-In mid-block. Notice what happens." She goes to punch me slowly and my arm blocks her punch. "I'm still here. I didn't have to run away."

"Now punch my face again, but harder." As she does, I blocked her punch faster and a bit harder. Now let's reverse roles. I'll try to punch your face very slowly and you try this new movement to block my punch."

As I go to punch her face, she's able to block my punch. I punch a bit faster and she's able to block me again.

"Excellent. Now this time, you try to punch me in the face again, but this time, you can try it with either hand. Notice I'll do the same block from both sides using the arm that's closer to your punch."

She starts punching me slowly. As before, I block her. She switches hands and so do I. She begins to punch faster and harder. I have no problem blocking her. Now we switch roles.

"This is fun."

"Here's the really fun part. I want you to take one swing at my head again and see what happens."

She swings, I block her punch and before she realizes what's happened, my fist stops just short of her nose. "Notice by blocking, I not only protect myself, but I can immediately clear a path to go on the attack. You did great for a first lesson. Let's get some rest. We'll have a busy day walking, picking herbs and then fighting for a while."

"What about the way we attacked each other last night in bed?"

"That's a type of attacking I think we both have to learn more about. We're both students, but I know I'm willing to practice."

At the end of a three-day walk, we find ourselves entering the city of Stockton. I pull out the paper with Li Ting's address. We knock on his door and an older gentleman wearing an elegant black silk robe with dragon and phoenix embroidery welcomes us in. "I've been expecting you. Won't you share my morning meal?"

Li Ting's shop is a model of efficiency. Jars of herbs are arranged by type and clearly labeled. I sense a slight lowering of Chi going to his Liver meridian. It's not a substantial blockage, but detectable. I look forward to balancing it for him. It causes him excess stress. I think as a Wood sign, Li Ting tends to be troubled by anxiety and anger, but he seems adept at hiding it from most people. It's like he's wearing a mask that he rarely removes and is comfortable within.

After a warm conversation and an extravagant meal, Li Ting says, "I didn't want to turn you away hungry, but I don't need an apprentice. Thank you for visiting me. I wish you both good fortune in your next endeavor." He opens the door and shows us out before we realize what's happening.

Chapter 5

As we're walking the streets trying to make sense out of what just happened we hear a man screaming and many men screaming back at him. We turn a corner, follow the sound and see the screamer standing on a large wooden box. We hide in an alley where we can hear everything, but avoid being seen.

"Many of you are here today because you don't have a job. Why? Cause some goddamn Coolie took it. He robbed you of the opportunity you should have to work. And this is not one Coolie and one job. There's thousands and thousands of 'em. Are you as fed up with this as I am?"

The crowd shakes their fists and shouts.

"These damn Coolies'll work longer hours for way less money. Why? Cause they got no families to support, no children to feed, no wives to come home to, no rent to pay. So they can work cheap ... and that means *you're* not going to be getting *any* work. That fair?"

"NO!"

"You can't even walk near that cesspool of a Chinee town they built here. The smell alone'll kill ya'. And have ya' seen how they lust after yer women?"

The crowd screams at every pause.

Our English is not very good, but we get the gist of what this crowd is yelling about. We stay hidden in the alley waiting for the crowd to disperse.

A man on the fringe of the crowd says, "Anyone seen Ryan? Anybody seen my kid?"

"He was runnin' down the street chasin' after his dog."

"Flasher, c'mere you little rascal." Ryan lost sight of his dog. I shove Mei Sam further into the dark alley until the dog and child pass. I keep stroking Mei Sam's hair to keep her calm. The small dog is sniffing and walks into the mouth of the alley.

Mei Sam says, "Isn't there a place on his spine where you can make him unable to bark?"

"Sorry, my father never showed me how to silence dogs."

"If the damn government won't protect us, we're gonna' have to protect ourselves so we're gonna' meet here tonight at midnight and we're gonna' have us some *real* justice. If you feel like we do, come'n join us. We're gonna' git our jobs back and make things fair again. America for Americans ... not Chinks!"

The little dog runs farther into they alley toward us. I try rolling a few small stones into another part of the alley away from us to distract him while I keep nudging Mei Sam farther in.

"Kill the Chinks ... kill em all."

The dog turns to look at the place where the stones land, then keeps following our scent. The boy sees his dog and runs toward him. Then we hear him yell, "There's Chinks hidin' here."

Several men come running over and pull us out. "A couple of Chinks been hidin' here listening. What should we do with em?"

As the group around us gets bigger someone yells, "Let's beat the crap out of 'em."

"Why not beat the crap out of the little feller here and have some fun with his girl."

I push Mei Sam behind me. I hold my hands up indicating I don't want any trouble. I speak on the higher side of my voice. "Please leave alone."

The men laugh as they drag us out of the alley. "Mei Sam, remain still. If we try to fight back we'll get seriously injured."

"Please no hurt us."

One of the men begins pushing me aside to get to Mei Sam. One of them throws her to the ground and two men begin fighting to see who gets to ravage her first. I wedge myself in front of her to shield her. Billy Carney, the man who was screaming on the wooden box walks up. "What's goin' on here boys?"

"Look what we found. They was hidin' here listening."

Carney sticks his finger in my chest. "What do you think of what I said?"

"Please no hurt us."

"I think they were hearin', but not understandin'. They's hidin' cause they didn't want us to find 'em. They's just in the wrong place at the wrong time, but that don't mean we can't have a little fun with 'em. He grabs me and pushes me toward one of the other men. That man pushes me toward another. The men have formed a circle and everybody's laughing and as they shove me around. Someone sticks out a leg and I trip and fall down. Someone picks me up and shoves me into the circle again."

"How about the girl?"

"We don't dirty our hands with their female trash. Do you want to get the clap? Do you want to make a half Chinese kid that looks a little like you? Look, we've got a big night tonight. Fun's over here." He punches me in the stomach and I scream, then begin to cough as I collapse. He grabs me by the shirt and brings his face five inches from mine. "You come round here again and we'll string you up from a telegraph pole." He turns back toward the circle. "Remember, revenge is on the menu at midnight." They disperse leaving me on the ground with Mei Sam crying over me.

I'm on the ground not moving. After the last man leaves, Mei Sam bends down to help and finds me smiling. "Are you alright?"

"Sure. They never hurt me."

"I saw that man punch you in the stomach really hard."

"I began falling backwards as he went to hit me so I only received a small fraction of the power of his punch. I tensed my stomach so the result is the same as if I slap you on the back to say 'hello. By moaning and coughing I helped him put on a show of hurting me.'"

"Why didn't you fight back?"

"If I had, there were fifty men who'd jump on me trying to destroy me. Those aren't good odds. I let them think they were hurting and frightening me so they could walk away feeling good about themselves, and I'm walking away without having gotten hurt.

"Why do you always talk like a fortune cookie?"

I grab Mei Sam's arm. "We have to hurry and warn the people in Stockton's Chinatown about what's going to happen."

When we get there we tell everyone we meet about the coming threat. "Those street corner mobs stand outside and yell all the time. Since these white men don't have jobs they have lots of free time for this kind of screaming." No one seems particularly interested in what we consider terrifying news.

Billy Carney enters his favorite bar and sits with three cronies. "Remember, we don't want any killin' tonight. What we want is to send 'em a message ... a powerful one."

"Then let's burn down a Chinese house or two."

"Nah, if anyone's in the house, they'll die. We don't want any murders ... tonight."

"Then let's find one or two Chinks walking the streets and beat the crap out of em'. We can leave 'em in a condition where they're unfit to perform any labor. Break some hands or arms ... or both."

"Yeh, now that's what I'm talkin' bout. And when we finish we can pin a note on em' telling em' to get out, or we'll have to teach 'em some more of these 'lessons.'"

"And we're damn good teachers." They all laugh and clank their beer tankards in a toast.

An hour later, Carney walks downtown looking over his shoulder to make sure he isn't followed. He ducks into Judge Sullivan's office. Carney looks out of place seated at a carved mahogany desk on a luxurious Sarouk Persian rug. Leather bound books line the oak paneled bookcases. The judge is wearing a stylish suit and silk tie with a diamond stickpin. Carney tries to sit down as lightly as possible on the leather chair.

"You're late Carney. I hope you have some good news. How did your rally go?"

"By the time I finished they were ready to eat Chinese food made out of real Chinamen."

"Remember, nobody dies tonight. Our goal is to rile things up. Enough to stimulate significant retribution by the Chinese. We need to stir things up, but not cook them. We want the majority of people in Stockton to demand the removal of the Chinese. Then, as their new senator, I can step in and lead that removal. This has to occur in stages."

"You know I'll do everything I can to help you get elected, but before I leave, I think you owe me a bit of money for expenses. And don't forget my salary ... here, you can give it to me under your table." Carney laughs at his own joke.

With no sign of appreciating the attempt at humor, Judge Sullivan opens a drawer, extracts an envelope, and hands it to him.

"We gave these people in Chinatown some crucial information and they ignored it. You know what? That's just what happened with Li Ting. We're going back to talk to him."

"What are you talking about?"

"Just follow me."

We knock on the door and Li Ting acts surprised to see us. "I thought our business was concluded. What can I do for you, *this* time?"

Your friend in Sacramento described you as an accomplished herbalist, but more importantly, told us you were a very kind man. Your behavior this morning didn't reflect either trait. It didn't make sense that a compassionate man would share a fine meal with us and then turn us out without providing any advice or encouragement. We'll come back to that point. A quick look around your store demonstrates your commitment to herbalism. Someone so dedicated wouldn't turn away a prospective apprentice before finding out if he had any skills that might prove useful ... especially given that there would be so little financial risk for you."

"And if you really are an exceedingly kind man, the way you were described, you wouldn't turn away two people with no resources who were new to Stockton and had no other alternatives. I suspect that you were testing us to see how we'd react. "

"How did you arrive at that conclusion?"

"Although I was doing the talking, I noticed you directed your responses to Mei Sam and your left hand was exhibiting a slight tremor the entire time. I was impressed with how well you hid it. More importantly, a good herbalist has a natural curiosity about anything that concerns herbs, yet you didn't ask us any questions about herbs or try to figure out if we had any information that might prove valuable to you."

"To put an end to this awkward conversation, permit me to make our request easier for you to grant. We don't require a definitive yes-or-no response. Just give us a short trial period and let's see how we progress from there. And if you do, as an additional incentive, I'm skilled at massage therapy. I believe I can help with some of the aches and pains I detected from observing your posture."

"Li Ting breaks into a smile. I'm impressed. You've succeeded in obtaining your trial apprenticeship. There's a little shed behind the shop where I store some old junk. We, meaning you, may clean it out and that'll be your trial accommodations. I'll find you a bed and give you some blankets. Go out and begin preparing your new home. I'll see you at the evening meal."

Mei Sam smiled at me.

———————————

At eleven that evening, Carney is guzzling beers with three of his friends. "I brought a pile of kindling, rags and lamp oil. I stashed it all behind the bar."

"Why'd you bring all that?"

"To burn down half of Chinatown."

Carney slapped his friend on the shoulder. "Whoa there. I love your enthusiasm, but I told you that's not our purpose tonight. If we burn down any part of Chinatown the trail'll lead back to us. Our goal is to provide a little justice so them Chinks will want to get them some revenge. When they cause trouble for us, we can go in and mop them up in response. Tonight's goal is to make them afraid and mad at the same time. This first step is to rile up all of our own people who show up at midnight so we can make our statement with enthusiasm."

By the time we showed up for dinner, we were drenched in sweat, grimy and exhausted. But, we had a place to live that was our own. We walked into the shop. Li Ting took one whiff and directed us to wash and change before we came to eat. We ran out behind the shack, undressed and washed. We'd never seen each other naked. Both of us were embarrassed and looked away, hurried to wash and rushed back for another of Li Ting's tasty meals.

"How'd you learn to cook so well?"

"I've been an herbalist my entire adult life. As an herbalist yourself, if you were asked to calculate the average taste of all the herbs you've sampled, what would be the result?"

"Although there are a few tasty, aromatic herbs, most range from bland to nauseating. I'll never get back the hours trying to persuade people to take them, even when they knew the results would make them feel better."

"Well put. I studied the culinary arts as my emotional antidote to their taste."

I got into bed right away, but Mei Sam fussed about in the room and kept peeking in to see if I'd fallen asleep. Noticing her discomfort, I rolled over and feigned sleep. After a few minutes, she got into bed. I rolled over, "Would you like to tell me what's troubling you?"

"Well...you know girls talk a lot. A week before I was taken to the mine, an older girlfriend had 'the talk' with me. She explained how babies were made. The other night you spilled your seed into my hand. It was a magical evening and that was a perfect way to end it. But the way my friend explained it, if you had put your tree in my dark mossy place and placed your seed inside me...well that's how babies are made. I'm fifteen years old and not ready to be a mother. Seeing you outside with no clothes on scared me. If you decided to rape me..." She began to cry. "I'm afraid of having a baby."

I laughed.

"Are you laughing at me because you think I'm a stupid little girl?"

"I admit to laughing at you, but it's a laugh of affection. First of all, I really do care for you, and I never will or would rape you. If my 'tree' were to ever enter your 'moss,' it would be by invitation only. Second you are not my wife and I don't want you to bear my child. That may change in the future, but certainly not at this time. If we ever do 'fulfill our marriage' by having my private parts enter yours, I'm smart enough to know that I must withdraw from you well before my seed is spilled. I may be naïve in my direct, firsthand knowledge about being physical with girls, but my knowledge about the mechanics of the process of fertilization is quite sophisticated. And, if you were to accidentally become pregnant, as a healer I know of many ways to end a pregnancy harmlessly before a child would ever appear...and with no injury to you. Please go to sleep tonight knowing that you're totally safe on at least this one account."

I gently kiss her cheek, move to my side of our little bed and begin my customary breathing ritual, but with a broad smile on my face. She rolls over and finds that sleep eludes her for several hours. Unlike me, she can't get her breathing under control.

At midnight, more than a dozen men show up at the town square. One man yells, "Let's go kill us some Chinks." The men begin cheering and Carney quickly raises both arms to quiet them. "Shhh, we don't want to attract any attention."

Carney continues in a lowered voice. "I'm proud to see so many brave White patriots here. Tonight we take real action, but there's not gonna' be *no* killin'. We don't want no police to get involved. We're gonna' be *creative*. We'll create fear, create anger and create confusion. We want every Coolie to look over his shoulder every time he walks down a street in Stockton. We want him to worry 'bout someone jumpin' out'a nowhere and cripplin' him so he can't ever work again. We want him to sh_t his pants every time he hears a strange noise. That's much better for us than killin' … *this time*."

"We wanna' provoke the Chinks into action. We want to get *them* to try to get revenge against us. That's what we want cause the minute they do, whatever we do back to them'll be self-defense." They were all nodding their heads and protruding their elbows into neighboring rib cages laughing.

"Our goal tonight is to catch us two or three of them Chinks, beat the crap out of 'em and fix it so they can't work for at least the next six or eight months. And if we're lucky, we'll piss 'em off enough so that some of 'em come into our neighborhoods with weapons. That's how we'll know we really succeeded. Remember, there's lots more of us than them. They'll bring rakes and we'll greet 'em with guns. Let's head on into Chinatown and have us some fun revengin'."

The mob walks through town until they reach the edge of Stockton's Chinatown. "Shhh … keep the noise down so we don't scare 'em into stayin' inside. There's a red shack down at the end of this street where they gamble. Chinks're fiends for gambling. Like animals who can't control themselves. They cheat you out of a job and that's where *your* money goes. We'll just wait for two or three drunk ones to come stumblin' out. They're the ones we're gonna' bust up."

Carney gets them to quiet down as they approach the red shack. They all hide behind nearby buildings until two Chinese men come staggering out. "Shh … let's follow 'em for a block or two to make sure no one else's around."

When they find a quiet spot, four of the men grab the two confused Chinese men. "Someone go through their pockets and see if they won any money." As one of the Chinese men tries to pull loose, a man backhands him across the face then another punches him in the gut. He slumps into the arms of the men holding him. A hand reaches into his pocket and pulls out a handful of coins.

"I guess this one was a winner. He'll pay for a few pitchers of beer tonight." He made a mock 'thank you' gesture toward the semi-conscious man. Seeing this, the other man tries to wrench himself away. He gets punched in the face and goes limp into another set of men's arms, but he has no money.

Carney says, "Lay each of them on the ground with their arms spread apart. Hold 'em there until we're sure they're both fully conscious. I want 'em to be aware of everything that's happenin' to 'em. I want 'em to tell their story over-and-over."

"I need four men who're wearing heavy boots." Four large men step forward. "OK, you two stomp on this one's hands and you two do the other's. Keep in mind that if you don't stomp hard enough, next week they may be stealing your jobs and your kids'll go hungry."

They gag the two men and begin stomping. Both unfortunate Chinamen try to scream as their hands are pulverized. They leave the two men on the ground weeping. "Everyone go home now, unless you want to join us at Clancy's for a pint. Good job … all of you. We struck a blow for America."

Police whistles are heard in the distance. By the time they get there, they only find the two Chinese men with bloodied hands and a note explaining what happened and why, pinned to their clothes.

Toward the end of our second week at the shop, Li Ting invites me for a walk to a nearby meadow. It's a place that has an abundance of herbs. "Lo Wan, see if you can locate some licorice plants. They look like this."

In a few minutes, I bring back some licorice and also drop some goldenseal into Li Ting's sack. "I think you might find this goldenseal helpful. When I first tasted it, I thought I should take up cooking myself."

"What's it good for?"

"It's bitter, but it can calm nerves. It also treats some skin diseases, intestinal infections and even helps relieve sleep problems. The biggest problem I've found is that in large doses, it causes diarrhea." We both laugh. "This meadow is amazing. It's full of all sorts of herbs. I can see Jie-geng, Huang-qin and she-gan. And I've only had time for a quick look around."

"Lo Wan, come here and sit down. Do I have to ask?"

"My father started teaching me about herbs when I was five. I'm sorry for my deception. I don't really need to be your apprentice to become an herbalist."

"Then why come to me?"

"I need this apprenticeship with you, just not about herbs. I've only been in America for a short time. I need to improve my English, especially my Business English. I have to learn how to operate a business in America. I have no idea how someone makes a living as a healer or herbalist here. I need to learn more about American social customs. For me, you're the perfect mentor."

"Are there other healing arts you know in addition to herbs?"

"Yes. I practice acupuncture and acupressure. And to keep the record straight, I really do practice massage therapy and will continue to use it with you if you find it helpful. Although I think of myself as being an accomplished herbalist, I've learned a great deal working here with you in the past few days so I can honestly fulfill the role of being your apprentice there too."

"Lo Wan, I think we'll have to change our relationship to us *collaborating*. I believe it'll be as useful to me working side-by-side with you. Consider your trial period officially at an end."

That night after dinner, I explain what happened in the woods and Mei Sam is so pleased she runs over and hugs me. That's what led to a long evening where we end up "consummating our marriage" … finally.

Over the following weeks, my English continues to improve to the point where I can engage in simple conversations. I'm not discussing Descartes and Spinoza, but I can be left alone in the store to deal with American customers. Li Ting is receiving two massages a week and can't remember feeling so good. I also improved Li Ting's Chi flow.

A large Chinese man knocks on the door of a noodle shop in Stockton's Chinatown. Pardon me good sir but I'm trying to locate my nephew Lo Wan. He's nineteen-years old. He's a short man. Works as a healer. Do you know him, or have you seen someone matching this description? He's married to a pretty young girl.

"Sorry, but I don't know anyone matching that description."

Mei Sam is euphoric about working in an herb store. Instead of being shown an occasional herb that appears by the side of the road, she now has two fulltime teachers. Earlier that afternoon she made a suggestion for re-organizing a section of the inventory to make it more efficient and Li Ting was so happy about it that he hugged her. This occurred just as I was returning from an errand.

I was not happy about this physical display and was curious about who initiated it.

Mei Sam's martial arts training, done in secret after Li Ting goes to sleep each night, graduated to mastering several kicks. She shows a natural talent for the arts. I decide to begin her rudimentary training in Wing Chun Kung Fu. Everything is going as well as I have a right to expect. And I breathe a sigh of relief knowing there is no way the Chancellor can discover anything about my new life since no one knows where I am.

———

Stockton's Chinatown is divided into four factions ensuring a conflict on almost any important issue. There are four older men who represent each of these four factions. They functioned as if they were the elected city councilmen of Chinatown. Two of them walk into Li Ting's shop. He runs to the storeroom to drag me out to meet them. "Gentlemen, this is my apprentice Lo Wan. I've been looking forward to you meeting him. I refer to him as my apprentice only to aggrandize myself. He knows as much or more about herbs than I do and he's a first rate healer."

"Lo Wan, there are four distinguished gentleman who direct Chinatown's interests here in Stockton. They occupy their positions not by virtue of their age but because of their wisdom and experience. I'd like you to meet two of them, Bo Mah and Ho Yup."

Bo Mah's Chi flow seemed to be operating smoothly. If there is any slight problem it would be along the Small Intestine meridian. Ho Yup appeared to have a minor disruption in Chi flow to his Heart Meridian. It was clear why these two men were drawn together as such close friends. Their two meridians are interdependent, responsible for traits such as leadership and strength. They were both Fire signs, which showed in their creativity and passion.

"Are the factions you gentlemen represent related in any way to the Six Companies?"

"Not really. They're located in San Francisco and deal with local events predominantly in their Chinatown, and with major issues generally representing the Chinese living in America. They don't deal in Stockton's affairs, but we keep in touch with them and occasionally consult with them when difficulties arise. Why do you ask?"

"I met a man who works for the Six Companies on board the ship that brought me to America."

"What's his name? Perhaps I've met him."

"Tu Chan."

"He's their Vice President and a good friend of mine. You were fortunate to make his acquaintance."

"Absolutely, he was my first English teacher. Li Ting is my current teacher, but don't blame either of them for my lack of progress. How may we help you distinguished gentlemen?"

Li Ting stepped forward, "Since the supply of herbs in Stockton is not abundant, they're forced to come here to this lowly establishment and I'll be proud to attend to them myself. It's a great honor for me that they choose this humble store."

We need some ginseng for tonight's meeting. We'll be discussing some intense recent events and how we should respond to them. I hope you'll both attend."

Li Ting nodded his head. "I heard what happened to those two men whose hands were broken. It's disgraceful."

All three looked at me, "I'm sorry, but I never involve myself in politics. I mean no disrespect."

"Please don't give it another thought. And if anything major is decided, Li Ting will tell you about it. It's our pleasure meeting you."

As the two men were leaving, it appeared to me that Ho Yup was staring at Mei Sam's backside a bit too long and she seemed to be encouraging it... or maybe I'm reading too much into a look.

A large barn located at the edge of Stockton's Chinatown has been converted to a meeting hall. Ornate paper lanterns and paper machete lions' heads serve as decoration. It's the largest structure in Chinatown.

The Four Elders sit down to tea at a large table in the center of the room. In Stockton's Chinatown such meetings are referred to as "The Stockton Tea Ceremony." Seated around the elders is practically the entire population of Stockton's Chinatown. The four had many administrative issues to discuss, but those were just a warm-up to the real reason everyone crowded into the hall tonight. They have to respond to the note pinned on the two men whose hands were destroyed, and who they now had to support financially, medically and spiritually.

The hall is packed with familiar faces. After looking around the hall, Bo Mah subtly motions his eyes and head toward three large men who don't look familiar seated at the edge of the hall. The other three elders gesture back that they don't know them either. Each of the other three elders responds with shrugged shoulders. They know everyone else in the hall.

Bo Mah stands and keeps waving his arms up and down in a calming manner. He waits until everyone quiets down. After they settle down he waits a few more seconds to add weight to his words. "This is just what they want. They hope we'll get angry enough to fight back. That will give them just the excuse they're looking for. They didn't come into Chinatown to destroy us with those beatings last night. Their goal was to inflame us so we'd respond in a stupid way and give them the excuse they've been waiting for. I believe restraint is the best course of action at this time."

Roo Ma, another of the four elders smacks both hands down on the table and begins yelling as he stands. "NO! We're *not* cowards so let's not *act* like cowards. No one respects a coward. I say we fight back ... hard."

People in the hall yell, "Yes, we must fight back."

Seeing the support he hoped for, he looks at Bo Mah and says, "You want to act just like the spineless Han Dynasty. They refused to fight the Mongols and let them conquer all of China.

We lost everything. You still wear your Mongol queue to show your obedience to the Qin conquerors even though you're out here in America. We're not whipped dogs. We have to fight back now." He hits the table with his fist.

People in the hall shout and stomp their feet.

Ho Yup stands and addresses the group in a soft, reflective tone. It causes the people in the hall to quiet down if they want to hear him. "There's a reason why the Chinese culture has survived for five thousand years. It's because we've always been smart, brave and patient. We act when the right opportunity presents itself, not before. This is NOT the right opportunity. Those of you who want to rush in and take on the White Americans in a fight… first come over to my house and play cards with me. I can use the money you'll leave on my table. If you can be baited so easily, I'll clean you out in a matter of minutes, then you may join us as we sit down and devise a more clever plan where we actually do get our revenge, yet the blame doesn't get assigned to us so easily that we'll be wiped out. We're smarter than them. Let's show it. The four of us will sit down and create a plan and we'll meet back here in five days. That's an auspicious number. Then you can tell us if you think our plan is a good one or not. But, whatever we do, it should be on our terms, not theirs."

The crowd in the hall doesn't cheer at this suggestion, but they don't shout it down either. They're disappointed that there isn't going to be a good fight coming soon, but realize that the elder is right. They leave quiet and disappointed, but with a glimmer of hope.

Li Ting shows Mei Sam the Goldenrod plants Lo Wan found and asked her to go to the meadow and bring back more of them. Then goes back to updating the herb inventory. A few hours later, a man runs into the store out of breath asking to see me. Li Ting asks what it's about and the man says he has an envelope for me. Li Ting asks for it, but the messenger says he was warned that he had to put it directly into my hands. Li Ting calls me in and the man hands me the letter.

I go back to our shack, sit down on the bed and open the envelope. It contains a small piece of Mei Sam's dress with the following words:

"If you would like to see your pretty wife with the rest of her dress still on, come down to the meadow where you found the goldenrod plants. Come immediately. Come alone. The longer you make us wait, the more we will enjoy amusing ourselves with your wife."

As the three men sit with Mei Sam tied up on the ground Ri Way says, "The Chancellor's orders are to torture and kill her while her husband watches. He wasn't very specific about what we should do to her before killing her...as long as she suffers and dies."

Ho Singh says, "She's very pretty and has a great body. It seems a shame to just kill her and waste all of that."

"How about if we screw her to death? It would make for an interesting report to the Chancellor about how Lo Wan had to watch *that* entire event, wouldn't it? I bet between the three of us, we could do it in a few hours. We'd probably get a bonus from the Chancellor for our creativity." All three laugh.

Hearing this, Mei Sam panics and becomes frantic trying to free herself, but she's bound too well. As she wriggles on the floor trying to undo her bindings Lee Yow said, "Look at her moving her ass and thighs. I think our idea is turning her on. Alright, it's time we draw straws to see which one of us hides in the bushes until her lucky prince arrives."

Six weeks ago, the Viceroy was smiling at the huge soldier he selected to lead the Chancellor's revenge mission. "I'm not sure why

I'm bothering to send two additional men to America for such a simple task. You can easily do it by yourself. All you're going to have to do is kill a young girl while a scrawny healer is forced to watch. Then, you rough him up a bit, without killing him, and you sail home to get paid a small fortune."

The Viceroy arranges a grand martial arts tournament to demonstrate that he chose the right man for this mission. He even hires an announcer for the event. He wants to insure that he impresses the Chancellor.

"This weaponless tournament has brought together sixteen of the best fighters in Peking. And now after four rounds of competition, we've narrowed it down to our two finalists. At this point, you'd expect to see these two superb, undefeated fighters face each other to see who's the best of the best. But no! Instead of fighting one another, our two champions are going to forge a partnership to fight Lee Yow, the Chancellor's champion. Your Viceroy has spared no expense providing you with a such a fighting spectacle." The two fighters grin at each other preparing to attack their solitary opponent.

The Chancellor's champion Lee Yow walks out and the crowd gasps at his towering height, chiseled physique and crisp movements. Without saying a word, the two fighters separate and prepare to attack as if they'd choreographed their fight strategy. Lee Yow bends under the attack of the first man, picks him up by the waist and swings him into the other man as if he was a war club. The entire competition takes less than ten seconds. Both opponents lay on the ground dazed.

Lee Yow tries to help both men up. The semi-conscious one says he's fine while the other man has to be carried a few feet away to be attended by several physicians. Within a few minutes, both of Lee Yow's opponents are conscious. They bow and congratulate him to the extent they're able to speak.

"I apologize. I know we weren't supposed to use weapons, but I don't consider that using a man as a club counts as a weapon." The two of them laugh, more out of fear than amusement.

The next day, the Viceroy introduces Lee Yow to his mission partners. "Lee Yow is our strongest and most skilled fighter. The little healer will take one look at him, fall to his knees and begin begging. We also know his intellect is as big as his physique. I know you can handle this task by yourself, but I didn't want you to get lonely." The other two men laugh because when the Viceroy tells a joke, you laugh.

"I'd like you both to meet Ho Singh. He has a knack for getting people to trust him and divulge everything they know hoping that he'll like them. Men tell him where their savings are hidden and young maidens wink as they tell him when their guardians go to sleep, and which window will be left unlocked. He came to my attention because he's a master of deductive logic. A fugitive escaped last year. Ho Singh discovered the man was arrested for stealing women's jewelry. He trapped him by making a list of all the women the man had consorted with. He figured out which woman he was currently besotted with and waited outside her residence until he showed up with a bag full of jewelry he stole from the women he lost interest in. Ho Singh is also proficient in several martial arts. Between the two of you, there should be no problem finding and handling the healer."

"Ri Way... I'm sending you because you're my wife's second cousin. When the Chancellor rewards you all with a great deal of silver, I want some of it to remain in the family." All three laugh. "Of course you also have outstanding martial skills, but more importantly, you're an entertaining fellow and will keep your companions amused."

I run down to the meadow and stop behind a tree a good distance away. I see Mei Sam on the ground with her hands and feet bound. Two men are guarding her. I wait for a while to see if there are any surprises and see a section of the bushes move. There's a third man hiding in position to ambush me. Knowing the reason Mei Sam is being held, I assume the Chancellor would only send men who are exceptionally well trained.

Rushing in and attacking would expose Mei Sam to harm. I think back to father's lectures from Sun Tsu, 'be underestimated.' I enter in a state of confusion carrying the letter and inquiring why they want to see me. I am holding the letter in plain sight, making no sudden movements using my slouched over posture.

The two men sitting with my wife are significantly bigger than me. They're also well armed. They laugh as I approach. "We asked for her husband, not her little brother. How old are you?"

I stammered, speaking on the high side of my voice. I make my voice crack as I say, "I'm nineteen. Are you the ones who sent me this note? What's this all about? Why is my wife tied up?"

"Greetings from the Chancellor. He received news that you were here and was surprised you were already married. We're here on a simple errand. We're going to torture and kill your wife while you watch. If you don't mind, we'll just come over and bind your arms. Then we'll sit you down so you don't miss a single minute of the entertainment the Chancellor is providing."

The two men called for their hidden comrade to come out of hiding while they reach out to grab my wrists. They see no reason for the big man to remain hidden. Judging by my size and the fact that I'm unarmed and scared, it's clear I pose no problem for them.

Chapter 6

The four Stockton elders sit around a table in Bo Mah's house sipping tea. Ho Yup, who said everyone at the meeting should sit and wait for the four elders to make a plan turns to the elder who demanded immediate, forceful action. "Well...Roo Ma, what do you think we should do my esteemed friend?"

"I think we should hit them where it hurts. We should do something strong and symbolic like burning down one of their favorite Irish bars. That would show them the kind of men we are."

"And what would such an act accomplish?"

"It'd be a show of strength. They'd learn that if they hurt us, some of them will get hurt in return."

"And what do you think they'd do to us in return for such an aggressive act?"

"It doesn't matter because whatever they do, we'll do something even worse in return for *that* act."

"That's an excellent idea because there must be at least one Chinese man for every fifty Whites. And we have sharp knives while they'll have to settle for guns and axes. I'd like to invite you to my card game."

"OK Ho Yup, what do *you* think we should do?"

"I'd like them to be afraid of us too, but not in a way where they could easily blame us for whatever we do in retaliation. Imagine if one or two of them were to disappear...without any proof connecting one of us to that disappearance. What could they do? They were foolish enough to pin a note on our boys letting everyone know who did it and why. But imagine if a few of them were to mysteriously disappear? Every one of them would become afraid to leave their houses. They'd only feel safe walking around in groups. And instead of admitting it was us so they'd know, they could only wonder."

"Who could we get to make these white men disappear?"

"In the hall there were scores of men who'd be proud to do it. It would be our job to select the right ones and instruct them in how we wanted it done in very explicit detail."

"You promised the group in the hall that you'd present a plan to them publicly and have them decide if they liked it. How'll you do that if the plan requires secrecy?"

"I think with a plan like this, everyone would agree that such a public announcement would be imprudent. But picture this. If you three agree we should proceed with this plan, we'll go into the meeting and say that by divulging our plan, we would make it inoperable. But, they'll know all four of us agreed to it. They know how rarely *that* happens. We'll explain the need for secrecy and ask them to trust us. I believe seeing our unanimity will convince them we're on the correct course. Do I have your agreement?"

The other three elders nodded their heads. Bo Mah said, "Then let's begin making our actual plans. How many disappearances should we plan? Do we want individuals abducted or should we take people in twos and threes? How shall we dispose of their bodies so they won't be found? How long should we keep this up?"

———————————————

As the two men move to grab my hands I overburden myself with all the ways I can attack them and am too lost in strategy to actually do anything. Again, my father's voice breaks through the logjam. "The reason you trained for so long was so you won't have to think … rely on your training and instincts … just react."

As they went to grab me I let the pitch of my voice rise, "No … this is too much for me, I'm, I'm going to faint." As I relax and let my body fall, the two men bend to catch me. I poke Ri Way in the eyes and I watch him fall down screaming. I turn to thrust my fingers deep into Ho Singh's throat and watch him fall down trying to make a sound while trying to breathe. I use my ridge hand to strike the back of his neck knocking him out. I ran back and also knock out Ri Way.

I see the big man Lee Yow jump back and pull out his long dagger. He is swinging in wide arcs and I work to stay out of reach. The big man moves quickly and is surprisingly agile. I use a series of feints and dodges to stay just beyond his range. This goes on for quite a while as he continues to assess me by striking from different distances and angles. After a while I notice Lee Yow has opened his mouth to catch a breath. He's beginning to tire. Being an intelligent warrior, he changes tactics.

It seems obvious to Lee Yow that I'm running away because I'm afraid of him and trying to tire him. Lee Yow stops, and turns toward Mei Sam. "Here's what I'm going to do. As I keep fighting with you, I'm going to be taking small steps toward your wife. You can step in to fight me like a warrior or enjoy the thought of how I'm going to kill your wife slowly as I take each step toward her. It's a nice game...no?

Although I move closer and farther from this large warrior, he keeps slowly approaching Mei Sam.

"As I complete the mission of killing your wife while you watch, I want to offer you best regards from the Chancellor. I'll kill her slowly so you won't miss a thing."

I pick up a large stone and hurl it at the big man's head, but his reflexes are too quick. As he ducks he says, "Just for that I will take *two* larger steps toward her. I like seeing the look on your face as I move closer to your pretty little wife. You can't best me because I'm too big and strong and I can't catch you because you're too quick, but I just moved another two steps closer to your wife. I can smell her now."

"I can see why you're moving toward my wife. You wouldn't be doing that if you weren't so afraid of me, and you have every right to be. You can move toward my wife and kill her before I can get to you, but there's something you clearly haven't thought about. If you're such a great warrior, why did they have to send two men to help you fight me?"

"As you can see, I don't need them."

"Here's something else for you to think about. If you hurt my wife even slightly, much less kill her; I will have you wishing you were dead within a few seconds. You're only safe while she's alive. You already know that I'm a healer, but you haven't really thought through what that means. I know how every part of your body works and I know every place in your body where I can inflict terrible pain. Pain so horrible that no man can withstand it. I promise to unleash that pain on you if you so much as touch her."

"You're a clever young man who's making a big assumption in your clever speech to me. You're assuming that in our fight, you will, or even could, be the victor. Permit me to introduce myself. I have been in countless battles ranging from organized wars to drunken fights in a bar. I have *never*; listen to the key word here, *never* been defeated. I'm strong, quick and very well trained. I have won every fight I was ever in. You, on the other hand, are a tiny healer without much experience in combat. If we ever stop talking and fight, I will crush you instantly. And, I will become a rich man for having defeated you and killing your wife."

The big man takes his dagger and slaps Mei Sam's stomach with the flat end. "I could have used the sharp end, but I just wanted to see the panic on your face. I hold all the advantages. It will be your stomach next."

"If you're such a powerful warrior, why don't you throw down your dagger and I'll throw down my tree branch and let's fight it out man-to-man?"

"That sounds like almost as much fun as screwing your wife … which I'll do right after we finish fighting. I agree, throw down your weapon and I'll throw down mine."

I throw down my branch and, true to his word the big man bends way down and drops his dagger. As he bends down to drop it he's shielding his hand so he can scoop up some dirt. He takes his arm back and throws the dirt in my eyes. I yell, "I can't see."

The big man laughs. "You're not a very experienced fighter if you fall for such an old trick." He rushes in and puts me into a chokehold. He's laughing as he drags me over to Mei Sam and holds the lock with one hand while grabbing her breast with the other another and laughs. Lee Yow is very strong and I feel like I'm losing consciousness. I try to squirm out of his grip, but I can't break the hold.

Since he released one hand to grab Mei Sam's breast, with the little strength I have left, I strike his elbow at the ulnar nerve. The shocking pain makes him loosen his grip and I'm able to escape. Holding his elbow he's able to rush in, bend down and scoop up his dagger. As I'm backing away he increases his speed chasing me. He stops to rub his elbow giving me the opportunity to plant a sidekick into his solar plexus. He's surprised as he runs into it doubling the force of the kick. As he bends over from the pain I use my outstretched fingers to poke him in the throat. He drops to the ground and struggles to breathe from the effects of the sidekick and blow to the throat.

This gives me the time to pick up my branch and create a little distance. As he's struggling to stand I taunt him. "If you're so confident in your fighting skills, you wouldn't have had to try throwing dirt in my eyes."

Losing his breath disoriented him so he jumps up and swings his dagger wildly. I use my branch to smash his hand causing him to drop his dagger and scream from the pain.

Out of the corner of my eye, I see Ho Singh beginning to stir and realize I don't have much time before he enters the fight. Ri Way is also beginning to move now. I don't know how fast they may recover.

I smile at the big man hoping to rouse him to anger by mocking him. "I warned you as a healer I know the workings of the body. Let me explain why your eyes are watering. Your hands have more nerve endings than any other part of your body. You know this because when you need to identify something by feel, you always use your hands to do it. You're now going to have to fight me without your right hand which is now all but useless." Lee Yow lets out a yell and reaches out to grab me with his left hand. I smash it with the branch and he screams again.

"Now you have two damaged hands. That's going to make it very hard for you to fight me or kill my wife. If you were hoping to stroke her breast, you'll have to do it with your foot."

He rushes in to kick me. I move just out of his reach. He quickly turns to move back to Mei Sam. I leap in and do a front roll to reach him just before he can reach her and I hit his instep with my branch as hard as I can making sure I break the bone. He screams and falls down.

I use my knife hand to knock him unconscious like his comrades.

I quickly rip the tunics off all three men to create enough material to bind their hands and feet. Then I checked to see if they have any other concealed weapons. Finally I run to Mei Sam. I untie her and she collapses in my arms.

I go over to Ho Singh, the man whose throat I struck, and use acupressure to restore his speech. "It's time for you to tell me a story."

I pick up a slight blockage of Chi flow to his Kidney meridian. Knowing this was the area controlling fear; this is the man I select to explain everything. As a Water sign, he'll be reflective, and recognize the situation he's in and be most cooperative. I count on the man's intelligence to tell him that after he sees how Lee Yow, a man much stronger than him, turned to jelly fit to be spread across a cracker. Both men are watching to see how Ho Singh behaves under duress. When they see his refusal they nod at him with pride.

Ho Singh stares at me for several seconds then says, "Go straight to Hell."

"Mei Sam, I asked this man to tell me the story about how they came to be here and his response was telling me to go to

Hell . . . I'm sorry, 'straight to Hell.' This is after suggesting that he and his comrades screw you to death. If you had an opportunity to express your feelings to him, think what strike and what location you would choose as I stand him up to provide that opportunity for you.

I stand Ho Singh up and Mei Sing delivers a front kick between the man's legs. Ho Singh falls down and begins to throw up from the nausea while he screams from the pain. I stand Ri Way up, and though his legs are tied, he tries to back away. Mei Sam laughs at his movements before she takes an extra little step and delivers her kick. He cries louder than Ho Singh as he's throwing up.

I'm not going to have you express your feelings to Lee Yow because he already has two broken hands and a broken foot. We'll leave him alone for now.

I think back to how I administered pain to Mei Sam's cousin. I was in conflict about inflicting pain on a weaker opponent to get my way, but this situation is vastly different. These men intended to torture and kill Mei Sam and then torture me all because some madman was going to reward them with treasure for it. I have the moral justification to inflict pain here, and to try to set them on a different path throughout the remainder of their lives. And if I'm going to be honest with myself, as I look at Mei Sam, they deserve a good deal of pain.

I stand Ho Singh up again and bring Mei Sam over for another kick. He shakes his head and begins to blurt out his story. "The Chancellor's Viceroy selected us for this mission because we have a set of complementary skills to carry out this task. As soon as the Chancellor found out about your wife, he decided it was time for your first installment of misery."

"How did the Chancellor find out about my wife?"

"The mining company telegraphed that you escaped with a pretty young girl. "The Chancellor has spies in every Chinatown in America. It wasn't difficult to find a young man travelling with a pretty underage girl. Our spy in Stockton let us know. Once we got here, it was easy to discover that a young healer was working at a local herbalist's store. I hope you're smart enough to realize that whatever you do to us, he'll send more men to find you. You may as well give yourself up to us and save everyone a lot of trouble."

"Perhaps you're right. It does make sense that since I have the three of you disarmed and tied up that I should just let you torture and kill my wife and then torture me. Hmmm, this is a tough decision, but I'm going to decline your generous offer of pain and death, and see how you deal with the same treatment, but thank you again for your thoughtful suggestion."

Mei Sam is laughing. She stands and throws a few practice kicks.

"I do think you're right. The Chancellor will send more men, but for now, I have a bigger decision to make. Maybe you can help me with more suggestions. I have to decide if I want to torture you first so that you beg to die, or kill you quickly or ... I can let you go."

"You, big man, what do you think I should do?"

"If you let us go, we'll be obliged to come after you again. That should narrow down your choices." Ho Singh gave the big man a look that said, "Are you crazy?"

"I appreciate your honesty, but it does leave me with a dilemma. I like to think of myself as a healer first. I hate to take a life unless there's absolutely no alternative. What if I get you to promise to leave us alone? Will you keep your word?"

"If I make a promise, I keep my word, but I would never make such a promise because I've already given my word to the Viceroy."

"Sometimes in life, there are circumstances that lead to re-assessing both our priorities and promises. You may find this is one of those times. I believe if I placed you in enough pain, you would make that promise to me to make that pain stop. I think you'd keep that promise for two reasons: First, I believe you're an honest man, unlike your friends here, and a trustworthy man keeps his word if given. Second, after experiencing *this* level of pain, I think you'd be terrified of ever being in this state again. What do you think?"

Lee Yow shakes his head, "I don't think you can get me to change my mind."

"Mei Sam, I think you might enjoy what's about to happen to one of the men who was going to screw you to death."

Let's just be clear. If you ask me to stop, *that* means you'll extend your promise to me. If you don't, I'll let you scream until your body can't take the pain anymore and you'll die, but let me warn you that may take a while."

"I accept your terms. I'm a warrior and not afraid to die."

"Here's where we disagree. I believe you're not afraid to die, but I think you'll be afraid of the pain."

I walk behind him and press on a spot between his thoracic and cervical spine and the big man begins screaming. It takes seven seconds of horrific screaming and crying before the man yells, "STOP!"

I stop the pain, "Then you agree that you won't come after either of us again?"

The poor man lays there … a quivering hulk, and manages to nod his head "Yes." Then he returns to his trembling state. He cannot not stop shaking and all this time he's whimpering.

I walk up to Ho Singh, "What about you?"

The man is pale and asks if he can just agree without going through the same pain. I shake my head, "I'm afraid not. You may feel that way now seeing what you've just seen and agree, but the effect of what you saw may wear off. This pain is something you have to experience personally. It'll help you remember your promise forever. But in the interest of mercy, I'll grant you a small courtesy. Your friend endured the pain for over seven seconds; I'll only give you four seconds of it. The man shakes his head from side-to-side.

"I'm afraid this is non-negotiable. Remember that a few seconds ago, you asked me to give myself up."

I hit the same points and Ho Singh screams much louder than Lee Yow. When I release the pain, he shakes much longer. His eyes are filled with tears. "So, do you still agree never to pursue us again?"

With watering eyes, he nods his head and emits a feeble "yes." With that, I turn to the last man and ask if he's ready.

From the moment I saw Ri Way, I noticed several Chi blocked meridians. This is not a strong man. He is clearly a follower and not worth much of my attention.

Ri Way also says, "no." I press the same point for the same four seconds. Ri Way passes out from the pain. When he comes back to consciousness it's difficult for him to form the words promising never to come after us again, but he finally manages it. His pants are soaked.

I turn to the three men. "You were going to kill a defenseless young woman. You even talked about raping her to death. And I shudder to think about what you were planning to do to me. You went through a total of fifteen seconds of excruciating pain. I would like to suggest that you use it to reflect on your decisions and actions. They are immoral. By the rules of combat, and any system of morality, I have the right to kill you … but I choose not to. You owe me your lives. I would like you to repay that obligation by reevaluating your actions."

"As warriors, you are not afraid to die, but now I believe, you are afraid of pain. I'd like you to use your experience with it to reflect on the way you've lived your lives and to each think of your futures. Strive to come back as better people with higher principles."

"To help you toward that end, I'm going to leave you with a lasting memento to guide your reflection. I notice all three of you are right handed. I'm going to break each of your right arms so that they'll work for performing menial tasks, but you'll never be able to use them to fight the way you were trained. Remember what you came here to do to each of us today. Then think of what you would be doing now if our positions were reversed. You won't like this, but I'm sure you'll understand it, and in time, see its fairness."

I quickly strike each of them in the same part of their right arm with an intense punch. "You will not have to see a doctor. You arms will heal without treatment, but you will always feel pain there. Fortunately, that pain will be bearable. I hope you use that pain to continually re-mold your characters so you can come back as better men."

"My advise to you is to avoid going back to China. I think you'll have a far better, and longer life here in America. If the Chancellor gets a hold of you, if you foolishly decide to go back…uh, just don't go back. We left the three shaken men on the ground. "You two will have to help Lee Yow to walk since his foot is broken. Please leave Stockton immediately. You won't enjoy the outcome if we meet again."

As we walked back to Li Ting's shop Mei Sam said, "Do you believe you've reformed those three awful men because you punched them in the arm?"

"No, but I want to think I tried in the best way I know. That way I don't feel as bad about breaking their arms."

"For a nineteen year old man, you've lived a very complicated life. Since I'm now a bigger part of it than I realized, there are probably a few more things you should explain to me."

"Well…I thought when we escaped from the mine, there was no way for the Chancellor to find me. I, meaning we, have just discovered we're no longer safe. The first question you're going to have to answer is, do you want to continue travelling with me or do you want to strike out on your own?"

"What a nice choice. If I separate from you, the mining company is still after me and so are the authorities for escaping from the mine. They'll send me back to become a prostitute…or, I can trail after you, always looking over my shoulder to see if this Chancellor has sent more men to torture and kill me…if they don't rape me first. Shouldn't there be a third option where I become a fairy princess? I guess I'm still stuck with you."

"In that case, I have to tell you how disappointed I am with your inability to subdue those three men by yourself. We'll have to train harder."

I received one of Mei Sam's newly mastered kicks. "When I told you I wanted to learn martial arts, you didn't tell me how much I'd need those skills if I stay with you."

Mei Sam took my arm. "If I'm going to stay with you, the least you could do is tell me you liked me a little."

"Fine … I do."

"Thanks."

It took almost two weeks until Stockton's first disappearance was noticed. It was so bizarre no one could figure out how it happened or who to blame. But it was the second disappearance that got everyone talking. Billy Carney asked Tommy Kirkpatrick if he knew anything about the disappearances. Tommy said he didn't. "Do you think it might be the Chinks?"

"I don't know, but I've got an idea how to find out." Early one evening, as it was about to get dark, Billy Carney and five friends hid behind a building while Freddie O'Reilly walked up and down the street alone. Freddie had bright red hair and was 5'9" tall, but weighed only about 110 lbs. His friends said he'd make a fine pipe cleaner. He kept walking up and down several streets not far from the edge of Chinatown. Carney was about to give up the plan because no one except a few local whores showed any interest, until the sun had just set. Three Chinese men dressed in black snuck up behind Freddie and hit him over the head with a club. Then they began to drag him away. They didn't see Carney and his men until it was way too late.

Carney's men hit them a few times to inspire their cooperation, then dragged them down to the police station. The Police Chief interrogated them with his translator. At first the three Chinamen said they were out for a walk, saw a little white man and decided to scare him just for fun. The clubs and the ropes they carried made their story sound a bit untenable.

The Police Chief tells the three men that they would usually be hung for the horrible murders they committed, but in this case their fate will be worse. They'll serve a life sentence in a jail with White men who'll be told they killed White people in Stockton. Every day will be Hell on earth for them. But that will be nothing compared to what they'll go through if they didn't confess.

The Police Chief smiles, "My translator tells me what they do in China to extract a confession when they catch a criminal. The man will go for days without food and water. Severe beatings. Being stuffed into a small, cramped cage and left out all night in the cold for as long as it takes." He laughs, "In China they know that once they want a confession ... they get it. They're very patient, just like I'll be, but I'll be eating, drinking a lot and sleeping in a warm bed while I'm waiting."

"I'm not really interested in the three of you. I know you three didn't plan these disappearances. You are just the dopes who were recruited to carry out the grunt work your leaders didn't want to dirty their hands with. I want you to lead us to the ringleaders who came up with this idea. If you do, we'll go easier on you."

It takes three days to get their confessions, and by that time there isn't much left of the three men ... but enough to drag into court.

Carney asks the Police Chief to wait a day before bringing in the newspaper reporters. He swaggers into Judge Sullivan's office. "You'd better get another envelope ready for me and this time, it's going to be heavier. You've read about these weird disappearances. I know you'd be pleased if the police found evidence showing that those disappearances are linked to the Chinese. I'm even surer you'll be happier if it was all planned by the Four Elders. .

Bring out that envelope. *It is and it is.* We have the confessions of three Chinese hoodlums caught in the middle of an attempted kidnapping. They identified the four elders as the ones who created the plan and helped carry out the kidnappings and disappearances."

Sullivan smiled as he opened his cash drawer.

Mei Sam and I go back to Li Ting's shop and he asks me to explain the mystery surrounding the messenger's letter. "Sit down, this'll take a while." I don't hold anything back and it's evident that both Mei Sam and Li Ting are worried, but for different reasons.

"I'm sorry, but this means we'll be leaving Stockton."

"Yes, of course. Now that the Chancellor knows you're here, and you dealt with his three men, you'll no longer be safe in Stockton. Next time he may choose to use stealth and send a group of wily assassins or an overwhelming force or even a combination of the two. And now he has an additional reason to exact vengeance. You've bested him. From your description, this man won't accept defeat gracefully. If not for your own safety, think of Mei Sam. I'll treasure the time we've spent together and I hope this money will help you."

When I refuse, Ting Ho says, "Hey, you still work for me. That's an order, take it or I'll fire you. You'll need it at some point. Besides, you earned it in your work here. And it'll ease my conscience as I push you out the door. I paid you almost nothing for all the work you've done here to help me."

As their talk continues into the night, there's a frantic knock at the back door. Bo Mah and Ho Yup are craning their necks to see if anyone is following them.

"The police have identified the Four Elders as the ones who've been organizing the disappearances. We're here to say a quick good-bye and to pick up some herbs we'll need for our trip. I don't know when or if we can return to Stockton. I only hope our departure will save lives."

"Where will you go?"

Bo Mah has a cousin who's been prospecting in the Sierras. It's in a remote area where I think we'll be safe."

Ting Ho hands the list of herbs to Lo Wan and asks him to bring them out from the storeroom. As soon as Lo Wan leaves the room, Ting Ho asks, "Would you consider taking Lo Wan and Mei Sam with you? They won't be safe in Stockton either. He's a highly skilled healer and a man of great integrity."

"Are you joking? We'd love to be travelling with two more companions, especially young, strong ones. Thank you. You're giving us a gift."

When I bring in the herbs the elders explain the benefits of hiding out in the Sierras. We immediately see the advantages and gather our small bundles. The four of us leave Stockton in the middle of the night.

The next morning groups of Irishmen pound on the doors of each of the four elders. Sadly, two of them answered and were severely beaten on the spot. Their remains were dragged down to the police station. Billy Carney banged on Bo Mah's door. When no one answered, he broke down the door and ran in to find an old servant. He screamed, "Where's Bo Mah?"

When the old man tries to explain that he doesn't understand, Carney uses the club he's carrying to smash the man's head in. Carney yells at the top of his lungs, "As you walk through the streets of this hideous place, if you see any fruit or other delicacies on their carts, grab 'em. I'm declaring it Free Food Day. Hell, if you see anything you like in a store, break the window and grab it. Today's Payback Day."

Their search turns into a manic looting spree. Every Chinese person who resists is beaten. Several buildings are torched. By the time the spree has ended seventeen Chinese lay dead, scores are injured and most of Stockton's Chinatown is destroyed. That's when the police arrive. There are no arrests.

One of the stores that are looted is Ting Ho's. Several men enter his shop and look around. They see nothing but bottles of herbs. "Sh_t, there's nothing in this damn store but twigs and stems."

"Those'll burn real good."

Ting Ho watches his store burn until there is nothing left but a pile of rubble. He grabs one of the Irish men and hits him. He's immediately attacked and brutally beaten by five men. Billy Carney is cheering them on. When they finish with him they leave him on the ground. One of his neighbors finds him and takes him to a local healer. He dies before morning.

As we trudge through a forest path, I'm pleased to see how easily the two elders keep up, and they never dip into their sack of ginseng. Fear of apprehension is an excellent motivator. It was around fifty miles to get to Sutter Creek where Bo Mah's cousin is.

Mei Sam pulls me aside. "We know how your Chancellor operates to track you down. Do you think staying in the mountains, far away from any organized Chinatown, is enough to keep us safe? If we're discovered, do you think you can really protect us?"

"My father trained me well. We'll pray it's well enough. We've got the advantage of having no better alternative."

Each night we huddle together for warmth going to sleep without the comfort of a fire. By the end of the third day, we find themselves at the foothills of the Sierras and begin to relax. All four of us are wearing our shabbiest clothing and we appear poor enough to avoid the interest of the few people we encounter.

On the third day we're about to circle around the small town of Jackson, the last town before we enter the high country. We figure we should probably buy a few provisions. We're the only Chinese there so we quickly find a general store and make our purchases; buy two small tents and leave. Three large white men greet us at the edge of town. "I hope you coolies don't plan on stayin' round here cause you won't find no work and we don't like you coolies much."

Ho Yup steps forward and says, "No sirs. We are on our way out of your town right now. You need not concern yourselves with us."

"The sooner the better. But maybe you'd like to consider selling us the girl. We probably need her more than you do and we'd sure as hell know how to use her better."

I step between the men and Mei Sam, bow and smile. "So sorry sir, this my wife."

The Viceroy did not sleep well last night. He had to report on the three men he sent to America and knows how the Chancellor receives bad news. He walks into the Jade Room, takes a deep breath and exhales slowly through his mouth. "Sire, I'm afraid I have some news you may find disturbing."

"My Dear Viceroy, I don't become disturbed. I like to think I'm a problem solver."

"I just received a telegram from America. The three men we sent to kill the Healer's wife did not succeed."

"Bring these men to me as soon as possible."

"I'm afraid that's not the end of the bad news. The three men have not boarded a ship to return."

"Viceroy, what steps have you taken to right things?"

"It seems that there's not much to be done sire."

"I want you to leave this room right now and return within the next ten minutes with some information for me. Bring me a list of the names and ages of the three men's daughters if they have any. Leave!"

Ten minutes later the Viceroy returns, "Ho Singh is the only one … he has a twelve year old daughter."

"Have her cleaned and in my bed at eight o'clock, and I mean scrub her really clean. If she's ugly, have her face painted to make it look prettier. I will make her a woman tonight. When I finish with her, you'll dump her out in the street. That should help me deal with my disappointment … a little. Also, find out if they have wives attractive enough for me to bother with. If they're ugly, give them directly to my soldiers as a gift. As for you, begin designing your next plan for this simple mission with the Healer now … Go."

Jackson is a small town where everyone seems to know everybody else. When they hear three townsmen raising their voices several people come out to see what's going on. As the three men laugh, one of the men goes to grab Mei Sam while the other takes a swing at me. I trip and end up causing the man's punch to end up connecting with the other man who's also reaching for me. My fall ends up with me rolling into the man about to grab Mei Sam. I stand and say, "Very sorry," to the man I tripped. The man gets up and swings a haymaker at me. I stumble and lurch away. The punch hits the third man as I fall again. I yell, "Ow," and limp away as if I'd been hurt. I hope that satisfies their egos.

Several onlookers are laughing at the three men on the ground. One of the three men gets up and yells, "You all better get the hell out of here before we really get mad."

As we hurry out of Jackson Bo Mah says, "Lo Wan, you are one lucky man. You almost got seriously hurt twice back there. Are you alright?"

No one seems to notice that I'm smiling and my limp is gone. "Your fear was fortunate because it caused you to trip. And if you hadn't fallen, those men would have given you a serious beating." The four of us walk away quickly before anyone else decides to participate in the entertainment they're watching. When no one is looking, Mei Sam smiles at me.

As we're walking, I begin to wonder about the trouble we had in Jackson. Did Mei Sam flirt with one of the men, or were they just three angry White men out to make trouble with any Chinese they meet?

As we continue to climb, I notice there are more trees and vegetation than I expected. Mei Sam is absorbed by the greenery. She expected arid conditions and is already in love with these mountains,

The next morning, after asking for directions in several mining camps, we find Bo Mah's cousin's encampment. Ya Min is in his early fifties and shows the effects of doing manual labor over the course of many years. The two men embrace, and Bo Mah introduces us.

Ya Min has a slight blockage of the Lung meridian. I sense a sadness beneath the surface. His Metal sign seems to indicate he is strong, honest and ambitious. I look forward to helping him clear his blockage. He appears to be a genuinely good man.

"There are twenty two miners working here. Each man works for himself. We're bound together into a loose collective. We each keep the gold we find, if any of us is in trouble or needs help, it's always available. As a community, we take turns cooking and doing laundry. We switch roles every two weeks. Sometimes we eat well and other times we wait until we eat well again. If you're all comfortable with this arrangement, you're welcome to join us."

That evening at dinner, there are introductions all around. The men's welcome ranged from mildly accepting to mildly suspicious. Our saving grace is that Bo Mah is a relative. When Ya Min introduces me as a healer that also stirs quite a bit of interest. The one detail that escapes no one is that there's now going to be a woman around. A young, pretty one. That fact is received with a wide range of emotions.

We pitch our tent in a remote corner of the camp. It's our first chance to be alone and we fall asleep in each other's arms. In the morning we eat our first communal meal and several men queue up to talk to me. Each man presents a list of ailments and asks if I can help. Most of my first morning at the camp is taken up ministering to minor injuries. It doesn't take long for a healer dispensing free care to become popular. Ya Min guides the other three to his mining site and begins teaching them how to pan and sluice for gold. Mei Sam takes to sluicing and spends the day at a stream with her pan alongside the two elders. She loves the clean air and fresh water. She thinks she's discovered her calling. It doesn't take long for her to find several small gold nuggets. The elders don't fare nearly as well, but they keep at it, trying without much success. In the afternoon, I finally join them.

Instead of immediately grabbing a pan trying to see if I can separate any gold from the sand and shale, I observe how everyone else is working. I don't like to rush into things. After a short time, I ask them all to stop and sit down with me.

"Over the years I've lived in a number of small farming villages. When people work the rice fields, they use irrigation techniques that are more efficient than the four of you holding and rocking small pans. Ya Min, would you and Mei Sam help me gather some wood to construct a small water wheel and some sluice boxes. Then we can pump and sluice water from the stream and the running water will wash the gravel from the gold, if there is any. It'll be much more efficient than each of you shaking a small pan for hours at a time in the hot sun."

"But before we begin, there's another consideration. Ya Min, you said each man keeps the gold he finds. If I'm correct, we may be harvesting more gold than the others in the collective. I suggest the five of us become equal partners in this little venture. To avoid problems, let's find a safe place to hide any gold we find and not let the others in the collective know how much gold we're finding. Ya Min, does that seem reasonable?"

"Yes. I've seen how greed changes people, and not in a good way. And, we can always change our minds down the road if we want. I agree, do the rest of you?"

The two elders nod their heads saying they both think it's a good idea. Mei Sam nods her head as she walks over to me and puts her arm around me.

The next morning, we set to work. The water wheel causes the flow of water through wooden gutters that function as sluice boxes. In the bottom are shallow fences that stir up the mixture of water and gravel. This causes small particles of gold to drop out of the solution because gold is heavier than sand and rocks. The gold dust and pieces are caught while the waste spills out of the ends of the boxes.

By the end of the day our sluicing system is functionally operational. Bo Mah pulls Ho Yup aside, "We are so lucky to have this boy with us. I was just happy to have a young healer with us on a potentially dangerous trip."

As we were walking back to camp, Bo Mah stops me, "I'm curious. When you first got to Peking, did you sit for the government examinations?"

In China, if you wanted to work in any meaningful enterprise, you had to take the national merit examinations. China was proud that every important position is determined by a candidate's capability measured by their elaborate system of testing. At regular intervals taking more and more advanced tests to continue their rise.

The landed gentry and rich merchants send their sons to study in Preparatory schools or, if they can afford it, they hire private tutors. This provides a huge advantage in raising their examination scores. That way the rich get richer and the poor remain in their place.

"When I first got to the Capital I did sit for the examinations and I was happy to pass them."

"How did you prepare?"

"Prepare? My preparation was asking for the location where the examinations were being given. I didn't even know about them until a few days before I took them. I was lucky someone mentioned them when I arrived or I would have missed them altogether."

Bo Mah stares at Ho Yup and shrugs his shoulders. "Even bright young men prepare for years to take their first examination. They complain about how grueling an experience it is. This fellow walks in, no preparation, and takes the examinations with the ease of answering, 'How's the weather?'"

The next morning all five of us begin the serious work of mining. Ya Min is stunned to see the amount of gold we're collecting. He pulls me aside. "This is so much more gold than I'm used to finding and we've only been at it for four hours. I suggest you and I take a walk and look for a suitable hiding place."

We walk deep into the hills and settle on a location. Ya Min suggests we go down to Jackson once a week to the assayer's office and convert the gold to cash and open a bank account in all our names. I agree. At the end of the day, we lead the other three to the hidden location and discuss the plans for a joint bank account. We all ate heartily that night. Each week, Ya Min alternated with each of the other men so everyone knows where the bank is. Females had few rights at that time so Mei Sam stayed behind.

On the fifth week, Ya Min and I go down to Jackson. On our way out, we bump into two of the men who created a problem about Mei Sam on our first visit. "Hey coolies, where's the pretty little girl? Have you decided on a price for her yet? We'll make it worth your while."

Lo Wan notices that the bigger man had a severe Chi blockage of his Liver meridian. He is prone to anger and doesn't handle frustration well. It seems to cloud his thinking. Being a Wood sign seems to lead to his irritability. He would be the one to make the first move. His friend seems to have a blockage of Chi in his Gall Bladder resulting in his sense of rigidity. His Wood sign seems to result in a poor reaction to anything that frustrates him. They're well suited to be friends so they can foolishly drag each other into dangerous situations.

Ya Min nudges me to keep walking out of town, but one of the men runs in front of me and another walks up behind me. "Hey, I asked you a question Chink, and I expect an answer."

The man behind me picks up a large rock and is about to hit me in the back of the head as the man in front goes to grab me. I trip and fall to the side of the man with the rock who hits his friend in the nose with it. The man drops to the ground bleeding and his friend bends down to help him. I gently push Ya Min's elbow indicating that we should just keep walking."

We quicken our pace and are soon out of town. "That was lucky. If you hadn't stumbled, that man would have bashed your head in."

"You're right. Let's walk a bit faster in case they decide to find more friends who want to continue the conversation. I'm lucky to be walking away instead of being the one lying on the ground bleeding. I think we're depositing a considerable amount of money in the Jackson bank. Perhaps too much. Let's find another bank in another town close by and begin an account there. I think it'd be a good decision financially and I don't know how these 'friends' of ours in Jackson will welcome us back next time."

Ya Min nods.

It was Mei Sam's turn to cook dinner. A young man named Ah Sook volunteers to bring her some fresh water for the soup she's preparing. Before she could gather kindling for the fire, Ah Sook appears carrying enough kindling for several fires. She thanks him. After dinner she begins collecting the dishes to wash them. Ah Sook appears and begins helping. When they're finished, she thanks him again for his help. Ah Sook blushes and walks away. Mei Sam notices how Ah Sook often stares at her, but he always turns away when she returns his glances.

The next morning, Ah Sook appears again when she begins preparing the morning gruel. He helps clear the dishes and washes them. He keeps asking her questions about her past and telling her about his family back in China. She thinks he's a friendly, but shy young man. When I walk over she introduces Ah Sook who doesn't appear nearly as friendly toward me. Mei Sam notices his attitude change.

During my introduction to Ah Sook I notice a pronounced blockage of Chi in his Pericardium meridian that seems to interfere with his clarity of thought. His Fire sign is evident outwardly by his skin rash and also shows up in his impulsivity and inability to hide his emotional reactions. I don't think this skinny man's interest in Mei Sam will end well. I'm happy Mei Sam's martial arts skillset is improving.

The next evening, another man and I cook dinner. Mei Sam is straightening up our tent as Ah Sook walks over. He asks if she'd like to take a walk. It's a beautiful time of day and she agrees to go for a short walk. Ah Sook tells her it's very lonely in the mountains and he's happy to have a beautiful young girl here for company.

"Ah Sook, stop right there. I'm a married woman and you shouldn't be speaking to me this way." She immediately begins walking back quickly by herself.

For the next week, she makes it a point not to be in any situation where she'll be alone with Ah Sook, but she notices he's still staring at her. She tells me about Ah Sook's flirtations.

"You may have the opportunity to practice your Wing Chun strikes and parries sooner than you expected."

Each day our mining quintet is finding more gold. We're starting to amass a substantial amount. One day Ya Min asks everyone to stop working so we can have a talk. "I'm worried that the others will find out about what we're doing. If someone happens by and sees what we've created, I'm not sure how they'll react, except that it'll be bad."

"I have the same fear. Help me cut down a few large bushes to use as cover for our equipment. Four or five bushes should be enough if they're big and full enough. We can take turns standing guard. Our mining area is pretty small and there's only one road coming in so it'll only take one person to guard it. If we have two or three minutes of warning, we can camouflage our setup. All it'll take is one of us standing down the road yelling an excited 'hello' from a distance to let us know someone is coming. Each night when we finish working and leave the site we can practice our camouflage skills."

We all agree and everyone breathes a sigh of relief. We eat dinner that night with a calm stomach and enjoy the food even though it was prepared by Ya Min who was nobody's favorite cook.

Just after sunrise, three White men come walking in during the morning meal. One of them yells, "Who's the leader of this outfit?"

One of the men who speaks passable English says, "No leader. Each man work alone here."

"How much gold you coolies finding here?"

"Not find much. Sometimes we eat only one time in day."

"Well, we'll just take a look around 'n see if yer lyin', and ya' better not be. The men walk into a few tents and begin shaking out random clothes and blankets. After a few minutes they come back out. We didn't find nothin' but that don't mean we believe you."

They walk up to one of the miners and backhand him across the face, knocking him to the ground. "What're you hidin' Chink?"

"He no understand you."

One of the White men bends down and looks through the man's pockets. When he comes up empty he spits in the man's face. "We'll check back and if we find out that you're lyin' n hidin' gold, we'll kill ya' all."

After they leave Mei Sam comes up to me, "Shouldn't you have done something?"

"These are stupid men who didn't really hurt anyone. They didn't find anything. They're dirt poor and desperate. I doubt if they'll return. If we fought with them, they might think we have something to hide and return with more men and they may even bring guns. This way we didn't make it worth their while."

The Chancellor was still fuming when he got to his bedchamber until his saw Ho Singh's daughter in his bed. She was wearing a short, transparent nightgown. Her body was hairless and she was shaking. The Chancellor laid down next to her and said, "Do you know why you're here?"

The frightened girl shook her head. "Don't be afraid. You're going to have the most wonderful night of your life. Now I want you to take off my clothes very slowly and then pull off your nightgown. When she began to cry and didn't follow his orders the Chancellor grabbed the leather riding crop he keeps by his bed and hits her across the thighs. "Nobody refuses me."

She was terrified and nodded. "Now do what I told you and then we're going to play a game called 'Horsey.' You'll be my horsey and I'm going to ride you. Get ready for the best game you'll ever play."

When the Chancellor was through with her, she was curled in a corner of the large bed weeping. He pulled up his sheet and called in his chief bodyguard. "Now bring her mother here to me. Make sure she's been cleaned up first. As a reward for your loyal service, I just finished playing Horsey with this little girl. You may now take her back to your room and also give her a ride. When you're finished with her, pass her around to your favorite men then dump her out on the road outside the castle walls."

After dinner, I was cleaning the dishes. Mei Sam was in front of the tent. Ah Sook walks up behind her and says he wants to apologize for his rude behavior. She nods, walks closer and as he begins to talk, he makes a sudden move to grab her shoulders and kiss her. He is surprised at how hard she slaps his hand away and more surprised that she almost simultaneously punches him in the nose. He falls to the ground with his nose bleeding.

"I let you off easy this time. Keep your distance from me because next time I may not be in such a forgiving mood."

When I return to the tent, Mei Sam can barely talk through her excitement. She describes each move in detail. "Now I understand why you have me practice each move so many times. When he grabbed me I felt like my hands had a mind of their own. They were thinking faster than my mind was capable. As

Ah Sook was walking away I saw him alternating between rubbing his nose where I punched it and his wrist where I slapped it away. Just a warning to you husband. Be careful. I'm a dangerous woman now."

I wonder if this entire incident was brought about by Ah Sook's loneliness or did Mei Sam play a role in inciting it.

Ah Sook's mind raced back-and-forth between his pain and his pride. He was just been beaten up by a girl.

The next evening after dinner the five partners went for a walk. Bo Mah says, "I came here for safety. I was being hunted by lots of angry White men. I had no intention of becoming rich, yet we're amassing quite a lot of money. Have any of you thought about what you're going to do with your earnings?"

Ya Min smiled. "I think I've saved enough already to buy my passage back to China and set up a store. I've always dreamed of becoming a merchant."

"What'll you sell?"

"I've always wanted more time to study and learn. I'll sell books and scrolls. It'll be a wonderful way to spend my golden years."

Ya Min asks Bo Mah what his long term plans are. "I'd like to go back to live in San Francisco. The Chinatown there is quite large and it's easy for a man to live the life he wants there if he keeps his profile low and knows how to avoid angering the wrong people. I have many good friends there."

Ho Yup says, "If you go there and wouldn't mind, that sounds like the perfect life for me also."

Bo Mah walks over to Ho Yup and puts his arm around his old friend's shoulder. "Nothing would please me more."

All eyes turn toward me. "I just recently came to California and have no idea what challenges and opportunities await me here. I long to return to China. I'm also happy to stay here and think through where I'd like to go and where Mei Sam would like to go. She and I have a lot to think about."

That night I whisper. "You've turned sixteen. I would like to stop raping you. I hope you'd like to become an honest woman. I was talking to Bo Mah and he told me that he can legally marry people in California. You would make me very happy if you would agree to marry me."

Mei Sam didn't say a word. She was too busy kissing me.

Chapter 7

The next two weeks are pleasantly boring. Each day starts with the same boring meal. We repeat the same tasks at our claim. We come back to camp and have the same boring dinner and go to sleep. After the tumultuous time I've been having since I came to America, boredom and predictability are treasured resources. One afternoon at their claim, I pull Bo Mah aside. When we finish talking he has a smile on this face as I assemble the quintet.

"Mei Sam and I were never *officially* married. Bo Mah is invested with the power to marry us legally in California and will do so now with the two of you as our witnesses. Please don't tell anyone else about this, but I'm so happy to have you three here to share this wonderful event with us." Bo Mah performs a simple, but moving ceremony next to the water wheel.

That night we consummated our marriage...legally.

A few nights later at an evening meal, Ah Sook introduces two new men who want to join the cooperative. They're both in their mid thirties and seem to be pleasant enough. Some of the men are a bit suspicious because they don't have any connection to anyone in the group. All of the other group members were brought in by someone who could personally vouch for them.

One of the new men is quite large and the other is of a more average size, maybe just a bit bigger. All the men sit in a circle and ask the two new men how they found their way to this collective. The smaller of the two says, "My name is Sun Ro. My friend Di Nu and I have tried to make a living in several cities, but each time there were many White men who beat us and accused us of trying to steal their jobs. They chased us out threatening to kill us if we stayed. We kept hearing that the safest place for men like us is in the Sierra Mountains where we could mine for gold, keep what we find and live in peace."

Sun Ro shows no apparent blockage in any meridian. He's an Earth sign with a penchant for honesty that seems hollow, like the type of person who could switch characteristics of one sign to another at will. The man seems to have no stable core. I would never buy an ox from a man like this.

His larger partner seems to have a minor Chi blockage in the Small Intestine meridian. His Fire sign characteristic seemed to project passion and enthusiasm, but it also appears to not run very deep.

Di Nu takes over. "We decided to try our luck and began hiking until we came to the mountains. Once we got here we just kept asking around for groups of Chinese miners and found mostly small groups of two and three men. We wanted to find a larger group because we've learned there's safety in numbers. Finally, we stumbled onto this camp."

Ah Sook says, "Tell them a little about what you'll bring if you join us."

"We're hard workers and if you don't mind us bragging a little, we're excellent cooks. That's what we did back in China before we were shanghaied and dragged here to America. It's how we've made a living since we got here. You don't have to say 'yes' or 'no' to us now. Just let us to stay with you for a few days, and if you like us, and our cooking, you might even hope we'll want to stay."

The men agree to give them a trial although several men don't appear to trust them. That was until breakfast. The new men got up early to pick fruit and baked dumplings using their findings as fillings. Everyone now seems infatuated with their new cooks. By the time dinner was over that night their trial was over. They're invited to join. Night-after-night as the two men become friendlier they pick different small groups of men and make special dessert treats for them and talk long into the night. They are both excellent storytellers and have become very popular in a short time.

On their fifth night after a particularly wonderful meal of dim sum with two sauces, the men come to our tent with a gourd telling us they prepared a special fruit drink and would love for us to be the first ones to try it. We said we'd be honored. Within ten minutes both of us are passed out and dragged into the woods. We're hauled out quite far so no one will be able to hear us. One of them drags Mei Sam up against a tree and takes off her long dress leaving her only in her undergarments. Sun Ro says, "Prop her up against that tree and I'll tie up Lo Wan and we'll wait for him to wake up so he can watch his bride die before his helpless eyes."

Li Wing comes back from the Capital late at night. "I spoke to a few people who knew Lo Wan in the capital, but none have any idea where he is now. I was able to track down the small living space he occupied and discovered that someone else has been living there for several months. Through this man, I found the landlord who said Lo Wan was a wonderful tenant and then he just disappeared. He abandoned his few belongings which the landlord threw away after several months."

As I broadened my search, I ran across several people he treated and they had nothing but wonderful stories to tell. When any of them went looking for him seeking help again, they were disappointed to discover he was gone without a trace. I'm afraid we're no closer to finding him."

"I went to the local authorities to see if they knew of his whereabouts and the police captain was curious about why I was trying to find him. I left the police station as quickly as I could."

"You didn't follow up about his curiosity? You just left?"

"I said I left father, but don't get ahead of my story. I hid and waited until the police captain left the station for the evening and followed him. He stopped for some wine on the way home. I followed him until I found a quiet street. I silenced him and had him accompany me to a deserted warehouse where we could talk. I restored his speech and he began threatening me until I stopped his right arm from working. That changed his attitude. We switched roles and I became the interrogator."

"He didn't know many specifics, but from what I could piece together, after a bit of coercion, Lo Wan made someone in an exalted position angry and was sent away in exile. Sadly, that's as much as he knew. On the positive side, I fixed it so the captain remembers very little of our conversation so I didn't make matters any worse."

After tying Mei Sam to a tree, Sun Ro grabs my hand to place it behind my back. The expression on his face changes as he feels his body go numb when I use my thumb to press where his neck meets his spine. Then I sneak up behind the larger man who was fondling Mei Sam's breast and the world goes dark for him.

Both men wake securely tied to a tree as I replace Mei Sam's dress and leave to find some herbs. I find some Tang-kuei that has some powerful properties for nourishing the blood and helping moisten the intestines. It also increases circulation, calms tension, and relieves pain. Within a short time Mei Sam is in a daze, but awake. She finds me standing over her and the two new cooks tied to a tree.

"What's happening?"

"Let's have our new friends tell us." I restore some movement in Sun Ro's upper body. He notices he's paralyzed from the waist down. Di Nu is in the same condition.

"Gentlemen, that was a very bracing drink you brought us. I must get your recipe. Which of you would like to explain your intentions?"

They react as if I asked the dumbest question ever. It was clear neither intended to talk.

The big man asked, "Why didn't it knock you out?"

"Before I even put my lips to the cup I could smell the ichacha. You probably call it 'knock out' drops. There were even traces of it floating on the sides of the cup. The second I put my tongue to it, it was clear what it was."

"Damn it, I told you to mix it really well. Wait till the Chancellor hears how incompetent you were."

Before you argue about how the drink was mixed, I've been suspicious about the two of you since you arrived. It was your hands. Although both of you are excellent cooks, you both have well-calloused hands, particularly your knuckles. They show years of martial training. I have a pretty good idea why we're all here tonight, but I'd really like to hear it from your lips. Which of you would like to start?

Since your intention was to torture then kill my wife and one of you already half undressed her, there's not too much to tell. I was awake the whole time you dragged us here, and heard your plans so there's not going to be much surprising information, but I would still enjoy hearing the story in your own words. Now who's going to start?"

The two men sat resolute, demonstrating pride in their obstinacy.

I respect your loyalty to the Chancellor. The one you were ready to torture and kill for. By the rules of any civilized system of warfare, I have the right, almost the obligation, to kill both of you, but I don't like to kill so I've come up with a more poetic form of justice for you both.

You can tell what kind of man the Chancellor is by the nature of this mission. Just to make it clearer for you, know that he wouldn't recognize me if I was standing right in front of him, but he's now gone to the enormous expense of sending five different men to kill my wife who he's *never* even met.

But we all know that frustration makes the Chancellor livid. Apparently, his motto is 'don't get angry … get revenge … in the most painful way possible.' So I'm going to send the Chancellor a telegram about how badly his foolish idea of sending you two bumbling fools turned out. I'll make sure to mention the badly stirred ichcha. Thank you for that nice touch. I'll let him know we're here laughing at him. An important part of this telegram will be that the two of you are being sent back aboard a ship. I'll provide information about which ship and the arrival date so you'll be welcomed on the gangplank. I'm not sure what he'll choose to do, but I'm certain I wouldn't want it to happen to me."

Sun Ro yelled, "No, wait, please. We heard you bested three warriors the Chancellor sent so the Viceroy decided to send us. In addition to our martial arts backgrounds, we have training as actors and we were taught how to prepare delicious food by some of the finest cooks in Peking. We were told the last place you were seen was Stockton. We began there. After gaining the confidence of several people we found out about Bo Mah's cousin Ya Min. We were very patient and talked to men in every mining camp we came across."

"How did Ah Sook happen to be the one who introduced you?"

"We met several of the men in this cooperative and they were close mouthed until we met him. He seemed to have a strong interest in knowing whether we were friends of yours or your enemies. It was evident he didn't like you so when he found the opportunity to bring in potential enemies of yours he was happy to help us join the group."

"Thank you for your honesty, but it still leaves me with the dilemma about your futures. You're sworn to kill my wife and I'm sure I was not to go unscathed. Although we'll keep our word and won't put you aboard a ship bound for China, there's still the matter of your intention to make my wife suffer and then kill her. What do you suggest I do with you?"

Sun Ro said, "You could let us go and I promise you'll never see either of us again."

"You really are a fine actor, but I can see a few pitfalls in going down that path. I was looking more at should I kill you slowly with the same kind of pain you were ready to leave us in, or should I be merciful and kill you quickly after exacting just a few bits of revenge?"

Di Nu said, "Just do what you intend to do and get it over with. We're both warriors and death doesn't frighten us."

"I admire your bravery, but it's not that easy. I'm a healer and I don't like to kill, but I don't like the idea that the two of you will have learned nothing from this entire episode. That's a terrible way to have your lives end."

Lo Wan walked over to Sun Ro and stood him up on shaky feet. "Mei Sam, this man dragged you here. That's why your legs are full of scrapes. That's also why your arms hurt. He also half undressed you while you were unconscious and even squeezed your breasts. Oh yes, I almost forgot, he planned to kill you. And to make me suffer, he was going to kill you slowly and painfully. How does that make you feel?"

"When you put it that way, I'd like to be part of their rehabilitation."

"You still have some of the ichacha they gave you in your system. A bit of exercise would help flush it from your system."

He helped Sun Ro stand. He needed the help because his hands and feet were tied.

Show me Gaun Sau."

Mei Sam unleashed her "splitting hand" on his shoulders. First one side than the other. Sun Ro howled with each stroke and fell to the ground.

"Not bad for someone who's just been drugged. Now let's stand him up and show me Biu Sau in the windpipe."

After she thrust her fingers into Sun Ro's windpipe he tried to scream, but no sound came out. He tried to breathe, but found it impossible and began to cough and panic. I use some acupressure manipulation on his throat to restore his breathing.

"Now one final strike. Show me your front kick. I think you know what target we both think you should aim for." The dazed man found the pitch of his voice rising as the simultaneous reactions of his body to pain and nausea resulted. As the big man watched all this he winced with each blow.

"Di Nu, let me help you up to your feet."

I walked over to Mei Sam and whispered in her ear. "Show me the same front kick and when he bends over, follow it with four Chung Choy blasts to his nose."

"Di Nu, since you're so much bigger and stronger than Sun Ro, we're not going to warn you what Mei Sam will do."

Mei Sam threw her front kick to add Di Nu to the soprano chorus and followed it up with her four blasting nose strikes. Both men lay on the ground groaning. Each had their hands between their legs massaging themselves. "That's my wife's payback for you planning to kill her, but it still doesn't solve the problem of what to do with you in the long run. I could ask you to promise not to come after us again, but even if you gave us your word, you're both actors which means your words are not to be trusted, but I'm going to ask for your words anyway because I'm a trusting man, but I'll accept your word with a twist."

"Di Nu, you told me as a warrior, you're not afraid of death, but you didn't mention how you'd react to pain. I think I'll feel better releasing you after I've given you enough pain to remember for the rest of your life. I will only make the pain last for five seconds for each of you, but you'll be afraid to ever experience it again. Di Nu, since you're bigger, I'll start with you."

The big man is still on the ground with a bloody nose. I walk up behind him and press a spot on his lumbar spine and he begins shrieking. I add a second spot in the cervical area and he howls. After five seconds, I stop the pain. The large man is quivering on the ground. He is convulsing and weeping.

As I walk toward Sun Ro, he tries to back away. I hit the same two locations and he screams and shakes more intensely than his partner.

Now I'm ready to hear you each promise not to come after us again. I believe you'll remember this pain and never want to have it repeated. If you break your word, the next, and let me add … the last time I will administer it, it will be longer, more intense and I won't stop it until …

I waited for each of them to regain a bit if their composure.

Well, we're almost done here. Although you both endured intense pain for a short time, and I'm sure you'll remember it, there's still the problem of equity. The pain you were going to leave me in would have lasted a lifetime so it's only fair that I leave you with a way to remember this bargain we're making forever as well. I'm going to punch each of you in the arm causing it to break in such a way that you'll still be able to cook and act on stage, but you won't be able to use that arm to fight the way you've trained. That'll help us sleep a bit more comfortably at night. You each should pay a lasting price for wanting to kill my wife and leave me in misery." I deliver a vicious punch to each man. "You will not have to have your arm set by a physician. It will heal by itself, but your days of using it for combat are over.

Since you're both trained actors, you know how to simulate the emotional reactions of others in multiple situations. From there, I believe, it's not a great leap to the practice of empathy. You've both just experienced feeling weak and helpless. I hope that what you've just gone through will help you develop your sense of empathy and keep you from hurting other people again.

As I told the last men the Chancellor sent, my advice is that you remain in America. If you return to China, the Chancellor will not be pleased with you since you failed him. I think you both recognize how deep the Chancellor's hatred runs and how he channels it. It's why you're here. I believe your life in China would be miserable and short. Here, with your skills, I believe you will both prosper. I suggest you begin walking downhill quickly before Mei Sam changes her mind.

In the morning, everyone was disappointed when they see gruel on their plates and no sign of the new men who cooked so skillfully. There are questions all around, but no answers. As the men are going off to work, I ask Ah Sook to take a walk with me. He is eager to get to his claim and suggests that perhaps we can talk later. As I put my arm around his shoulder, we look like good friends to the few men still around, but the searing pain Ah Sook feels there convinces him perhaps he should hear what I have to say.

"The cooks you introduced to the camp were not very nice men. They told me the role you played in their introduction. I'd like you to think back to the beating my wife gave you. Wouldn't it be embarrassing if everyone in the collective knew about it? It would be more embarrassing if she did it again, this time in public. The pain you're feeling in your shoulder now is from two of my fingers, not using much pressure. I'd like to think we can make this entire episode disappear with two promises. First, never approach my wife unless I'm with her; and second, none of the events we're discussing here have ever happened. Do I have your assurance on both accounts?"

Ah Sook nodded his head and said, "Yes, thank you for letting me go."

"If you go back on your word, my wife will give you a public beating, and that's before I get to you."

———

The Viceroy walks into the Chancellor's Jade room with his midday meal churning in his belly. He has to give another distressing report that his overlord will not like.

"Ah my Viceroy, I used to place a great deal of confidence in you, but it's evaporating daily. You told me we lost three talented men who were sent after an undersized healer in a country where he doesn't know anyone, and cannot speak the language. A country where everyone hates him. And you told me those three men we sent didn't choose to return to China with the news of their failure. Have you received any word of their whereabouts?"

116

"No my Chancellor. I'm investigating their disappearances as we speak."

"I hope today's news will be more to my liking. How did the two talented actors fare?"

My Lord, I'm saddened to report that the new story is eerily similar to the previous one. They failed. We're also investigating their disappearance as well. They haven't returned."

"I don't accept anyone besting me. Certainly not a flyspeck of a healer." The Chancellor smiled. "My esteemed Viceroy, you know I don't get angry when I'm disappointed. I choose retribution as my source of consolation. I'm afraid that soon I'll have to decide which is more important... retribution against the young healer or you. Please spare me from having to make such an arduous decision. Before you implement another plan, confer with me about it... even though I shouldn't have to bother with such trifling matters. I remind you that I don't have infinite patience. I also know the location of all your relatives. I will leave you with one word of motivation... *Macau*."

"I think you know the next immediate steps you're to take. See if the two actors have young daughters or exceptionally pretty young sons. Next, see if they have attractive young wives. If they do, bring them to me, if they're not attractive, have them entertain my soldiers. If they don't have wives or children, let me know what other relatives are available."

The Viceroy leaves the Jade Room trembling. His chief bodyguard is shocked to see his condition. The Viceroy says, "Every day I walk in to give him bad news... I expect to be my last."

The Viceroy decides that some wine might provide some needed therapy to soothe his nerves. His bodyguard knows if the Viceroy is happy, his own job is easier, just as the Viceroy learned the same lesson with the Chancellor. After their fourth glass, his trusted bodyguard asked the Viceroy how the Chancellor developed such a violent temper.

The Chancellor's father was married to a beautiful woman from a powerful family. She bore him three beautiful daughters.

He consorted with four gorgeous concubines who came from well-placed royal families. They also bore him daughters. When he was in his fifties and losing all hope, a miracle occurred. His wife produced a male heir. He became the proudest father in China.

"No expense was spared in raising his son. If the boy pointed to a toy, it was his. It was the same if he pointed to a pony ... his. If he didn't like a tutor, he was whisked out of the room and replaced by another. Every effort was made to keep him happy. This made it impossible for the little Chancellor-to-be to find happiness because life had no challenges. The summary of his life was, 'I want it ... mine ... eh.'"

"As he grew older, they brought friends in for him to play with. By the age of six, if a friend displeased him, he screamed, 'Kill him.' Of course that wasn't ever done, but he never saw that friend again and was told that child was killed on his orders. When the Chancellor was nine years old an unfortunate incident occurred. The young Chancellor saw one of the boys he had ordered killed running on the castle grounds. He had a tantrum and demanded to see his father."

Taking his son by the hand, they went to one of the Castle Captains and asked for an explanation. The Captain, caught off guard, managed to say that an old gardener was supposed to have taken care of the execution. The young Chancellor-to-be, holding on to his father's hand, demanded to go to the Gardeners' Shed right away and confront the guilty man. He screamed at the Captain to point him out. The frightened Captain pointed to an old gardener who was asleep in the corner on a cot. The boy yelled, 'Kill him ... kill him now while I watch.' The Chancellor ordered the Captain to behead the gardener. The Captain obeyed. The young Chancellor-to-be clapped his hands and cheered. Then he said, 'I'm hungry' father, and they all left."

"Sadly, there are countless similar stories. You don't want to hear what happened when he discovered his sexual urges. No young girl he saw was safe. Neither were occasional pretty young boys. I'll leave you with this advice. Don't disappoint him."

A quiet week passed and gold kept accumulating. Late one night, I told Mei Sam I needed to have a talk with her. "I've put your life in danger twice now because of a history you played no role in. The good news is we've put away enough money to permit us to do almost anything we want, but I don't think we should stay here much longer."

"If things are going so well, why should we leave?"

"The two men sent by the Chancellor were able to find us, just like when we were in Stockton. We're no longer safe here. I also think that at some point, our prospecting scheme here'll be discovered and it'll lead to bad feelings. I'd like to see more of this country and resume my studies. But more important, I'm certain the Chancellor will make another attempt on your life fairly soon. It seems like we're not as well hidden as I thought we were. I believe each attempt will be more sophisticated. I couldn't bear to have anything happen to you."

"You said you can handle these attempts. You did very well with this one."

"Yes, but I may not be as lucky next time. The Chancellor has a big advantage having unlimited resources. And remember, we're both still wanted by the authorities. I was deluding myself thinking I could handle any situation that arises."

"Having a lot of money gives us a number of options. Let me begin with the most important one. I want to give you the opportunity to remove yourself from your marital vows. If you went out on your own, you'd have enough money to open a business in a community that's more accepting of Chinese people, you could even buy a farm, and never again fear being sold into a life of prostitution, and you won't have to look over your shoulder for someone who wants to get back at me through you. What would you like to do?"

"As I look back on my short history, my life began the night you tore off my dress and gave me your shirt to wear. Our lives are intertwined. I choose to go wherever you go if you'll have me."

"Mei Sam, thank you for letting me exhale. I was praying that'd be your choice, but I had to hear it from you. I think we should go to San Francisco with Bo Mah and Ho Yup. I have an influential friend there and of course we'll have our partners as well."

"Won't going to one of the largest Chinatowns in America make it easier for the Chancellor to track us down?"

"Yes, but that may be an advantage for us. We were surprised on both of his previous attempts. In San Francisco, we'll be vigilant every minute and it won't be so easy to surprise us again."

The next morning the five partners discussed their futures and all agreed that San Francisco was an auspicious place to begin their new lives. They also realized there was safety in numbers and their finances would be safer if all five of us travelled together. I suggested that we go to all four banks and withdraw everything tomorrow. Then, keep moving until we reached San Francisco. We also decided to destroy our mining setup so that it wouldn't be discovered and fought over.

"We should stop outside the last town after withdrawing the money from that bank and find a remote spot. There, I'll sew each person's money into the lining of their clothing leaving only few dollars for expenses. That will keep our money safer."

Everyone cheered Mei Sam's idea.

Early next morning each of us packs a small bundle of necessities to make travelling easier. We leave everything else. After our morning gruel, when everyone went their way, the five of us headed for our claim. We destroy every trace of it and then move on to the bank at Jackson.

The bank withdrawal goes smoothly but as we reach the town limits we run into the two large White men who keep trying to buy Mei Sam.

"Did ya' come to town to sell the girl?"

I was ambivalent. I didn't want a confrontation, but I sort of did. "Yes, men come with us. We go just outside town so no one see. You bring money and we make good deal."

The three travel companions are shocked, but Mei Sam has a pretty good idea what is going to happen and smiles. The Jackson men catch her smile and are encouraged to follow. They all hurry out of town. The two men slow down, but I say, "No, more far from town. Nobody see. Nobody know." I lead them into a clearing in a forested area, "I change mind. No sell."

"You God Damn Chink. You're right. You ain't sellin' her. We're just takin' her right now."

One of the men goes to grab Mei Sam. I yelled "Fook Sau."

Mei Sam's hand folded over the top to control the man's hand to stop it from grabbing her. Then she continues to push her hand higher to hit him in the face with a palm strike.

I yell, "Chung Choy Blast."

Mei Sam delivers a series of short, piston-like strikes to the man's nose breaking it and leaving him on the floor holding the nose that is now gushing blood.

I yell, "Go get other man." The other man hears that and runs to scoop up his friend and the two of them stagger back to town. Their three friends are smiling as they hold their arms up with palms facing outward as if to say, "Don't hit me." Then they begin to laugh and applaud. Mei Sam takes a deep, theatrical bow and then assumes her fighting stance. "Not to worry. If someone tries to take our money, I'll take care of them."

The next three bank withdrawals are much easier. We find what seems to be a safe place to make camp while there's still plenty of daylight. Though Mei Sam is an excellent seamstress she takes a long time because she wants to distribute the cash evenly throughout their clothing leaving no unsightly bulges or obvious shapes protruding. When we put our jackets back on everyone is stunned that so much money can be distributed and hidden so comfortably.

Bo Mah called us together. "It's over a hundred miles to San Francisco. It'll be a nice five or six day walk. Another alternative is to get on a stagecoach, but that would present problems that are better avoided. The weather's pleasant this time of year and we'll arrive in San Francisco in good health having gotten plenty of exercise. We can also avoid travelling through cities by taking less popular rural roads. The fewer people we see the better. And if we run into trouble, we have Mei Sam to protect us."

We set a good pace and at dusk each night we select a pleasant campsite and prepare an evening meal. Each night, as far as the other three know, Mei Sam and I like to find a quiet spot to sit and talk. What we actually do is continue Mei Sam's martial arts training. She has a voracious appetite for learning and loves to practice. During the day as we walk, I point out new medicinal herbs and plants. She puts them in a small sack she carries. For the two of us, this was not a trek; it was our first real vacation.

As we sit around the campfire, I ask Bo Mah to tell us about Chinatown in San Francisco.

"Well, if there's such a thing as old money in Chinatown, it's represented by the Six Companies. They do a lot of good, charitable things, but also have their hands in anything that brings in money legally and some businesses that are right on the edge of legal."

"Like what?"

"If someone is shanghaied and comes across the ocean against their will and now is forced to go into involuntary servitude, the Six Companies get a piece of that. If someone's work contract is sold from one company to another, the Six Companies are part of the deal. If you want to sail home to China, you'll have to go through them."

"So they're a terrible organization? And corrupt?"

"They're more of a necessary evil. As Chinese, we can't deal directly with the steamship companies so it's good to have the Six Companies acting as a broker. And they see to it that we don't get cheated. At least not from the steamship companies. They look at it as their fee for the work they do."

"Next, we should go on to discuss the Tongs. I can summarize them in one short sentence. They're gangsters. Each Tong has a boss. Each member has to prove both his loyalty and value to the boss. Their initiations often involve committing brutal crimes to prove both their loyalty and usefulness."

"Each Tong has its own style of dress so it's pretty easy to tell which one they belong to. When you learn to identify them, which won't take long, it's best to walk the other way when you see any one of them. Stay out of their way and they generally stay out of yours. They try to be very careful not to interact with the police so the Tongs mostly quarrel with each other."

"So far, you don't make San Francisco's Chinatown sound very inviting."

"Oh, I'm telling you the worst parts first. Now if you like good food, there are no finer places to eat except perhaps the Emperor's table. If you love Chinese Opera or Chinese Theater they feature some of the best performances. There are also fine Chinese Boxing matches. There are shops that rival the finest merchants in our homeland. And of course, there are many so-phisticated people who live there with whom you may talk, play chess or Go or just share a glass of wine. And there are people from almost every part of China that you'll run into ... if you don't go looking for trouble."

Chapter 8

As we begin getting closer to San Francisco Bo Mah pulls me aside. "I don't know if you've thought about this, but in the eyes of the authorities, you're a wanted man. And, you told me that to rescue Mei Sam, both of you had to escape from the mine that owns your contracts so the authorities are after you both."

"You said Tu Chan is your friend. Do you know that he doesn't just work for the Six Companies; he's their Vice President. That's the second highest position in their organization." Legally, if Tu Chan sees you, he's obligated to turn both of you in to the authorities. If it's discovered that he saw you and didn't, he could be arrested and lose everything he's worked for. Worse still, if the authorities find either of you, they'll arrest you. We have to find a way to have you pay off your debts to the mining company. Coordinating this transaction without the authorities being involved will prove difficult if not dangerous for you. The good news is the amount you'll have to pay will be tiny compared to what you've earned from our mining work. I would consider it an honor to broker the situation for you with Tu Chan's help. I'm sure we can clear your name, but during that time, you two can't set foot anywhere near San Francisco, especially Chinatown. On our way to San Francisco, we'll have to find a safe place where you can hide until we can bring you both in."

Bo Mah asks Ho Yup to join them and asks where he thinks Lo Wan can stay. Ho Yup smiles, "I have a nephew who lives outside Fremont. It's a small city about forty miles from San Francisco. He lives on a farm with his family. We could stop there on our way and ask if he would be able to accommodate you and Mei Sam until we can clear everything up."

Ho Yup's nephew Foo Hai is in his late thirties. He lives in a small house with his wife and two children. They all work to keep their farm running by selling produce to restaurants in Fremont, Oakland and even San Francisco on occasion. They don't have much, but seem comfortable and happy.

Foo Hai hugs his uncle and says he'll gladly have the young couple stay with them as long as they like ... if they're willing to work on the farm to earn their keep. It seems like a perfect solution all the way round.

Foo Hai has no detectible Chi flow problem. As a Water sign, he seems to display a tendency to adapt and remain tranquil. The man has a lovely family and he seemed devoted to them.

The first morning Mei Sam wakes early to help Soo Wei, Foo Hai's wife, prepare the morning meal and begin the long list of chores Foo Hai has prepared. He goes out with me and we work side-by-side so he can gauge what kind of a worker I might be. He wants to determine how best to use this opportunity of free labor. He discovers I'm capable of doing anything he asks and is overjoyed to have this free labor for the price of a bit of food. That's why he's so surprised when I stop him to talk.

"I'm very grateful you've taken us in. I'd like to help out with the additional expenses that we're costing you for food. Do you think four dollars a week is fair?"

Foo Hai was afraid I was going to suggest that we get paid for our labor. For his family, an additional four dollars will be enough for a month's food costs, seeing how they grow almost all their own food. He's overjoyed. Each evening after the children are put to bed the two couples sit around the fire and talk. Some nights Mei Sam gives Soo Wei some sewing tips. The first two weeks go by in a pleasant blur.

Bo Mah goes to the Six Companies to talk to Tu Chan. He's surprised that Bo Mah and I ever had the opportunity to meet. Once Bo Mah explains the whole story Tu Chan looks down and draws a deep breath. "If it was just one person, I think I could fix the situation easily, but the complication of Lo Wan and his young wife as a runaway Singsong girl with a contract makes the situation more complicated."

"The Sam Ping Mining Company is part of a powerful syndicate. They have close ties with a large bank and I hear they also deal with several Tongs. They've had some financial problems recently that'll make them even greedier. I'll have to tread lightly if I'm to negotiate our way out of this. I can tell you now that he'll have to buy his way out and it won't be cheap. Tell me where you're staying and I'll begin making inquiries. I'm so happy to see you old friend, and I'll be happy to see Lo Wan again, but you didn't bring me a very nice gift on your arrival."

Foo Hai asks me to walk outside with him one evening after work. "Since you and Mei Sam have been working here with us we've never been more productive. I know your time is limited here, but we've never grown and sold so much produce before which makes what I'm going to say even more awkward. My cousin explained why you're staying here and that if the authorities in San Francisco found out you were here you'd get arrested. I also know that you have some money put away so if you give me fifty dollars, I won't turn you in to the authorities.

"Foo Hai, I thought that although you agreed to do us a big favor, which I very much appreciate, I thought that we've also become friends. You disappoint me greatly."

"I need to think of my family first. As a courtesy, I'll give you two days to decide what you'd like to do."

When I tell Mei Sam she asks, "Did you punch him first or kick him? I would have kicked him."

"He has a family to provide for. He's a greedy man and sees this as a rare opportunity. Fifty dollars is a princely sum for him. We have enough money so that if I did give it to him, we'd barely notice it, but that's not the point here."

"What are you going to do?"

"He's given me two days to decide so I'm going to think about it. I don't know if he's told Soo Wei his plan so I'd like you to avoid discussing it."

———————————

Tu Chan went to see Bo Mah and Ho Yup. He told them the fee that Lo Wan owes is quite expensive. It amounts to seventy dollars. They said the girl would cost even more. They want one hundred dollars for her. I negotiated with them and got them to agree to both fees for a total of one hundred and fifty dollars. I'm sorry, but that's the best deal I could get."

"That's a great deal of money. Would they accept one hundred dollars now and the rest to be paid over the next six months?"

"Let me go back and see if they'll accept your offer. I'm not optimistic."

The minute Tu Chan left the mining company office they sent off a telegram to the Chancellor informing him that they located Lo Wan.

———————————

The next morning Foo Hai's young daughter was having a difficult time removing some thick weeds. She went into their shed and brought out an old rusty scythe that her father had warned her against using, but she was not going to let the weeds win. As she was using all her weight to swing it, she lost her balance and the rusty tool cut deep into her leg. By evening it was clear that the cut was infected. She was running a high fever. Soo Wei kept putting cool compresses on her head. Mei Sam ran to get Foo Hai and me.

Mei Sam pulled me aside and whispered, "What are you going to do?"

"Karma is an odd force. No one knows when it's responsible or an event is just a coincidence."

Mei Sam frowned, "He's an evil man who turned on a friend for personal gain. He's being punished for his actions, but if I had to choose, I'd help the girl."

I hugged Mei Sam. "Despite your anger, you're showing a true healer's compassion. Go to the nearby forest and bring back the following herbs." I went over the list twice to make sure she knew what to bring back, then ran into our room to locate my needles.

I yelled, "Keep placing those cold, wet rags on her head." I pulled out the acupuncture needles the old herbalist had given me in Sacramento and asked for some alcohol. I began placing needles into her head, neck and near the wound.

Foo Hai screamed, "What the hell are you doing to my daughter?"

"See these red stripes coming from her wound? Feel her head. She's running an extremely high fever and those red striations means she has a severe infection. The fact that all this is happening so rapidly is also a troubling sign. I sent Mei Sam out to find some herbs."

"What the hell does a young girl like her know about herbs?"

"I've been teaching her. You never asked my profession. I guess you assumed I'm a miner. I'm a healer and if we all cooperate and Mei Sam gets back soon enough, we may be able to save her. The next few hours are crucial. Please stay out of my way. We're doing everything we can to help her."

A half hour later, Mei Sam runs into the house drenched in sweat and throws a bunch of what looks like scraggly leaves on the floor next to where I'm sitting.

I hand some of the herbs to Soo Wei, "Grind the leaves of this one up into as fine a powder as you can. Mei Sam, boil those plants and bring them back in the water you boiled them in. They'll make a tea that'll help her."

Foo Hai asks, "What can I do?"

"Take your little boy into another room and stay out of our way. If I need you, I'll call."

I keep placing needles into various sites. I wrap some in cloth and set them on fire, others I just leave in place and still others I twist after they've been in place for a few minutes. Foo Hai puts his son to bed and returns. Soo Wei and I help the girl drink the medicinal tea that Mei Sam brewed. I form other herbs into pills with rice and honey. I use other herbs to make poultices I place directly into the wound that I cleaned out.

We battle the infection well into the night and by morning, the fever begins to break and the red lines around her leg begin to recede. "I know we're all tired and want to get some sleep, but we'll have to take turns caring for her. If there's any change for the worse, wake me immediately. Mei Sam and I will rest first. It's best when she wakes that she sees her parents."

By the second day, the little girl was able to get up and walk a bit. "Don't let her move too much for the next few days, but it's good for her to walk around a little every few hours. It'll increase her circulation."

Toward evening Foo Hai asks me to step outside. This is where I expect him to return to the subject of paying the fifty-dollar ransom. I play through several scenarios about how to handle the situation. I still haven't settled on my final action. I'll make it based on how I feel when the final moment arrives. I'm surprised that before Foo Hai says a word, he begins weeping.

"I don't know where to start. I treated you shamelessly and by all rights you could have paid me back by letting my daughter die. Instead, you stayed up all night using your skills to cure her. I'm so ashamed. Know that I was only thinking of my family. Please find it in your heart to forgive me and try to forget I ever opened my selfish mouth. Every time I look at my daughter, I'll see your face and gratitude will fill my heart. If you don't want to forgive me, I understand."

I'm happy I was able to help and I'm going to walk away believing that I healed both your daughter and you."

That night, I began my breathing ritual and found it easy to drift off to sleep.

At five-years-old I was playing with Pao when the dog scratched me and my arm began to bleed. I hit him and my mother ran over and said, "Lo Wan, why are you are you hitting Pao? Don't you love him?"

"I do, but he scratched me."

"I watched the two of you playing and you were pretty rough with Pao. He was playing back. He loves you and would never hurt you on purpose. How can you be a great healer if you lose your temper so easily? How can you become a great healer when you want to hurt someone ... especially a poor creature that you say you love? I'm so disappointed." She put some salve on Pao's paw and fed him some herbs. "I forbid you to play with Pao for a week."

Later that night, I went to my mother's bed with tears streaming down my face. "Mother ... I'm a bad person. I love Pao, but I got mad and hurt him. I'm afraid I'll never be a good healer. I have a bad temper that I can't control."

She hugged me and said, "Just coming in here and apologizing is the first step toward learning to control your temper. You're five-years-old, it may take you until you reach six to fully control it. Go and find Pao and let him sleep next to you. He loves that."

As they left Tu Chan's office, Ho Yup asked, "Lo Wan and Mei Sam have many times that amount of money. Why didn't you just grab the deal Tu Chan offered and be done with it?"

"Because if the mining company believes that Lo Wan grabbed that deal, they'll think they should have asked for more. They might think Lo Wan has much more money. Then they might send Tong members to hunt him down and rob him. Let them think he has to work hard to scrape together one hundred dollars, which is a large sum of money and have them wait to get the rest. That way they'll be glad they got something now. They'll think it's a good deal for them … especially because they never expected to get anything."

Ho Yup and Bo Mah waited two days before Tu Chan returned to say the mining company was angry, but finally agreed to the deal. With that, Bo Mah went into the other room and brought out one hundred dollars and gave it to Tu Chan.

Tu Chan asked, "Why are *you* paying for Lo Wan's freedom?"

"We all worked the mine together and chipped in to buy he and his wife's freedom. I want to thank you and the next time we see you, Lo Wan will be with us.

The next day Soo Wei runs out in the fields to get me. "You have company." My first reaction is, "Did Foo Hai change his mind and turn me in for a reward?" Bo Mah, Ya Min and Ho Yup are standing just outside the house and Mei Sam is in tears hugging them.

"You're both free. We're taking you back to San Francisco to start your new life. We found you a room in the same house where we're all staying. You're welcome to remain there as long as you like. Of course, if you find accommodations more to your liking, you're also free to leave whenever you want. Tomorrow night you're having dinner at Tu Chan's house."

Bo Mah explains the financial terms of the release from their contracts. He says they all shared in paying off those debts. I try to object and am shouted down.

When all five of us arrive at Tu Chan's house, he runs out to hug me. He clasps me tightly until he notices Mei Sam, then pushes me aside and runs to hug her. "Don't any of you pull me away until I'm ready to let her go." We all laugh and go inside. It was one of the warmest nights I would remember not counting my first night in Sacramento with Mei Sam. Tu Chan treats me like a returning lost son and immediately adopts Mei Wan as his new daughter-in-law.

After an elaborate dinner with many courses, we sit around the fireplace and talk late into the night. Tu Chan asks what plans we have.

"We've made a firm commitment to spend the next two days walking around and exploring the city of San Francisco. It's only after that our plans become murky."

"If you could do whatever you dreamed of with your life here, what would it be?"

"I just want to do what I was trained to do. I want to continue being a healer and improving my skills."

"That's what I was hoping you'd say. I have two old, very dear friends, Chan Lee and Tang Po I insist you meet. They're healers as well and they're always complaining about how over-worked they are. I'm really tired of hearing them whining ... so I told them about you and they're overjoyed. Take your two days of sightseeing and on the third day I'm taking you to meet them. Like you, they share a devotion to life-long learning and feel fortunate their skills help so many people. You'll find the environment stimulating because they're forever arguing, but not over petty issues. You'll feel like you're attending a university."

"And Mei Sam, what would you like to do? I understand you're quite a good seamstress."

"Lo Wan has been teaching me about herbs. I'm not very skilled yet, but I would love to work with the same two men you described and continue my studies."

"I'm sure they'll find a place for you, and like Lo Wan, they love teaching. It'll be an ideal environment for you."

"It feels like we're in a dreamlike version of China. The shops and restaurants are wondrous." We walk around sampling the tastes and textures and smells. It seems like we're in a fantasy state. Neither of us has ever seen anything like it, until we arrive at a street on the outskirts of Chinatown. A man on a large wooden box is yelling in a way that reminds us of the hate filled speech when we first arrived in Stockton.

"How much do you hate the Chinks?"

"Kill 'em all!"

"Why can't you get a job?"

"The damn Chinks!"

"They been here for a long time, but they don't want to learn English. They don't want to talk to you. They don't want to be your friends. They just want your job and your money and your woman. And they'll get it by undercutting your pay and working longer hours. They have nothing else to do. They live like pigs, nine to a room. Of course they can work cheaper than you. They eat slop and wear the same clothes every day. Of course they can work cheaper than you. They never get a haircut. Of course they can work cheaper than you. Do you think they care if your kids starve?"

"NO!"

Do you think they care if they put your families out in the street?"

"NO!"

"So what're we waiting for? Let's send them all back to China. And if they don't want to go?"

"Kill 'em all."

We walk back into the heart of Chinatown, but its luster has dimmed substantially. I suggest we might brighten our spirits if we could discover where Chan Lee and Tang Po work before we're formally introduced. We begin walking down each street looking in every store window and examining every building. When that doesn't yield any positive results, I walk up to a middle aged man on a street corner and ask, "Hello friend, I hurt my leg. Can you recommend a good healer?" We're taken to the offices of several healers, but not the ones we're looking for. I walk up to another old man standing near us and try again.

He smiles. "You're making an excellent choice. I highly rec-ommend both of them. Follow me and I'll show you where they work. You'll never find it on your own." He leads us through a grimy alley to a door that opens to a flight of shaky stairs.

The old man knocks on the door then walks back down the stairs. A servant opens the door into one of the most wondrous rooms I've ever entered. One wall is all book shelves filled with every manner of Chinese medicine books. Another wall has neatly labeled jars of herbs organized by type. The furniture is intricately carved and there are beautiful hand woven rugs on the polished wood floors. The other walls are covered with elaborate scrolls and paintings. The servant asks us if we have an appointment. When we say we don't he asks us to sit down then disappears into the next room.

We sit until the door closes. I spring up and begin scanning the volumes on the shelves. I grew up in a house with a collection of medical books, but this is like an imperial library. I immedi-ately find a volume that arouses my curiosity and begin leafing through it pointing out things to Mei Sam. We didn't notice two men entering the room.

Chan Lee asks, "How may we help you? I notice you've selected a Portuguese medical book that's been translated into Chinese. Are either of you hurt or did you come here to do some light reading?" Both men are smiling.

As soon as I see Chan Lee, the word that pops into my mind as I evaluate his Chi flow is "perfect." His Earth sign suggests nurturing and security. Then I see Tang Po and register a similar Chi flow, but as a Fire sign he seems to exude enthusiasm and passion. They seem like a perfect pairing. Like they would always support yet challenge each other on a daily basis.

Tang Po looks at the book and says, "I think this book was originally written in Spanish not Portuguese. You always make snap judgments without careful examination. The beginnings of words in Spanish and Portuguese are generally the same, but look at the derivational suffixes and conjugations."

"You may be right…this time, but who really cares?"

I clear my throat. "Pardon me, my name is Lo Wan and this is my wife Mei Sam. We heard about you from…"

"Tu Chan. And he described you both accurately. I'm impressed you found us on your own. We work very hard to keep ourselves out of view of the general public. We have no signs and people only come to see us by recommendation. Would you like a cup of tea?"

Tang Po calls out toward the kitchen and asks for four cups of tea. "It's an auspicious sign that you didn't choose to wait for a formal introduction. You took matters into your own hands and came to find us."

After a short conversation, both men say they're impressed that I was so well informed given my age.

I've never met such impressive healers who clearly believe in ongoing learning and mention cures and techniques that almost have me drooling. In my mind I give them the highest compliment possible, they both remind me of my father. Both old men are charmed by Mei Sam. They ask her several rudimentary questions about herbs to gauge her level of interest. They're impressed by how much she's already learned in such a short time and are excited to have her energy in their quarters.

Chan Lee said, "We're planning to meet you tomorrow when Tu Chan introduces us. I have a favor to ask. After the introductions, ask us a few rudimentary questions about acupuncture. Tang Po or I will act as if you have offered us a grave insult and we'll tell Tu Chan that there's no place for such arrogance here. I can't wait to see the look on his face as we throw you out. Then we'll all sit down to a fine meal. It's our duty to remind him of the importance of humility."

With our moods considerably lightened, we decide to locate the best restaurant we can find and have an exotic meal to celebrate our good fortune. As we're walking into a restaurant, from a distance I recognize Doy Low and immediately cover my face. I hope the Tong member from the ship didn't see me.

After a good night's sleep, we wake early and go to the small outdoor area behind our house to continue Mei Sam's martial training. I'm surprised to see Bo Mah, Ho Yup and Ya Min, all wearing loose fitting clothes. "We'd like to train with you. Is that possible? When I was younger I practiced some Chinese boxing. All three of us think the way our lives will be progressing here, learning some self-defense skills may be helpful. After we saw the results of Mei Sam's progress, we're sure of it."

This is the beginning of my more formal martial arts classes. They're all willing to get up as the sun rises. I'm surprised to see how the two Stockton elders take to it. They're surprisingly strong and agile. Ya Min is the slowest student, but even he begins to make steady progress... though slowly.

When I arrive to begin working with Chan Lee and Tang Po, the first thing they want to do is to sit and chat. They ask me a lot of questions and it becomes clear this is really a screening exam. Within a half hour they call for tea. Their broad smiles indicate they're reassured. "We're pleased we can treat you as a peer rather than a student or apprentice."

When it's time for their first patient, I'm surprised to see a well-dressed White man rather than a Chinese enter. They introduce him as Timothy Finn, a member of the San Francisco City Council. He has low back pain and the old healers tell him today, I am going to work on him.

"No! I don't want some young student learning on my back. I want one of you two. That's why I come all the way down here. Remember, I have to travel down here wearing a disguise to make sure no one recognizes me. I go to a lot of trouble to come here because you two are the only ones who ever really help me. I'm not going to let some wet behind the ears student practice the skills you're teaching him so he can try them out on me."

"Mr. Finn, you know our work always meets the highest standards. Do you really believe we would offer you anything but top quality treatment?"

"No, but..."

"Then we suggest you permit Lo Wan to treat you and see if you aren't happy with the results. I assure you that if you aren't, one of us will gladly assist you further. We consider you to be an intelligent man, but we find ourselves shocked by your discourse. Are you telling us you are now able to see into the future? Is that how you know that Lo Wan is incapable of helping you?"

"No, but ... "

"Then I suggest you remove your shirt and pants and lie down on the table so Lo Wan can begin his treatment."

"But ... "

"Was I not clear?"

As I completed his acupuncture treatment, the Councilman got off the table smiling. "My back feels wonderful. Young sir, permit me to apologize for doubting you. Chan Lee and Tang Po, will both of you please forgive me for questioning your judgment. Coming to see you is always worth the extra effort. I thank all three of you."

I hand the councilman a small sack of herbs, "Brew tea with herbs and drink with breakfast for one week. I think it help."

Tang Po asks, "Why did you light three of the needles you placed in his thigh?"

"It was clear that his pain radiated through the sciatic nerve. I wanted to increase the flow of Chi in that meridian. Do you get many white patients here? I thought the Whites don't like us here in Chinatown."

"Most don't want us here at all, but there are a surprising number of well-educated whites who are quite open-minded. The one you just treated is an important man in this city. I hope you never have need of his help."

One afternoon a man walks in and bows to Chan Lee, who bows back, and then the two men walk into his office together. A few minutes later they come out again and I notice the man putting a wad of bills into his pocket, smiling as he leaves.

"Pardon me, but people usually pay you, why were you paying that man?"

"It's the cost of doing business here in Chinatown."

"You're always so clear and open when you explain something to me. Why are you giving me less than half an answer?"

"That nice man was from the Lo Ji Tong. Every month we pay them ten percent of the amount of money they claim we earn and they provide us with protection."

"Protection against what or who?"

"Mostly protection from them, but also protection from other Tongs and criminals."

"What would happen if you didn't pay them?"

"Let's just say bad things *could* happen."

Tu Chan and my friend Bo Mah told me a bit about the Tongs here in Chinatown. I find them very disturbing. Based on my one interaction with a Tong member aboard the ship I plan to steer clear of them wherever possible."

On their way home Mei Sam says, "Listen, another rally." We find cover behind a building so we can hear them.

The same man we saw when we first got to San Francisco was standing on the same wooden box yelling the same kind of hate speech. When the crowd is about to boil over, he stops and raises his arms. "I'd like to introduce a good friend who'd like to say a few words to you. I'd like you all to meet Billy Carney. He came all the way from Stockton to talk to you so make him feel welcome."

The crowd cheered as Carney took his place. "I fought in the war against the South. Lost a lot of good friends, but back then, I thought the war was worth it. We ended slavery. But what was our reward? All them freed ex-slaves began taking away our jobs. Then the railroads, greedy mining companies and farmers started importing these damn job-stealing Coolies. How many of you fought in the war?"

Loud cheering.

"How many of you lost friends and loved ones in the war?"

Another chorus of cheers.

"Did we lose our loved ones and suffer injuries so Chinks could take away our jobs?"

"NO!"

"I'm here with one of my heroes, Judge Andrew Sullivan. He's running to be your next Senator from California. I want you all to vote for him. Tell yer friends. We need someone in Washington to help us get rid of the damn Chinks. But does that mean you have to wait for him to do it for you?"

"NO!"

"In Stockton, we took matters into our own hands. You can read about it in the papers. Think about it the next time you're walking with a few of your friends and see a Chink or two walking toward you. Strike a blow for liberty. Strike a Chink in the gut … or the face … or both."

Loud cheers and laughter were heard.

"I'd like to introduce a man dedicated to removing these Chinese troublemakers legal-like. He's working for you every damn day. Here's your next Senator from the great state of California, Judge Andrew Sullivan. Let's make him feel welcome. San Francisco."

"White citizens of San Francisco, I don't have to stand up here and tell you what a menace these yellow Chinese devils are. You know that. So let me tell you what I've *already* done to help you fight the 'Yellow Peril.' I'm proud to have sponsored the "Pigtail *Ordinance*." You see those long pigtails those Chinamen wear. To us, those pigtails look stupid, but when *they* lose them, Chinamen consider it a huge disgrace. They think it's part of their manhood." Because of my law, any Chinaman who's arrested is forced to having his hair cut within an inch of his scalp. And they don't even have to be convicted … just arrested!"

The crowd cheers.

As he said the word 'manhood' he reaches into his pocket and pulls out a long Chinese queue and holds it aloft. The crowd goes wild. He spits on the queue, throws it on the ground and stomps on it.

The crowd gets wilder.

"But hey, I didn't stop there. I also co-sponsored the *Cubic Air Ordinance*. This is a San Francisco law requiring 500 cubic feet of space for every person living in a rented room. That's like an eight-foot by eight-foot room. These Chinamen crowd nine people into a room that size. They stack three sets of three beds one on top of the other. That's nine Chinamen to a room meant for one person. Because of my new law, if there's not enough space for them in a room, they get arrested for it. Now here's the part the best part. Once they're arrested, we throw them into a jail cell that's even more crowded than where they were living when they first got arrested for not having enough space."

The crowd screams.

"I've been working on the Chinese problem for quite a while. Ten years ago, I'm proud to say I helped get the Page Act passed. Notice you don't see many Chinese women here. Because of this law it's now almost impossible for a Chinese female to enter our great country. That means they can't start a family here and increase their numbers by dropping their kids here."

"Right now I'm busy on a much bigger piece of legislation called '*The Chinese Exclusion Act*.' I think that name speaks for itself."

Before the crowd stops cheering, Sullivan says, "Now I want each of you to vote for me to be your next California Senator. America for Americans!"

Mei Sam and I run home to tell Bo Mah and Ho Yup who we just saw and make them promise not to leave home for the next week. "If you need anything, Mei Sam or I will get it for you."

The next day as I'm walking home from the clinic, three men with black felt hats, each carrying a short-handled hatchet step in front of me to block my path. As I turn to walk away, I find myself staring into the eyes of Doy Low.

"Lo Wan, how nice to see you again." He held up one hand. "Do me a favor and listen to what I have to say before you do or say something you'll regret forever. No one here will move any closer to you now so you're in no immediate danger. I want you to know that I have a very long memory. The first time we met, I asked you for a coin or two and we both know how that ended. Well, I'm here to try again, but in a more enlightened way. I've taken some time to learn about you and your time here in Chinatown. How much do Chan Lee and Tang Po pay you each week?"

"How did you find out I'm working for them?"

"Chinatown is really a very small community that I know how to get around in. Now, how much do they pay you?"

"Why would I tell you that?"

"Well, it would save a lot of time and no one would get hurt if you do. It will be a simple matter for me to find out. I suggest you save us some time."

"They pay me ten dollars a week."

"I suppose, like most businesses here in Chinatown, they pay you on Friday afternoon. So every Friday afternoon, I'm going to wait for you to leave work and meet me right here on this corner where you will pay me seven of those dollars. I don't want to take all your money. As you can see, I'm demonstrating generosity of spirit…just like you taught me."

"And why would I do that? Have you forgotten the history of you trying to extort money from me?"

"Oh no. Believe me, I haven't stopped thinking about any of it since it happened. Be glad I'm letting you keep three dollars a week. And the reason you'll pay me the money is for protection."

"Do you really think I need to pay for protection from you? Do you think these three men are enough to keep me from ripping your arms out of their sockets?"

"Your answer is a bit short sighted. If it was just you and me, we wouldn't be having this conversation. I'll give you the courtesy of explaining how protection works since you're new here. Let me pose a mathematical problem for you. While I've seen how good you are at protecting *yourself*, how good are you at protecting three people at the same time ... while they're in different locations?" Let me make it more interesting. Make that six people. If you don't pay me, I might begin with your lovely young wife. We could certainly have some fun with her. Or would you prefer we attack Chan Lee and Tang Po. They might even try to heal themselves as we're beating and maiming them. Or, how about your friends Bo Mah or Ho Yup or Ya Min? Let's throw you into the mix and make it an even seven. That's a more auspicious number. We know where to find any of you ... day or night."

"And if you're thinking of attacking me right here, you might be able to kill me or make me suffer, but my Tong brothers from the Moo See Tong, have all sworn that whatever you do to me here will be returned ten times worse on any and all of the people I've just listed. Now you understand the concept of protection. I'll meet you right here every Friday afternoon to collect your payment. I look forward to enjoying this over-and-over every week."

"This isn't a very nice way to keep your promise to me for sparing your life."

"Oh, I forgot to tell you, in America, there's a long tradition that if you have your fingers crossed when you make a promise, it doesn't really count. It was dark and you probably didn't notice my fingers that night. I look forward to seeing you here next Friday afternoon."

The next morning, I cancel the morning martial arts class. Mei Sam tries to find out what's on my mind. "I have a lot to think about." For the next three weeks I meet Doy Low and hand him the seven dollars as arranged. Doy Low responds by giving me a smile and a head nod, just the way I had ordered him to respond on the ship each day, but his smile is now much broader.

As Mei Sam watches the change in my disposition, she keeps trying to find out what's causing it. I'm irritable and have trouble focusing on anything but the most menial tasks. "I'm your wife, you have to let me in here. What's going on with you?"

"I know I'm very small, but I've always felt like a man. Now I don't. Now just leave me alone."

She takes the hint and stops asking. I'm used to handling problems as they occur, but this is different. I've had little experience when my low frustration tolerance was fueling my thoughts. I'm always prepared to be responsible for myself and doing what needs to be done. Now I'm responsible for the life and safety of six other people I care about. I can't be with each of them all the time. This is a problem with no solution. There is no one for me to turn to for help.

I resume the morning self defense classes, but they lack the intensity they previously have. Slowly, with each passing day, I work to bring my energy back. And each day the only variation is just how badly I'm failing at it. I notice my concentration is difficult to channel and I have no sense of humor. The best I can do is apologize to Mei Sam and the others. My nightly breathing routine is failing me.

One afternoon Chan Lee asks me to come into his office. "You seem to be out of sorts. You look disheveled and have totally lost what little sense of humor you had. Clearly, something is troubling you. Would you like to talk about it?"

"Thank you, no. It's something I have to work out alone."

"Here, doctors have an expression, 'Physician, heal thyself.' It's an ironic statement because they're describing a problem the doctor has that he cannot heal by himself … he needs the help of others. Look, you're in a new district of a new city in a new state in a new country. There's a lot you don't understand about the culture you find yourself in. I've been here for a long time and may be able to help you. My roots run deep here."

"This is something I need to solve alone, but since you're immersed in it, I'll trust you with it if you'll keep it confidential."

The only person I will discuss it with is Tang Po. We keep no secrets from one another. Is that acceptable to you?"

"I guess so since he's also involved."

"I'll call him in."

I take my time explaining the entire story. When I finish Chan Lee smiles. "I think we may be able to help you. As far as you understand, our relationship to the Lo Ji Tong is one where we pay and they provide protection for us and leave us alone. Our actual relationship with them is a bit more complicated. We pay for protection so they save face. The amount is actually trifling. Joo Wei, the head of the Lo Ji Tong sends for us when he's in pain. We've been very close to him for years. The Lo Ji Tong and the Moo See Tong have a complex relationship where they often find themselves in a position where they must cooperate with one another. I've never heard of this man Doy Low. That means he's not a significantly important member of the Moo See Tong. That's good because it means it'll make for a less complicated negotiation."

"I'll talk to Joo Wei and ask him to set up a discrete meeting between the heads of the two Tongs, the two of us … and of course, you."

It takes a week for the meeting to be arranged. Joi Lin, the head of the Moo See Tong brings only two hatchet men with him as he was asked. Joo Wei also brings only two of his hatchet men. For both of them, this is "travelling light," although these four men are the equivalent of ten normal Tong warriors. Still, this small number of men is an auspicious sign because it demonstrates a significant level of trust between the two men and their respect for the two venerable healers.

When I see Joi Lin he shows a continuous, unimpeded Chi flow. His Fire sign indicates a great deal of strength. He seems to grasp the essence of any situation he is in immediately and appears to be decisive. Joo Wei is almost a mirror image of Joi Lin. Strong Chi flow, A Fire sign and very bright. It's clear why they are both leaders of powerful Tongs.

"Esteemed gentlemen, I know how many more pressing issues require your attention so I'm deeply honored that you agreed to grant me an audience."

Joi Lin says, "I don't know you. I'm here as a favor to Chan Lee and Tang Po. They keep my tired body working so I may accomplish what I must do, so I'll listen to what you have to say only as a courtesy to them."

Joo Wei says, "Apparently, I'm going to be asked to grant a favor here. Know that part of the negotiation from my end will require Joi Lin granting me access to these two exceptional healers. Your prowess in Chinatown is legendary." Joi Lin smiles and nods.

Tang Po says, "We will sweeten the deal a bit more by adding access to Lo Wan's significant talents. He's also a gifted healer."

After I explain the situation, both men ask what I would like from them. "I would appreciate the opportunity to settle this situation man-to-man with Doy Low. I would not like to see the Moo See attack my wife, my friends or my employers here."

Joo Wei says, "First of all, I would never permit anyone in my Tong to harm Chan Lee or Tang Po in any way. That would not even be a consideration. I think what you ask for is fair. Here is my proposed solution. This Friday afternoon when Doy Low comes to collect his seven dollars he will find two senior Moo See and two senior Lo Ji soldiers waiting to make sure that things are settled fairly between the two of you and that will be the end of it. Joi Lin, is that acceptable to you?"

"That's a very fair solution and I agree unconditionally. Lo Wan, is that acceptable to you?"

"Yes of course. Thank you both. I don't want to appear ungrateful, but I would like to have one more person in attendance. I would like my wife to be there."

"You want your wife to witness Doy Low take a beating?"

"No honorable sir, I would like my wife to administer the beating. Furthermore, I would appreciate it if the four men witnessing the event would agree to keep the results to themselves. I think that humiliation and the threat of it becoming public will stop Doy Low's further attempts at revenge."

Both men laugh and nod in agreement. The meeting ends on this note with everyone in high spirits laughing. Both Tong leaders say they are tempted to come and witness this meeting themselves, but will have to settle for hearing about the event from the men they send.

I bow deeply to both men and they leave. I thank Chan Lee and Tang Po for their invaluable help. "I owe you a debt I can never repay."

When I return Mei Sam can immediately sense the difference in my mood. I tell her the entire story and for the first time, she shows some doubts about her martial arts skills. I tell her we have three days to train and I have designed her fighting strategy for the encounter. That lightens her spirits a little.

After dinner we begin training in earnest. I tell her, "Doy Low will be overconfident because you're a girl, and you're small. He will rush to attack first in an attempt to intimidate you. You'll let him feel like he's succeeding by running straight back several steps to avoid being hit. You'll be running away from him like a scared rabbit. Do this the first two times he attacks. Just run straight back to avoid having him reach you. This will establish the pattern that you're a runner. But, on his third attack, run two quick steps back as you did before, stop, quickly turn sideways and plant a sidekick straight into his solar plexus. As he's running hard into your kick, he'll double its intensity by moving forward so fast. His arms will be at his sides to help him run harder to catch you so he'll be open for your kick. As soon as he bends over from the pain of your kick, you'll deliver a series of Chung Choy blasts directly into his nose until he's on the ground and unable to breathe because of the bleeding. If you're in any danger, at any time, I'll step in immediately."

The next three days go by in a blur. We practice the routine endlessly. The goal is to have no thinking involved on her part once the fight begins. At the clinic, Chan Lee comments that it's nice to see me back again. At night after our workouts, I work with Mei Sam on breathing and relaxation skills so she can go to sleep conquering her tensions. I remind her that if I think she is in any danger at any time, I will jump in. Then I remind her that she was on Doy Low's list to be hurt, raped or killed if I didn't pay. That engages her anger.

I notice that whenever Mei Sam thinks she's alone, she practices the form of her sidekick. She begins slowly working on her balance, particularly when she's chambering her right leg. Then she works on extending her right leg as she pushed up her heel and lowered her toes so her heel will make solid contact. She is meticulous in her preparation. Each kick is delivered fast, hard and with snap. I'm proud of her work ethic and the results she's getting.

Chapter 9

The Chancellor calls for the Viceroy. "Have you planned the next attack on the healer?"

"Yes my Liege. Until now I didn't take it seriously enough. I assumed he wouldn't put up any resistance. This time I've done my research and designed a foolproof plan. There is no way it can fail. Would you like me to lay it out for you step-by-step?"

"If it works as well as you say it will, you have my full confidence. I don't feel the need to check up on you. In the event that it doesn't, however, we may have to consider sending you on a trip to visit your uncle in Macau." The Chancellor smiles and waves the Viceroy out of the Jade Room with a flick of his wrist.

Every day he goes in to work, Lo Wan thanks his two friends for helping him resolve what he saw as an insoluble problem.

"You solved it, all we did was give you the opportunity by setting up a meeting. We're so happy to have you back. We were very upset seeing the morose visage that was inhabiting your body here daily."

The week crawls by until Friday afternoon finally comes around. Doy Low is waiting at his corner alone. His level of confidence is so high he no longer asks his Tong brothers to accompany him. He's surprised to see that Lo Wan doesn't show up alone. He's with a beautiful young girl.

"Doy Low, I'd like to introduce you to my wife Mei Sam. Or, as you know her, one of the six people on your list to rape and kill if I don't pay you."

"Don't you think this is a bit awkward? I have a good mind to raise your fee to eight dollars a week for this insult...maybe even nine."

"Let's renegotiate. I would like you to lower your fee to zero dollars a week and have you never speak to me again. That seems fairer to me. What do you say?"

I'll tell you what I have to say. I'm leaving now and telling my Tong we can begin working through the list immediately. Instead of me saying 'hello' to your wife now, you might as well be saying 'good-bye' to her. I must say I'm surprised that you don't show more loyalty to people you're supposed to care about, especially when they're so pretty."

With that, Doy Low turns around to leave and is surprised to see two Lo Ji hatchet men blocking his path. He turns 180° and begins walking in the other direction only to see two hatchet men from his own Tong. He smiles, points at Mei Sam and me and says, "Let's get them."

"Pardon my bad manners. I should mention that there's been a change in the organizational structure that you and I have been proceeding under. I spoke to the heads of two Tongs, yours and the Lo Ji, and they both thought that you and I should be able to settle this matter by ourselves because the issue seemed to be so personal and petty. It's silly to have any one else get hurt because of your vanity."

Doy Low turns to his Tong members and says, "Get them!"

They smile and shake their heads.

"You threatened my wife's life and you even threatened to rape her. I don't think she likes you very much and thinks that you and she should fight."

"I don't kill girls...unless it's for Tong business."

Lo Wan turns to the two Moo See Tong men and says, "How would you react to a member of your Tong who was afraid to fight a girl."

Both laugh.

With no warning, Doy Low screams and charges Mei Sam. She runs away moving straight back. Then she moves to the side a bit as he charges her again. Once again she runs straight back as she'd practiced. On Doy Low's third furious charge she stops after running back two steps, turns sideways, chambers her leg and released her sidekick into his solar plexus just as she's practiced. Doy Low runs into her kick doubling its force. As he bends over in pain fighting to breathe, she bends her knees to get better leverage and begins delivering her Chung Choy blasts. It was the fifth punch that landed him on the ground with blood oozing out of his nose. He is struggling to get air. I push down on a pressure point to help restore his breath. I turn to the two Moo See Tong members and ask them to remember that an oxcart ran into him in case anyone in their Tong asks. They smile and nod. The Lo Ji tong members smile as well. Then they all applaud Mei Sam.

I kneel down next to Doy Low and grab onto the short hairs growing where his head and neck meet. As I pull hard on those hairs, watching Doy Low wince in pain, I whisper, "I want you to remember two things: I didn't have to tell her to stop hitting you; and, I didn't have to help you restore your breathing just now. In thinking back, I should have killed you on the ship when you attacked me with your puny knife and I should kill you now. Remember this, I never make the same mistake three times. If you trouble me again, you will beg me to kill you … and I will oblige, but it will be a long, painful oblige."

"As a courtesy, although you don't deserve one, I've asked that the four Tong members here today as witnesses keep the beating you took from a girl a secret between us. If you act on the slightest thought about revenge again, know that everyone in Chinatown will hear about today. How you were beaten up by a girl. That may affect your reputation here … no? And that's before I get to you.

By the way, you owe me twenty one dollars which I expect you to deliver next Friday afternoon here on this corner."

As we all leave, I smile as I look to the Tong men, bow and say, "Thank you and remember … shhh."

They all bow and smile back.

I ask if her hand hurts. Mei Sam smiles and shakes her head. "His nose was soft. Thank you for making me practice so many times. I felt like I was dancing. Let's eat. Beating up a man makes me hungry."

We go back to collect Chan Lee and Tang Po. The four of us go out for an extravagant "Thank You" dinner.

Over the next few months, I'm happy, particularly on Friday afternoons. I never saw Doy Low again after he paid me the $21. More interestingly, I've had several opportunities to work on both Joo Wei and Joi Lin. I'm careful not to be overly familiar and make a point of showing each a great deal of deference. What surprises me is that each man, in turn, shows me a great deal of respect for my skills. I discover a new way of looking at the Tongs. They have their own form of honor. Although they are involved in many nefarious activities, given the hatred shown by Whites toward the Chinese, I come to see them as a necessary balancing counter force. They aren't as evil as I previously thought.

Returning from an afternoon of gathering herbs, Mei Sam walks up behind me. I'm absorbed in one of the several books I'm poring over. She's surprised she can sneak up on me so easily and looks over my shoulder to see what book is so captivating. It's a Japanese Pillowing book. An illustrated sexual instruction book presented in story form. These books are designed to teach rich young Japanese girls what they have to know to please their future husbands. Sitting next to this book are several illustrated Chinese sex books and a copy of the Kama Sutra.

When I look up and see her I blush. "This isn't what it looks like."

"Really, what is it? I like to read. Would you like to share your books with me?"

"This is so embarrassing. I've been studying to … eh, learn how to pleasure you better."

"Now that the subject is out in the open, I've been hearing rumors that you've been seen walking out of pleasure houses on more than one occasion. Have you been cheating on me? Am I no longer appealing to you? Am I just too young and in-experienced for you?" As she questions me, tears are dripping down her face.

I put my arm around her and ask her to take a walk with me. "When we first got together, I told you I wasn't very experienced being with girls. I'm using the term 'Not very experienced' as a synonym for being 'a naïve virgin.' Every time I see a man show interest in you I imagine that you're flirting with them because I'm not holding your interest … uhm, physically. I get jealous and worry I'm not an experienced enough lover. So whenever I have the opportunity to learn more from books, I take it."

"More importantly, since I've developed a close relationship with the bosses of two Tongs, I've used the opportunity to fre-quent their brothels, but I've never had sex there … ever. I've been paying their prostitutes to give me instruction in lovemaking so I can be a better lover for you. The thought of being unfaithful to you does not interest me. I look at those women as teachers. They're quite adept in that role and I've actually become friends with a few of them once they realized the nature of our relation-ship. I'll always be faithful to you."

In the middle of my story, Mei Sam begins to laugh. "You've been seeing whores for education? You really are a bizarre man. Weren't you ever tempted to lay with any of them?"

"No. I look at making love as just that. You're the one I love, so you're the only one I want to make love to. Case closed."

"I have to admit that I've been enjoying sex quite a bit more with you. I just assumed it was because I keep falling more in love with you. And that's still true. But now that I think about it clinically, you have become a much better lover. But let's agree that you've graduated and no longer have to 'attend school.'"

At dinner, Ya Min said, "I have an announcement. I've talked to Tu Chan and he's helping me get a ticket on a steamship back to China. I'm going home at last. As my partners, I want you to know this wouldn't be possible without your help, trust and encouragement. I'll keep a special place in my heart for each of you. I'm also pleased that I'll no longer slow down the progress in the morning martial arts classes. When you come to my store in Peking, I'll give each of you a free book."

Everyone laughs and hugs Ya Min. A week later, he's gone. I'm very happy for Ya Min, but this opens a place in my mind to think about my own possible return to China. Since Mei Sam says she'll be happy anywhere as long as we're together, there's nothing tying me here except my own curiosity about America.

At first I was ecstatic after completing my adventure with Doy Low. Then I noticed that melancholy was replacing my sense of relief and serenity. On Monday I told Mei Sam to go to the clinic without me. I would be along later.

I'm still lying in bed when Chan Lee knocks on my door. "When you didn't come in to work today I was surprised at first, and then concerned. Do I need to set up another Tong meeting?"

I laugh a little and explain my concerns. "My adventure with Doy Low resulted in a triumphant outcome that pleased everyone but me. I'm happy that he no longer threatens the people I care for and I no longer have to pay 'insurance' money to him, but my real goals for Doy Low failed on a spectacular level."

"I knew he was a bad man, but I thought that by a combination of administering physical pain, paired with a show of forgiveness and generosity of spirit would bring about a moral transformation in this spiritually bereft Tong member. He promised he would reflect on his previous behavior. I got him to come by everyday to renew his promise, even though I did it through fear and physical pain."

"I thought, hoped, that I might have the influence to bring about his moral transformation. I failed miserably. Now the questions I'm wrestling with are: can such people be changed from the outside, or can it only come from within? Do I have the skills to perform such a transformation? Can I learn them? Sadly, I have answered those questions. Now the question is are some people intrinsically bad and incapable of change and should I invest any more of my time toward this end?"

Chan Lee listened patiently. He's the opposite of the people I've been fretting about. He exudes empathy and combines it with scholarship. I always think I should be taking notes when we speak. He suggests that we walk back to the clinic.

"You're not the first person to ask these questions or try to undertake such transformations. You would have saved yourself some anguish if you'd gone to our bookshelves and done a bit of research. The term you are looking for is *Psychopathy*. It was first used by a German psychiatrist named Koch in 1888, but before that there were terms in use like 'perversion of the moral faculties' coined by Benjamin Rush and 'Moral Insanity' used by James Cowles Prichard that go back to the early 1800s, and I'm just scratching the surface."

"It's a mental disorder, one that no one has ever found a cure for. You're a pretty ambitious healer who at the age of twenty thinks he can cure a disorder that has run wild for centuries and has been documented by scientists for almost a century. Whoever has studied it agrees on one thing. It doesn't have a cure. Perhaps when you're finished curing it, you can discover a way to reverse gravity. At my age, I'm tired of falling down."

I had to laugh. When Chan Lee and I get to the clinic he gives me some books to read just to solidify my understanding, and I begin accepting the fact that perhaps bad people aren't curable…no matter how hard I hit them.

Chan Lee and Tang Po invite us to another elaborate dinner at one of the finest restaurants in Chinatown. It's the end of our fourth month working together and they're always on the lookout for a good excuse to have a celebration. Chan Lee raises his glass, "Lo Wan, having you come to work with us was a very auspicious event. We're proud to work with you as a peer. Mei Sam, saying that your disposition brightens up our place of work immeasurably would be an empty compliment. Your continuing desire to increase your knowledge of herbs has made you a useful contributor to our work, and your endless curiosity and thirst to learn makes Tang Po feel like there's still some use for him. Ganbei."

Tang Po lifts his glass, "Tonight we have some good news to celebrate. Our dear friend and colleague Shu Ping is coming to visit from Seattle. Lo Wan, you know that we consider you a colleague and think of you as an equal. There are not many men," he looks at Mei Sam, "or women, that fit into this august group. Shu Ping is one of those elite few. Once a year we visit him and he in turn visits us. We think of him more like family than as a colleague. I look forward to the two of you meeting. If there are any questions you have about healing that we haven't been able to answer to your satisfaction, he'll be the one to ask."

A cleaning frenzy begins and lasts three days. Every corner is dusted, every rug is beaten and every piece of wood is shined. "We do this as a matter of respect, but it's also a good excuse to clean everything. It's another reason why we look forward to Shu Ping's annual visit."

On the appointed day, we rent a large carriage and go down to the railroad station to meet Shu Ping's train. It's lucky we rented a large carriage because Shu Ping arrives with a young colleague named Jo Fan. He is in his late twenties and impresses everyone with his charm, wit, experience and knowledge.

I was no longer surprised to meet another man with perfect Chi flow. As an Earth sign, nurturing was a key trait that Shu

Ping radiates. Jo Fan appears to be a young replica of Shu Ping. I like them both from the moment I meet them.

Shu Ping hugs his two friends, bows to Mei Sam and me then introduces Jo Fan. "He came to work for me about a month ago, but it soon became obvious that he should be treated as a colleague rather than an employee."

Tang Po laughs, "That's just what happened when Lo Wan came to work with us."

Jo Fan and I become instant friends. It's not often two young healers with similar skills and backgrounds meet. We talk together late into the night on many occasions. We enjoy taking walks into the woods with Mei Sam and teaching her about herbs.

We particularly enjoy sharing healing information and working on each other. Both of us love learning and sharing new techniques and have insatiable curiosity about healing. Every evening, all six of us go out to a different restaurant then go home and talk into the late hours or split up into smaller groups to continue our conversations. Everyone is sad when Thursday night comes around, because Friday is the day Shu Ping has to return. Jo Fan insists on one final walk into the woods that night. It's the last time we'll be together until Mei Sam and I would visit him in Seattle months from now.

After a while the three of us sit down under a tall tree and Jo Fan says, "There's one final treatment I was saving to show you. I learned it from an Arabic mystic. He is the most gifted healer I've ever met. He travels around the world learning from every culture he comes across. I've revealed this technique to very few people, but it would mean so much to me to share it with you. I know you'll use it wisely. It unlocks Chi more quickly than any remedy I've found. He digs the knuckle of his middle finger into a place by the second thoracic spine and I find I can't use my arms and legs."

Jo Fan stands, bows and smiles. "My greetings from the exalted Chancellor. I feel a bit distressed about this because I was really getting to like both of you, but sadly, my allegiance lies elsewhere."

"Run Mei Sam, run." She remains frozen like a frightened deer. Jo Fan smiles, "For tonight's entertainment, I plan to rape Mei Sam while you watch. Although she will initially resist, but as you watch, I plan to bring her to ecstasy against her will before it's over. Then I will torture her before I finally, and I'm reluctant about this part, have to kill her. You will be the audience for all this. Then I will have to hurt you, but you will survive the experience to reflect on it and wait for the Chancellor's next visit."

———————

Shu Ping lifts his third glass of wine and proposes a toast. "Now that we all have some young blood invigorating our lives, perhaps two visits a year will not be enough. Perhaps we should form the small, elite society of preeminent healers we've been talking about."

Tang Po says, "That's such a worthy idea. If we set a goal of adding a new member once a year with the stipulation that all three of us agree unquestionably about that member's qualifications and temperament. I think Lo Wan and Jo Fan should also have a vote." All three nodded.

Chan Lee adds, "Perhaps each new member should write a paper which would be shared between us. If we all write papers when we had new techniques, or other vital discoveries our field will grow even faster."

Tang Po laughs. "For all the good we'll do, we could think of ourselves as a force to oppose the Tongs. That would make us the 'Untongs.'" All three laugh and prepare themselves for their fourth glass of wine by finishing their third."

———————

I continue screaming, "Please Mei Sam, I'm begging you, run." She remains frozen in place. Jo Fan smiles, then jumps up and runs to strike her and she runs back several steps to evade him. He charges her again and she runs back several more steps to evade him again.

Now he's angry and the third time he charges her furiously and she runs back two steps, plants her left foot, chambers her right leg and catches him in the solar plexus with a perfectly timed sidekick. As he doubles over from the pain, she bends her knees a little and begins the first of five hard Chung Choy blasts to his nose and then ends with a brutal front kick to his groin.

I yelled, "Rip off his tunic and use it to tie him up tight. Then come over here. Now move your thumb slowly down my back just to the left of my spine until I tell you to stop. Right there. Now push your thumb in hard moving it in a tight circle clockwise as hard as you can." Within five seconds I'm able to stand and move my arms and legs.

The first thing I do is hug her as tightly as I can and kiss her over and over. "You saved my life. We are forever in each other's debt." Then I turn to Jo Fan. I retie both his hands and his feet. Then I revive him.

Jo Fan asks, "Did you train her? I was certain she would be numbed by fear, not turned into a fierce warrior. Even if I had expected it, I'm not sure if I could have defeated her." He looked toward Mei Sam, "You have earned my admiration. You fought magnificently."

"Jo Fan, I've met many despicable people, but you've disappointed me more than anyone I've ever met. You intended to rape and kill Mei Sam while I watched after we let you into our hearts. If anything could be worse than that ... you learned and trained to become a skilled healer only to use those skills to kill instead of help. For me, that's the ultimate unforgivable sin. The Chancellor sent two other groups of assassins after us. I set them free. I did hurt them, but I let them live because even though they were despicable men, I found something in them that I thought might be redeemable. And I abhor killing. I've always tried to redirect people to the right path. Until tonight."

"If you'll indulge my curiosity, have you killed many others before this attempt?"

"Within the higher echelons of the Chinese government, I've been given the name 'The Healing Assassin.' I've had a successful career. My healing skills have taught me to create many accidental deaths of influential people. Until tonight, I've never failed."

"Your subterfuge combined with your perversion of the healing skills indicates you deserve no mercy. I will extend to you the courtesy of killing you quickly. Do you have any last words?"

"You can kill me. I understood the risk I was taking and I came willingly, but know that it's only a matter of time before the Chancellor takes his revenge on you. When I arrive in the other world, I will patiently wait for and savor when that day arrives."

"Jo Fan, thank you for making my next task so much easier and reducing any guilt I may have had."

I walked behind Jo Fan and snapped his neck severing his spine. It takes only a second and he was spared any pain. Then we discover a high cliff perfect for throwing him onto some rocks in the ocean. It's a quiet walk back to explain what happened. We didn't have to pretend being upset.

"We have some tragic news. Jo Fan had more to drink tonight than we realized. He was running along a mountain cliff, tripped and fell hundreds of feet down onto some rocks in the ocean. His body was washed out to sea."

"I'm stunned. I've only known Jo Fan for a month, but he was with me constantly. We became very close. And he was so excited about coming down here for this visit. He asked me endless questions about all of you ... especially you Lo Wan. Did you secure the body?"

"No. We tried wading in, but he was washed out into the sea. When I saw him staggering on the edge I tried to reach out and pull him back, but I was too late."

Shu Ping said he wanted to be alone. The rest of us sat in an adjacent room. No one spoke. A half hour later, Shu Ping emerged and said, "I have said my prayers. I don't pretend to understand the ways of Karma. We all have to accept and adapt."

The next day, we took Shu Ping back to the railroad station and said our good-byes. On the way back, Tang Po said, "Am I correct in assuming there is much more to this story than what we've heard so far?"

"You know about the two attempts made on Mei Sam's life from men sent by the Chancellor. Jo Fan was the third attempt. We took a walk outside of the city to a deserted area and he told me he wanted to show me an important, powerful treatment. With total trust, I permitted him to do it. He paralyzed me, tied me up and was preparing to rape, torture and kill Mei Sam as I watched helplessly. Fortunately, Mei Sam repeated the attack strategies she used on Doy Low perfectly and beat him unconscious. She followed my instructions and was able to undo Jo Fan's manipulation and then untied me. He confessed everything and unlike the other attempts, I chose not to spare his life."

"I did not kill him out of anger. He was a devious, evil man. Under any other condition, I could perhaps have forgiven and tried to redeem him. But for a healer to attempt to take the life of another healer, someone he didn't even know for the sake of someone else's petty revenge was too much to bear. This was the first time I've taken a life. I feel wretched about the entire experience, but I feel no regret for the action I took. If you'd like me to leave now, I'd understand and leave with nothing but good feelings about you both."

Chan Lee spoke first, "I would have done the same thing if I was in your place." Tang Po also nodded his head in agreement.

"Tang Po said, "What do you plan to do now?"

Lo Wan said, "I know we can't remain here. The Chancellor will just send more men and continue trying. I have only one choice. I have to return to China and take the battle to the Chancellor." Mei Sam looked at me realizing her life was also about to take an abrupt shift.

"Tomorrow I'm going to see Tu Chan and prevail upon him to arrange for passage back to China for Mei Sam and me. I'm excited to see my family again and to have them meet my wife. I will leave her in the safety of my family while I go after the

Chancellor. Parts of this trip will be wonderful. If everything goes well there, I hope to return to San Francisco and continue working here with the two of you … if you'll have me."

Both men nodded their heads and reached out to embrace Mei Sam and me.

"Tu Chan. It seems every time we meet I'm asking for a favor."

"Let's not forget all the times you've fixed my back. Tell me how I can help you."

"My favor comes in two parts. I'd like you to arrange the purchase of two tickets on a ship to China. Then I'd like you to make it out for two different names and help me obtain some accompanying falsified identification. If the Chancellor discovers my name on the ship's log, we'd never make it off the gangplank."

"Why do you need to leave so abruptly?"

I explain my situation.

Tu Chan smiles. Obtaining false identifications is the kind of favor I do on a daily basis. How soon would you like to leave?"

"As soon as possible."

"There's a steamship leaving for Tianjin in three days. Show up here that morning and I'll see you off."

"Tu Chan, meeting you was the luckiest thing that happened in all of my American experiences." Mei Sam kicked me in the ankle. "I mean the second luckiest thing."

Chapter 10

The ship that Tu Chan selects for our passage to China is a considerable upgrade from the one that brought me to America. That ship had over 100 men sleeping in the same room with bunks piled three high. If there was a way to weaponize the smell it would have been outlawed by international convention. On this trip we have a lavish stateroom with a large, comfortable bed. Where the trip to America had food that would have to be improved to be considered unpalatable, this ship's fare is haute cuisine. I consider it an auspicious omen that there have been no attempts to club or stab me while I sleep.

We're making a point of treating our ocean crossing as a honeymoon. The trip is blissfully uneventful and we arrive relaxed, anticipating our journey to unite with my family.

The ship docks in Tianjin and our first order of business is to go to Peking and find Ya Min's bookstore. Ya Min walks in from the back room and is astonished to find the two of us casually browsing through his bookshelves. He runs over and embraces us. "What are you two doing here?"

"It's not often someone offers you a free book just for coming into his shop. We're here to collect." That evening we have dinner together and spend the night with Ya Min. We leave after the morning meal.

It takes two days to travel to my family's village and I'm relieved to discover that my father and brother are still living in the same house. I walk up to the house and yell, "Is anyone home?"

I'm surprised to see a third occupant come running out with my father and brother. We are all screaming. Li Wing raises his arms to quiet everyone. "As your elder brother, I claim the right to begin."

"Eight and a half months ago I took Lee Shin as my wife." A quick glance was all it took to see why any man would be taken by his new bride. She is nineteen years old and beyond beautiful. Although Li Wing tries not to embarrass her, he blurts out that she's intelligent and kind-hearted. There is too much excitement for subtlety. I can see that she was just the type of woman my brother would marry. She's perfect. Li Wing put his arm around me, "Brother, I want you to meet my wife Lee Shin. Her father is an herbalist and taught her a great deal about his healing art. She continues her study with father and me."

Lee Shin walks up to me, smiles and without waiting to be invited, hugs me. "I have heard so many wonderful things about you. I'm so excited to finally meet my brother."

I take Mei Sam's hand and lead her forward. "This is my wife, Mei Sam. I have been teaching her about herbs and she has taken to their study with a voracious appetite." Li Wing and father step forward and hug her and then the two brides hug one another. Each girl later says that it was like meeting a fully-grown sister for the first time.

The awkwardness and formality lasted a very short time and the re-uniting became a long series of hugs accompanied by a great many tears. Finally we all sit and father says, "Son, you left without a word. Our efforts to locate you turned up nothing. We had no idea what happened to you. Why didn't you write?"

"If everyone will kindly sit, I'll tell you my story. Get comfortable." It will take hours to complete, and I'm only going to give you the short version. "I didn't want to risk writing to you for fear that the Chancellor might intercept a letter and place you and Li Wing in danger."

"Why did you choose now to return home?"

"The Chancellor has made three attempts on Mei Sam's life. Each attempt was closer to succeeding. I realize that although it takes six weeks to physically travel from China to San Francisco, it only takes a matter of minutes to send word back to China from San Francisco by way of the telegraph. Each time there was a failed attempt on Mei Sam's life the Chancellor found out about it quickly and immediately began preparing a new plan for my misery. It's clear from the third attempt that the assaults will keep coming and each new one will be more sophisticated if I don't do something about it. As you know, I'm not very good at being passive. So, I'm here to take the fight to him."

"Did you really think just you and Mei Sam can defeat someone as powerful as the Chancellor?"

"Of course not. I'm going to do it alone. I brought her here because I know this was the safest place to leave her while I attempt it."

Lo Wan's father laughs, "I'm afraid you've got this all wrong son. If you go, we all go."

"No! I won't risk any of you getting hurt or dying on my account."

"You're responding as if you have a say in the matter. We're family and we'll always protect each other. We'll begin Mei Sam's martial arts training this evening."

"I'm afraid that's impossible. I've been training her already and she's become quite accomplished. When the healer-assassin paralyzed me, it was Mei Sam who fought him off and saved my life."

"I stand corrected. We'll *continue* Mei Sam's training starting tonight. You'll be pleased to know that Lee Shin is also becoming a skilled martial artist. Let's eat a light meal so it won't slow down tonight's workout."

During dinner, Lee Shin and Mei Sam sit together and begin what is obviously going to be a close lifelong relationship with an ease that rarely occurs between two young, attractive women.

After dinner we all go out to the barn. I pair with Lee Shin and Li Wing pairs with Mei Sam. After ten minutes of light sparring, Li Wing and I share a warm hug and words of congratulations. Then we begin the real workout.

After training, we begin formulating a plan. The first thing we should do is look for someone who's familiar with the layout of the Chancellor's castle."

Father smiles. "I helped Woo Yi's wife deliver their third son. There were serious complications during the birth. A midwife came to get me in the middle of the night. I was there for days. Tomorrow morning I'll ride out to see him. He worked on the chancellor's Castle renovation a few years ago. Perhaps he can provide some useful information."

As father enters the village he's happy to find Woo Yi living in the same house where he helped deliver the baby. He's welcomed and Woo Yi insists he stay for the evening meal.

"My elder son's taken an interest in becoming a builder. He's developing passable carpentry skills and is interested in designing houses. He works mostly in local villages so there's no opportunity to create larger projects. I remembered you telling me you had the opportunity to work on the Chancellor's castle in the capital. Would it be possible for him to visit you and have you teach him some of what you know about larger scale works?"

"It'd be my pleasure. As far as I'm concerned, he can begin tomorrow morning. I'm working on a magistrate's mansion. He's welcome to assist me."

Early next morning Li Wing is at Woo Yi's door waiting for signs that the family is awake. "I'm pleased to see you're so eager to begin. Would you like to see the plans we've drawn up for the mansion?"

"Yes I would, but I'm embarrassed to say that I've only worked on small projects that didn't have plans. Would you be willing to teach me how to read building plans?"

"Sure, it's quite simple once you get the hang of it. Come in and share my morning meal and by the time we finish eating, you'll be an expert with construction plans."

Woo Yi is astonished at how quickly Li Wing picks up reading building plans. He also finds that for every point he makes, Li Wan comes back with two questions. "It amazes me how you can represent three dimensions on a flat piece of paper."

"I can tell from your background you've studied mathematics and understand how the X and Y coordinates work in algebra. Let me introduce you to the third coordinate … the Z-axis. Take this room where we're having our meal. Show me what it would look like if you were constructing it and wanted to show the depth of each section by including the Z coordinate."

Li Wing struggles and Woo Yi makes a few corrections and soon, Li Wing is able to represent the space in three dimensions.

Li Wing asks Woo Yi lots of questions about larger scale projects ending with the Chancellor's Castle. "You make the Chancellor's castle sound magical. Do you have any of the plans so I can see how some of these features are represented on paper?"

"Sorry I don't, but if you ever find yourself in the capital, I'm sure my cousin Ri Loo has the full set. He is one of the master builders who worked on re-constructing it years ago. He was the one who hired me to work on it."

"If I go to the capital, I'll ask you for a letter of introduction. I've already learned so much from you and we haven't even gone to the magistrate's house yet. I don't know how to repay your kindness."

"Your father's already done that for you. I'll never forget his skill and his kindness. I'm happy to repay just a small fraction of my debt to him. Let's go see the Magistrate's mansion."

"Viceroy, I just received word from our spies in San Francisco. The bad news I have to report is that our third attempt failed, but I have some wonderful news that will make you forget all about it. Lo Wan and his young bride have booked passage back to China. Wherever they go, we know they'll end up here. I'll send word to our castle spies. I'll get a report of any people coming to look for work in the castle. Buddha be praised. He's delivering them to you as a gift. Maybe they'll arrive in time for your birthday sire. The Chancellor laughed.

"OK girls, I want both of you to put on these padded gloves and padded shin guards. I'm going to be wearing them too. They'll limit the amount of damage we'll do to each other. Now, I want you both to gang up and attack me at the same time."

"But that's two-against-one. It won't be fair."

I yelled, "Just do it ... now!"

Being yelled at got the two girls to attack me, but they were being playful as they tried to hit me. That was until I smacked each of them hard enough to show that this wasn't going to be a game. They each got angry and began to attack me in earnest. What they soon discovered was that they were constantly in each other's way so that only one of them could attack me at a time. I had no difficulty defending their tandem attack.

When I called a stop to the training both girls were drenched in sweat. "What did you notice in that drill?"

Lee Shin said, "I noticed that you never stood still and that we each seemed to be in each other's way instead of being able to attack you at the same time."

"Why do you think that happened?"

"You didn't give us enough time to formulate a plan of attack."

"That's correct, but did you notice what I was doing?"

"You kept moving in circles and you never stopped."

"Good, but there was something more important. Did it occur to you to attack me from two different sides?"

"Yes, but we kept getting in each other's way."

"By circling I always kept one of you in front of the other. I only had to face one of you at a time. Now let's have you try out this new strategy. Lee Shin, it's your time to face the two of us alone. Remember to keep circling so that one of us is always be-hind the other. Mei Sam, don't get too comfortable. You're next."

We worked on the two-against-one movement strategy for hours until everyone felt exhausted, but comfortable with the idea.

"Now let's make it *real*." An expression they learn to hate. "Make it real," at our house means 'try to cause real damage.' Pain and its avoidance are two of the best martial arts instructors.

At dinner Li Wing is excited and tells everyone about his good fortune. He learned a lot about carpentry and reading construc-tion plans. Even a bit about creating them. More importantly, he tells them about Ri Loo in the capital. The girls and I don't have to say too much about our training, but our bruises provide an eloquent story.

"Mei Sam, Lo Wan says you're an excellent seamstress. Can you also embroider?"

"Yes, but I wouldn't say I was great at it. "

"I suggest you begin practicing. The Chancellor has a size-able army in his castle. I'm sure there's always a demand to have uniforms repaired. We'll look for a way to get you a job there. Lee Shin, I also have an idea for you. I like the way you cook, but I've only tasted a few dishes you've made, and we eat very simply here. Can you cook more elaborately, and no offence intended, but more with taste in mind?"

"Sadly, what you referred to as 'simple dishes' are at the peak of my skill level."

"With your knowledge of herbs, if you can learn a bit more about creating delicious meals, we can get you a job in the castle kitchens. We can tout you as someone who specializes in cooking tasty foods that increases energy and vitality. What army com-mander wouldn't like his men on that kind of a diet? I'm going to introduce you to two sisters in the village who are excellent cooks. They'll be happy to help you improve your skills. Well, maybe not happy, but they'll be willing."

The next morning Lee Shin meets a pair of spinster sisters in their mid-seventies. They didn't like their given names so one adopted the name "Dumpling" and the other chose "Rice." If you wanted their attention, that's how you had to address them. There were more stories about them than there were spices on their kitchen racks.

When the sisters were in their early twenties, a man came to town and met Rice. He was immediately smitten and began an affair with her. One day he came to the house when she was out and he met Dumpling and was similarly intoxicated with her. He tried to pick the one he wanted to be with, but the closer he moved toward one, the more he wanted the other. He begged each sister to keep her relationship with him a secret because he didn't want to lose either one.

Each sister noticed the odd behavior of the other, but since they'd never had secrets from one another life became odd. They each attributed the strangeness to the fact that they had a boyfriend that they didn't tell the other about. This was each sister's first secret.

The object of both their affection was able to keep his charade a secret for a few weeks. All during this time, when he was with either sister, he dined like royalty. It was a big part of both attractions. The people in the small town kept noticing that the man was becoming enormous, but he always looked happy.

The sisters never suspected that he was deceiving them, but both had a vague sense of guilt because they had a secret from the other. One day, there was a mix-up in schedules and all three appeared in the kitchen at the same time. He cried and confessed everything to both sisters. Instead of being angry, they were overjoyed to hear the truth because now there was no reason to sneak around anymore. They could all be together and enjoy each other's company. They were ecstatic at not having to keep any secrets.

The fellow stayed around and continued to amass weight because both sisters were now cooking for him daily. He kept growing fatter until he couldn't walk down a street in the village without huffing and puffing. One day, he just disappeared. A popular theory was that he was poisoned, but another was that his heart exploded from eating too many fattening foods. Either way, he had the distinction of being the first man they shared. There were many more that followed.

Everyone knew that the sisters were close and shared everything in their lives so the series of men that came and courted both sisters was odd, yet came to be accepted as a force of nature. This made for stories that evolved into local legends. Now, many years later, the sisters have gotten older and they just cooked. These stories didn't make the villagers afraid of the sisters … it just made them very very respectful.

"I want to thank both of you for agreeing to teach me. I confess that my view of food is that it's only necessary to provide energy to fuel the body. If the food isn't 'useful,' I don't eat it. I'm hoping you can change this crippled view. I want everyone to enjoy eating the food I prepare. I want them to salivate at the sights and smells coming out of my kitchen."

"Your father-in-law has been very helpful to us over the years so we're happy to be able to pay back his skill and kindness. Let's begin. Sit down, close your eyes and open your mouth. We're going to put some different tastes on your tongue. Respond to each with one of these two words: 'pleasant' or 'not.'"

They put a noodle cooked in a sweet sauce into her mouth. Lee Shin smiled and said, "Mmmm."

"We didn't understand you. 'Pleasant' or 'not?'"

"Oh I'm so sorry. I meant to say, 'pleasant.'"

"Thank you. Let's try another one."

This time they put a salted almond on her tongue.

She began to say, "Mmmm" but caught herself, "Pleasant."

After trying twenty different tastes they asked which were her favorites.

"I liked the ones that were a little sweet, but not the ones that were too sweet. I also liked the ones that were a bit salty, but not too salty."

"Your taste preferences are going to make our work very challenging. Your father-in-law said you wanted to cook food that's going to taste heavenly to most people, but it's going to have a lot of herbs in it. To us herbs taste like grass, twigs and dirt. Only really strong tastes can mask them and those are the tastes you don't find pleasant."

"Please help me recognize what tastes good to most people. I won't let myself be limited by my own tastes. I'll work hard to change."

"That's good enough for me. Dumpling, does that work for you?"

"Sure. I like her attitude and willingness. Let's start with the basics. There are three tastes all people," she looks at Lee Shin and smiles, "…I mean almost all people love: sugar, salt and fat. If you want to please them, you'll have to include generous amounts of them in any meal you create. The worse your herbs taste, the more of these three ingredients you'll have to include to mask their taste. The more herbs, the more intense the disguises have to be."

Lee Shin said, "To make the problem a bit less difficult, the herb I'll use most is ginseng. It energizes people. It'll fool soldiers into thinking that I'm somehow giving them something special to invigorate them. I'll use red ginseng. It's less bitter than other forms of ginseng so I'll need less sugar to hide it. I'll also serve ginseng in the form of tea and accompanying it with sweet cakes and cookies to help disguise the taste. I'll use two other herbs, jujube extract and licorice. They also don't taste too bad. Certainly better than dirt."

"It sounds like you won't need us for much. You seem to already have most of your problems solved."

"Thank you, but I need you both desperately. I can disguise the taste a little, but I'm a failure when it comes to making food taste delicious. Everyone who tastes what I make points out how 'healthy' it seems. That's the closest I come to receiving a compliment on the taste of the food I prepare. That's where my needs and your talents will have to come together."

After the first week of training, Dumpling says, "It's time for a test." She goes to the door and yells out, "Tasting time." Three young boys are soon waiting in line. They get there almost before she finishes yelling.

Rice gives each a small bowl of food that Lee Shin prepared. Each child greedily shoves some into his mouth. That is the only bite each one takes. They each hand back their bowls and walk away without saying a word. "They may be young, but their palates are very sophisticated. Don't get discouraged, very few pass their first test."

Over the next week and a half, Lee Shin shows up in their kitchen every day learning how to turn ordinary foods into delicacies containing ginseng. By adding combinations of sugar, salt or fat to every dish, mouths begin watering. What really begins to frighten Lee Shin is that she tries every dish she creates and they begin tasting better to her. She vows that after all this was over, she will return to her austere eating program … if she can. Rice takes a dish that Lee Shin has just prepared, opens the door and yells, "Tasting time." The same three kids are at the door. When they see it's Lee Shin they stop smiling. Rice hands each of them a bowl and within a few seconds their bowls are empty and they hold them out for more. Within a few days, more kids are jamming into line to get a taste.

Dumpling says, "You've just had your graduation ceremony." They each receive a hug from Lee Shin who leaves with a deep feeling of pride. The only drawback to her training is that at home, everyone now insists that she do all of the cooking. "I'm not sure if you sent me to Dumpling and Rice's kitchen to be able to help Lo Wan or to become your new cook."

After dinner Lee Shin sits with Mei Sam and watches her practicing embroidery. "You have a gift for representing nature using needle and thread."

Mei Sam holds up a long piece of silk with a beautiful scene of plants growing by a stream. "Do you like it?"

"It's beautiful. It looks like a painting. I can't wait to see it on you."

"Why would I be wearing your shawl?"

"My shawl?"

"Yes, sister. This is a gift for you."

"I don't know what to say."

"You can repay me with a story. How did you and Li Wing find each other?"

"Both Li Wing and his father bought herbs at our shop when they couldn't go out and harvest them locally. I was frustrated by the fact that Li Wing showed more interest in the herbs than in me. When I flirted with him, he didn't seem to notice. He was fixated on the herbs. Other local boys were always flirting with me, but I paid little attention to them. I spent my time learning about herbs and running our family business. I was reading esoteric books about herbs so I could engage Li Wing in conversation about them. Herbs were the only thing he seemed to enjoy discussing. I tried stumping him with questions to impress him. I wanted him to take me seriously. My reward was unending frustration. He always knew the answers to the questions I asked. He explained the answers and then seemed to be in a hurry to leave."

"One afternoon as he was rushing out of the shop I walked to the door to say good-bye as three of the local boys were walking down the road. One of them said, "Lee Shin, there's a Moon Viewing celebration tonight and I'd like to invite you to go there with me."

"No thank you."

His friends began to laugh, making him angry.

"I'm not asking you, I'm ordering you. You're going with me. I know you're just playing hard to get. Fine, it worked. You win. We're going together tonight. Let's seal it with a kiss."

"He ran over to the door and tried to kiss me. I pushed him away and that made him angrier and he grabbed me. Li Wing saw what was happening and ran over, "Please let her go."

"This isn't any of your business herb boy. Get out of here before I beat you to a bloody stump."

"All three of the boys surrounded Li Wing. I yelled for them to leave Li Wing alone."

"No, he asked for it. Now we're going to give it to him. He threw a punch as Li Wing appeared to trip so the boy who grabbed me punched his friend in the face knocking him down. All three of the boys went to grab Li Wing who appeared to be afraid of them and kept stumbling around while the three boys kept banging into each other and punching each other while trying to hit Li Wing. After another minute or two, all three were a bloody, dirty mess. They stormed off cursing and threatening to come back with more friends to hurt him. Li Wing's clothes were dusty from tripping, but he wasn't hurt."

"I thanked him for helping me and asked him to come to the office in the back of our store. I helped him dust himself off. Later he confessed that the dusting got him very excited."

"I saw what you did there. You pretended to be clumsy and let those three foolish boys destroy one another without you ever having to throw a punch. They never came close to hurting you. It was like watching a ballet. You were amazing. But now that you're here, I want to ask you something. Why didn't *you* ask me to go with you to the Moon Viewing celebration tonight?" I jumped up and couldn't hold back my frustration … it came out in the form of anger. "I've been flirting with you for what seems like forever and you barely seem to notice me. Aren't you interested in me … even a little?"

"Usually, when I come in here it's because someone's sick or hurt and needs my help. I try to finish my business as fast as I can so I can rush back and help them, but I have a confession to make. This is really embarrassing. Please be kind and don't tease me, and please don't laugh. I think about you all the time, but I'm just really shy. My work is my life and I've never spent much time around girls. I've had no experience with you, I mean them. I'd like to spend time with you, but I don't know how to even ask you about doing that."

"I began laughing, which hurt his feelings because he thought I was mocking him. I quickly pulled him out of the chair and put my arms around him. I began kissing him. 'Now you have a little experience with girls. I want you to come back here tonight after you finish your work so I can give you a lot more experience.' We've been together ever since that night."

Mei Sam told Lee Shin the full story about asking Lo Wan if he was going to rape her and the night they spent together in Sacramento. They both laughed at sharing such similar experiences.

At the morning meal Lo Wan's father said, "I've found a boarding house where we can stay in Peking. It's just outside the capital and run by an old friend of mine. We'll leave in two weeks."

Everyone knew that meant for two weeks martial arts training was going to become very "real." Each morning they all laughed when they noticed everyone nursing their bruises from the previous night as they limped to the table.

Each of them packed a small bundle containing one good outfit for the castle, one everyday outfit and a shabby one so they wouldn't be troubled by people they met on the road while travelling to the capital. On their second night they set up their camp and left the two girls to begin preparations for the evening meal while the men went to gather wood and hunt. When they came back, they found the girls surrounded by eight leering bandits.

Three had knives drawn, four had large clubs and the leader carried a large rusty sword. They were so taken by the two attractive young girls they failed to see the three men closing in on them. After the tension of the past month, we were sort of happy to find these bandits. Father walked up and said, "If you drop your weapons and empty your pockets now we'll let you just walk away in peace. Make up your minds quickly because in another few seconds this generous offer will no longer be available to you."

Surrounded by so many men, Lo Wan didn't bother to analyze any of their Chi states. Like the rest of his family, he was going to relish this moment to release as much of his pent up tension as the situation permitted. He did feel a bit sorry for these eight men who had no idea what was about to happen to them.

The bandit leader laughed, ran toward Lo Wan's father and found himself on the ground with his sword now poised over him about to strike his neck. Two more bandits ran to help their leader. I tripped one of them and then landed my elbow in the man's stomach knocking his air out. Li Wing grabbed the other bandit's arm with one hand while he grabbed his club in the other. Then he bend down and smashed the club on the man's instep. He howled while hopping around on the other foot.

Lo Wan's father turned to the five other stunned bandits and said, "This is your last chance to drop your weapons and empty your pockets. You will not be able to leave now because your leader stupidly turned down my first offer, but we won't use your weapons against you. We're just going to use you as exercise."

The five men dropped their weapons and emptied their pockets. "Lee Shin, stand up please. Which one would you like to fight?"

She pointed to the biggest man. "I'll take that one. He's the fattest."

The man grinned and walked to the clearing to face the young woman in front of him. He said, "I think we should wrestle." He grinned at his cleverness and the other men laughed. One of them said, "I'd like to wrestle the little cute girl when you're finished with this one."

The man walked up to Lee Shin and threw a haymaker at her head. She ducked under it and punched him in the stomach. He doubled over and she took a step back to watch him react. She was in no hurry to end this exercise. The man fought to regain his breath and lumbered toward her. She said, "Do you still want to wrestle with me?"

He smiled and charged her using his shoulder to knock her down. She moved slightly to the side, grabbed his arm, and twisted it as she redirected his forward force now to drive him to the ground. As he was falling, she used the knife blade of her hand to deliver a strike on the back of his neck. He fell down and remained there motionless.

"Mei Sam, I'm sure you're getting a bit restless being the only one who hasn't gotten any exercise yet. Please stand and walk over here."

Then Lo Wan's father pointed at the man who said he would like to wrestle with her. "You, the other wrestler. Stand up and walk over here. You have the advantage of competing against the smallest one of us. Do you still want to wrestle with her?"

"With this one. Oh, yes." He turned to Mei Sam and said, "Come here sweetheart. I'll show you how it feels to rub up against a real man."

Instead of charging, he walked over to Mei Sam who moved in a backward direction. The man lunged at her and she moved just out of his grasp. He took a few bigger steps and went to grab her again. She knocked his hand away and in a continuous movement, her block became a strike with three fingers that struck his throat. He fell to his knees and rubbed his throat as he fought for a breath. Now angered, he lunged at her and was met with a roundhouse kick that struck his outer thigh so hard that he fell to his knees. She stood over him and said, "Come on and stand up so we can wrestle." With that she walked over to him, bent down a little and grabbed his crotch. She squeezed and twisted as the man howled. As she let him go she asked, "Do you want to rub that part against me some more?" She took a step toward the man who fell over and covered his crotch with both hands. He was weeping.

Even his fellow bandits were laughing. Lo Wan's father said, "Well we have each fought and five of you have fought. That leaves three of you to go. You two at the end, stand and come here. I want the two of you to fight each other. The winner gets to fight Lee Shin." He pointed at her.

The two began to fight with no intention of hurting one another. When Father saw this he said, "Sorry, I wasn't thinking straight. I used the wrong incentive. The loser has to fight Lee

Shin." The two men now grabbed each other, punched, scratched, kicked and pulled each other's hair. After five minutes of the least graceful fighting any of the family had ever witnessed, one of the men finally lifted himself on his elbows and threw a punch that knocked his comrade out.

"I guess neither one of you is in any shape for a real fight now." He points to the last man and asks him to stand.

"That's not fair, you said one of them would fight her. It shouldn't be me."

"You're right. You shouldn't have to fight Lee Shin."

"Thank you sir."

"You didn't let me finish. You're going to fight both Lee Shin and Mei Sam at the same time."

Before the man could say a word, the two girls stood and faced him. One stood in front of him and the other behind him. Each time he moved to attack one, the other smacked him on the head, or kicked him in his rear end. Everybody was laughing so hard they were all in tears. The angrier the frustrated bandit got, the harder they smacked him.

Then the fun began. As he attacked one girl, the other grabbed hold of his tunic and began to tear it. Within a few minutes, he was wearing only his loincloth. This made attacking his backside much more fun. They continued to hit him hard enough to hurt, but not enough to damage him. Finally, he laid down and curled into a ball and began weeping.

Lo Wan's father called a stop to the fighting and asked the men to stand. "Do you all agree that if we let you leave, it's with the promise not to return?" The men all agreed. Do you also understand that if any or all of you return, we won't play next time? We'll kill you all." The men nodded again. "Then leave now, as quickly as you can. You've delayed our evening meal far too long as it is." The men scrambled to get any clothing they may have dropped and ran as quickly as they could.

The rest of the trip was uneventful. At dusk two days later we arrived at the boarding house of Lo Fay. He showed us to our rooms and invited us down for our evening meal. Li Wing said, "Tomorrow morning I'll visit Ri Loo. I have the letter of introduction from his cousin. I hope he'll take me on as an apprentice or employee."

The next morning, Mei Sam walks around near the outer wall surrounding the castle and notices that many of the soldiers' uniforms are ripped or worn. She walks around the wall until she finds a sentry station and asks one of the sentries, "Who's in charge of mending torn uniforms?"

"The Chief Tailor."

"May I see him please?"

"The Chief Tailor's much too busy. If you're willing to wait, I'll try to get one of his assistants."

It's a warm day and she's kept waiting for over an hour, but her wait attracts a number of young soldiers offering her a chair, some water and a shady spot to place her chair. A young man finally comes out, annoyed at having been disturbed. His mood changes when he sees Mei Sam. "How may I help you young lady?"

"I'm looking for a job. I'm an experienced seamstress. I'm new in the capitol, and I mean no offence, but as I was walking around the city, I noticed a lot of your soldiers wearing uniforms that are in tatters. It's clear you need someone to help restore them."

"You'll have to wait while I ask the Chief Tailor if there are any positions available." The young man runs off. He comes back a short while later out of breath saying they will offer her a trial job for one week. Then it's up to her and her skills. She didn't know how hard this young man begged the Chief Tailor to take her on. He was smitten.

She's escorted to a building a quarter of a li past the outer wall. "Does the Chief Tailor work in this building?"

"Oh no. He works in the castle. But he stops in here to check up on us every day or two."

He brings her into a large room with racks of uniforms needing repair. "Grab one and start sewing. Our goal isn't cosmetic. Sew each uniform so it doesn't fall apart and looks fairly presentable from a short distance then get to the next one. The Chief Tailor demands quantity, not quality." He turns to walk away then turns around. "May I escort you home after we finish working today?"

"Thank you for your kind offer, but I have a very jealous husband. I don't think he'll like it. He's very big and has a bad temper."

Late in the afternoon the young man runs in yelling, "The Chief Tailor's coming. Look busy."

A middle age, overweight man chugs into the hall. On closer examination, he isn't that old. He's just fat and has years of worry adding to his appearance. After walking down several aisles he sees Mei Sam. He looks at her and smiles. "You're new here. Do you have much experience as a seamstress?"

"I've been sewing since I was a young girl. My mother taught me."

He turns toward the young man who was still hanging around, "Bring her a large piece of white cloth."

His assistant runs to find a piece of cloth and hands it to her. "Let me see you perform a Running Stitch." As soon as she complies, "Now let me see a Back Stitch, now a Basting Stitch, now a Cross Stitch."

She performs each stitch quickly, carefully and most importantly, with competence. That was until his final request.

"I don't know what a Cross Stitch is. Can you show me what it looks like?"

He grabs the cloth from her hand and sews several Cross Stitches with efficient, bold movements. He is well suited for his job.

She smiles and says, "Oh, like this? My mother just called it an X stitch."

He smiles back and says, "Do you know many other stitches?"

"Oh, quite a few. I had to learn them when I was practicing embroidery."

"You embroider as well? You don't belong here with these amateurs. You're coming back to the castle to work with me. Your talents will be wasted here." As he talks, his eyes move back-and-forth between her face and her chest.

They walk out together and get into his carriage. Within a few minutes they are at the castle and she's shown into a lavish hall known as the "Silk Room." There are twenty people all working. Each is at a table with a collection of needles, scissors, threads and a wide assortment of fabrics … mostly silks. Every one of them, except for the Chief Tailor is attractive. Each wears stylish robes like the one the Chief Tailor has just changed back into.

He introduces her around. Each one seems to be an expert and they are all friendly. They are secure enough not to suffer from the burden of envy and unflattering comparison. Mei Sam is grateful for her good fortune landing here. She introduces herself as Lu Chow.

The Chief Tailor leads her to a rack of stylish robes. "Select one to work in today. Wearing finery adds to the ambience of the space and enhances the quality of our work. When you arrive each day, walk over to this rack and select your outfit for the day. Let me help you put on your robe." He made it a point to accidently rub his elbow across her breast as he smiled at her.

Later one of the young women asks, "Did you attend an embroidery school?"

"No, my mother taught me."

"You must have a wide repertoire of skills. It took most of us the better part of a year to progress to the Silk Room. I can also see why he's taken a fancy to you. That's the other way some of us got here. The Chief Tailor has a wife and two concubines, but he's always prowling after pretty young flowers. Prepare yourself. The good news is that if you don't return his affection, he'll threaten to send you back to one of the outer sewing rooms, but he won't actually do it. He's afraid you'll tell his wife."

In the morning, Li Wing goes to find Ri Loo, the builder who supervised the Chancellor's castle renovation. He arrives just as the builder is on his way out. Li Wing is uncharacteristically nervous because of this man's importance to their plan. He reported feeling like a salesman knocking on a door in front of a 'No Peddlers' sign.

"I'm sorry to intrude upon your morning's tranquility good sir. Would you be kind enough to peruse this letter from your esteemed cousin?" Li Wing hands him the letter of introduction from Woo Yi then wipes the sweat from his face.

"Please relax. Do you always talk this way?" Ri Loo stifles a laugh. "How's my cousin? I haven't seen him in years?"

Li Wing exhales. "He's prospering. When I left, he was completing a mansion for a district magistrate. When I told him about my interest in construction he was kind enough to take me on as an apprentice. He taught me a great deal. He also teased me about asking two questions for everything he taught me. When I told him about my ambition to create larger structures he said if I ever found myself in the capital, I should seek you out. That's when he wrote the letter you're holding. I've found very few men who had his generosity of spirit."

"You're in luck, I'm on my way to supervise the framing of a massive mansion in one of our most exclusive neighborhoods. I don't want to be viewed as competing with my cousin to see who has greater generosity of spirit, but would you like to come along?"

"Only if I wouldn't be intruding. Warning, I really do ask a lot of questions."

"Anyone who is fortunate enough to have skills has an obligation to pass them on. If you become bothersome, I promise I'll let you know, and perhaps not as politely as my cousin did. Since it's such a beautiful day, I prefer to walk rather than ride. Is that agreeable to you?"

"Yes, unless you'd prefer to run. Walking is my second favorite way to travel."

"We'll walk and use the time for you to tell me what my cousin taught you."

"All the projects I've done before meeting him were small ones that didn't need plans. I'd never seen a building plan before I met him. He taught me how to read them, then how to draw them and then how to lay them out in three dimensions. He told me you helped renovate the Chancellor's castle and might have a copy of those plans. If we ever have the opportunity, I'd love to see how a project of that magnitude can be set down on paper."

"A project that large could only be created by first laying it all out on paper. Today's project was thoroughly laid out in plans first. I have those plans with me. Once we get started, I'll be happy to show them to you. For reasons of security, I was never allowed to keep a copy of the plans for the Chancellor's castle."

When they got to the project, parts of the wooden frame were already in place. The mansion was larger than anything Li Wing had ever seen. "Where did you find such enormous pieces of lumber to construct those huge beams?"

"If you look more closely, you'll see each large piece of wood is actually several smaller pieces that've been tongued, grooved and filed then sanded so carefully they look like one large piece of lumber, even to the trained eye. Look closely enough and see if you can tell where they're joined."

"You're not a builder, you're a sculptor."

"I think you'll learn a lot if you have the patience to come to this site for the next few weeks. We're just constructing the shell of the mansion. The main rooms will be the height of six men. Come to my house early each morning and we'll walk here together. Let me assure you we'll never run."

Lee Shin went to the castle, and walked up to one of the sentries. "I'd like to speak to one of your military cooks please." The two soldiers at the guardhouse looked at each other and began to laugh. They said they'd never heard of such a thing.

"Then may I speak to an officer please?"

One of the men in the guardhouse goes inside and walks into the barracks. She waits by the side of the guardhouse until the guard returns with a sergeant who she smells before she sees.

"Who the hell's been asking stupid questions about military cooking?" When he sees the beautiful young girl standing in front of him, he straightens up and smiles. "What can I do for you young lady?"

"I'm the one who's been asking the stupid questions. Being a sergeant, perhaps you've read what the famous French General Napoleon Bonaparte said, 'an army travels on its stomach?'"

"I have no idea what you're talking about. I'm going to get my captain. Wait here." It takes half an hour for the sergeant to return with a tall, good-looking man who he introduces as his captain.

"Good day Captain. I'm a cook and an herbalist. I can prepare food that'll provide more energy to your men. It'll improve their performance and their health and the best part is I can make it taste so delicious they won't know it's good for them."

The captain nods and asks her to come into a small room next to the barracks. "Your idea intrigues me. Like all good ideas, even though I've never heard it proposed before, as soon as I heard it, it seemed obviously clever. Let me introduce you to our Head Cook. For you to work here in our kitchens, he'll have to approve it. After that, I hope you'll let me take you out for a fine dinner."

"I appreciate the offer, especially coming from a handsome captain like yourself. Will it be possible for us to first go to my house and bring my husband, or should I send word for him to meet us?"

"I'm sorry. I meant no disrespect. Let me find the Head Cook."

"What can I do for you young lady?"

"I'm sure that as a well-trained and experienced cook you've noticed that some foods seem to make men sluggish and other foods energize them. I'm a trained herbalist and a cook. I can prepare a diet that will energize your men so you can get a higher level of performance out of them."

"I've never heard such an idea. We feed our men as much meat as we can afford to keep them strong, but herbs? Herbs? I never thought about using them, but it sounds like it's an idea that's worth trying. Come in tomorrow morning. If you can provide the herbs, I'll supply the food. We'll try it out on a small group of men without telling them what we've done."

"The captain slaps his hands on his thighs. "What an excellent idea. It's like a science experiment. We'll look forward to seeing you tomorrow. You'll be introduced as just another cook, although you look quite a bit more attractive than most of our other cooks." The Head Cook glares at him. The captain walks up to the cook and puts his arm around his shoulder and smiles.

The next morning, Lee Shin arrives at the castle with a small bag of ginseng and another bag with a mixture of jujube extract and licorice which helps promote a good night's sleep after a day's stimulation from ginseng. The cook asks her what herbs she is going to use. She smiles and says, "I've brought in a special mix and notated them in my journal. Once we've tried them out and get enough information, I'll share all my information with you, but for now, we're conducting research, like you and the Captain said. I can assure you that above all, I will do no harm."

The cook smiles and says, "This mystery intrigues me. How soon do you think we'll see some results?"

"If my calculations are correct, after the two meals we'll be serving today, we may already see some changes. If not, we'll probably see something by tomorrow."

Lee Shin begins preparing a large pot of fried rice and also decides to make some congee because most men she knew like rice pudding. All of the flavorful spices she adds mask the taste of the ginseng that she crushes into a fine powder. She sees nothing but smiles at her table. She also receives several winks. One man yells out, "Can you come to our dormitory with a late night snack?"

Another yells, "Can you be the late night snack?"

Although she blushes and responds with a smile, the captain walks over to both men and smacks them on the back of the head. "We'll have no more talk like that. If you're stupid enough to insult a cook you might deserve the poison she puts in your next meal." All the men at the table laugh.

The captain makes a list of the men who eat at her table. He makes a point of following them during the day to observe their energy levels and dispositions. He is impressed with the changes he sees within an hour of their morning meal. The cook is also impressed with the results and wants to taste the meal.

"I don't think that's a good idea. It might influence your objectivity. I promise to have you dine with us after the first week or two, but for now, you must be a dispassionate scientist and gather your unbiased data through observation so you arrive at a proper, scientific conclusion."

The Head Cook says, "You sure don't talk like a beautiful girl, but you make good sense."

After the first two days both the Head Cook and Captain are stunned by the results. They began telling their superiors about it. A general asks to meet with Lee Shin. "What you've done with this new diet is remarkable. I'd like you to begin doing it on a larger scale."

"I'm flattered that you're happy with my work, but I wouldn't feel comfortable expanding my work on a larger scale alone. I'd prefer to consult with my mentor. He's one of the most brilliant herbalists I've studied under. I'm sure, with his help, we can create a diet that would save you money and deliver even more effective performance. That is, if I can persuade him that this is a worthy project. Would you like me to ask him?"

"Yes, by all means. Bring him in. See if you can get him here tomorrow morning. We'll pay you both a handsome fee. I think this could be a revolutionary idea."

"I'll discuss it with him tonight, and if he agrees, I'll bring him in. Here's a suggestion that'll make him more likely to cooperate. He's very devoted to his craft and has no desire to become wealthy trading on his skills. Offer him something like a charitable contribution to a cause he favors, or perhaps setting up a school to teach herbalism. Also, if he asks about what the soldiers who his work will affect do, understand that he tends toward the Buddhist philosophical path of Pacifism. Emphasize the fact that your men keep the peace, protect the weak and help keep enemies of the people at bay. He wants his work to serve a higher purpose."

The next morning at the sentry gate there was a carriage waiting to take Lee Shin and her father-in-law Soo Lin to the castle to meet with the General.

"General, I'm proud to introduce my teacher Soo Lin."

The General bows slightly. "Soo Lin. I'm honored to meet you. You should be very proud of your student. In just a few days, she's already made her mark here. And if you do a fraction of what she says you can do, you'll help revolutionize the way soldiers are fed. Tell me what you need and I'll move heaven and earth to provide it for you."

Father brushed away the compliments. "Please provide a list of all the foods these soldiers have eaten in the past three months so I can determine what toxins we'll have to purge from their systems. Then I'll need a list of the duties and activities that the soldiers have to participate in for a typical week. This'll help me determine the specific types of herbs to place into their diets. You're fortunate to have obtained the services of Lee Shin. I've never met anyone so gifted in disguising the taste of herbs to produce succulent meals everyone enjoys."

When Soo Lin asks for the list of the soldiers' duties, Li Shin winks at the General, who nods and smiles in return. "I'll have both lists ready for you in a short time so you'll be able to begin your calculations. Later we can also discuss your compensation. Lee Shin told me about your charitable work. I'd be proud to support any cause you favor."

"Thank you General."

Li Shin pulls Soo Lin aside that night and asks, "Why did you make yourself so difficult to work with when you met the General?"

"I had the choice of appearing needy and hoping he'd hire me as a favor to you or to require that he court me and feel gratitude and relief that I agree to work with him."

Li Wing continues to work with Ri Loo. With every passing day, he receives more responsibility and finds himself enjoying his work. Li Wing had never seen a structure to compare with this mansion. He spends all his free time studying the plans. During his evenings, he practices creating his own building plans and brings them in for Ri Loo to critique. Ri Loo is a skilled teacher and is impressed to find as time goes by, Li Wing's plans needed less critiquing.

"I asked your cousin if he had the plans to the Chancellor's castle he said he didn't but you did. I'm surprised to hear you say you don't have a set either."

"When we were redesigning the castle I asked the Viceroy if I could have a copy of the plans to study and store with my records. He laughed. "These plans are top secret, they're never allowed out of the castle. Can you imagine if they fell into the wrong hands?"

"That's a shame, I was hoping to take a peek at them to see what plans look like on such a massive level. I was curious about all the secret passageways he told me about. Well, I think I can survive the disappointment about not seeing the plans, but I don't think I can survive my current state of hunger much longer. You must be as ravenous as I am. Let me take you out to dinner."

"Fine. I know a wonderful restaurant close by as long as it's your treat." He goes on to order an elaborate meal with many courses. "And, let me suggest a fine wine to complement our dinner." It's clear that Ri Loo is no stranger to extravagant living. To establish the suitable ambiance, this restaurant employs beautiful young girls to sing and dance for their clientele. Ri Loo and Li Wing relax as they eat and drink.

Li Wing sways into Ri Loo's shoulder and his speech is now a little slurred. "I know this is an indelicate question, are there many builders who're level of expertise in Peking?"

"Oh sure, quite a few."

"My dear friend and mentor, there're just the two of us here, tipsy and talking. Nothing you say will leave this restaurant, even if I was able to remember it. I've seen the respect people have for you at the mansion site. They hang on your every word, and you're the first one selected to supervise the biggest projects in Peking. I've had a chance to observe some of your peers. Between you and me, are there really any who come even close to your level? I swear, whatever you say will remain here in this restaurant and you can deny it tomorrow and blame the wine, but really…?"

"O.K., I admit to being one of the better builders here at the capitol. Now are you satisfied?"

"Who in the capitol would you say is truly your equal? Name one." I filled his cup with more wine.

"Alright dammit." Ri Loo whispered, "I'm the best by far, but you didn't hear that from me. No one could've built some of the huge projects I did. Certainly, no one could have created all the secret hallways and tunnels in the Chancellor's castle that I did. And I'll let you in on a little secret. I was so proud of those designs that each night when I got home, I re-drew some of my most creative Castle plans from memory just so I'd have a record for my archives. I've got em' safely locked up tight in a secret chamber behind the room where I keep my collection of past projects. Sorry, but I can't show them to you or anybody else. No one's supposed to know I even have em'. Shhh."

When Li Wing gets back to the inn, he tells us about the hidden plans. "I think soon it'll be time for me to quit Ri Loo's service. To honor him for his help, I'll bring my brother, who's an incredible cook, to his home. There we'll offer a meal fit for an emperor to him and his entire family as an expression of my eternal gratitude. We'll have Lee Shin and father help you prepare and serve a delicious meal suffused with enough herbs to knock out several horses giving us enough time to search his study, find the plans, read them and put everything back in order. When they wake up we'll all laugh about how much they all ate and drank. We'll thank them again and say "Good Night."

Two days later, Li Wing looked sad as he told Ri Loo that his family needed him to go back to work so he'd have to leave his service. "Before I go, I want to show my thanks for all the help you've given me. Knowing how much you appreciate fine food, my brother is a wizard in the kitchen and has agreed to prepare a feast in your honor. We'll be here at sundown tomorrow."

"I'll be sorry to see you go. I've truly enjoyed our time together. Your thanks is enough for me. You really don't have to go to the bother of creating a banquet."

"Master Ri Loo, I'm not *offering* you a banquet, I'm *insisting* on it. You seem to believe you have some say in the matter. I know it's just a symbolic gesture because I could never repay what you've given me, but in my own way, I'd like to make this token gesture."

All five family members are out in the nearby forests harvesting herbs. We gather jujube extract and licorice that promote relaxation. In addition, we harvest many other herbs that help put and keep people down. We were now gathering for two events. First we have to knock out Ri Loo and his family, and soon after, gather way more herbs because we have to make a small army comatose. We rent a neighbor's barn to store the herbs we collect.

On the night of Ri Loo's banquet, Li Wing introduces his brother. Lo Wan bows before Ri Loo and is pleased to see a confident man whose Chi flow seems unimpeded. Possessing a Metal sign that shows considerable confidence and self-discipline.

He is shown into the kitchen and places the food on the counter and begins to warm it. He brought both Li Shin and Soo Lin to help. Ri Loo's cook asks if he can assist them. Li Wing insists that everyone in the household sit at the table as a guest at this banquet. The cook is happy to comply.

From the first course, Ri Loo and his family can't stop praising the food. "Then eat and drink some more. This is your night. I'm so pleased that your entire household is here to share in this celebration. I only wish I could have prepared a more elaborate meal."

"Are you kidding? We're being treated like royalty. I'm so stuffed, I can barely move."

I laugh inside. Ri Loo had no idea how correct he is. After the meal knocks everyone out, we began looking for the secret chamber. We look for half an hour and can't find a trace of a hidden door, hinges or a lock. We're down on our knees examining every wall and corner meticulously. We keep pushing each other to work faster before someone in the house wakes up.

Li Wing stops me. "We've been going about this the wrong way. Ri Loo can join two pieces of wood so their fusion is undetectable. Let's try using our ears instead of our eyes. "We'd better hurry because they're not going to stay knocked out much longer." Li Wing begins a subtle tapping on every section of wood making up the wall until he detects a hollow sound. "This must be it, but how do we open it? Ri Loo said it was locked."

Ri Loo picks his head up and manages to say, "More wine please." Soo Lin runs over and fills his glass and helps him gulp it down." The family is beginning to stir. It appears the herbs' effects are beginning to wear off and we still haven't found the chamber.

The Viceroy meets with several castle spies and discovers that three of Lo Wan's family members have penetrated the castle. Ironically, they are all quite productive. At present, there is no need to apprehend them. The more they believe they are succeeding, the easier it will be to catch them when they make their move.

The Viceroy's spies also discovered that there was a new man working on a large mansion with Ri Loo, the man who'd been in charge of the Chancellor's castle renovation. After a bit more digging, this new man is discovered to be Lo Wan's brother. The Viceroy is enjoying this game of intrigue. As the Chancellor has said, "We're all playing a game of Go. We'll see who's a better strategist.

The Viceroy decides that the best course of action is to have the Chancellor believe he was the one controlling the game, even though the Viceroy knows who's really the master strategist. His goal is to have the Chancellor figure out how instrumental he is so that he'll be well rewarded for his efforts here. "I wonder what a suitable reward is for saving a Chancellor's life?"

———————————

One-by-one, the members of Ri Loo's family are moaning as they are slowly coming out of their stuporous states. Fortunately, Soo Lin has created a special bottle of wine into which he put small amounts of ichacha. While unscrupulous people used this herb as "knock-out drops" he uses only a tiny amount to keep them mildly, but adequately sedated. It would do them no harm. He also massages several acupuncture locations to promote additional relaxation. Lo Wan has to laugh because this scene reminds him of his childhood when his father used to take him and Li Wing to the circus.

Lo Wan loved everything about the circus, but his favorite attraction was always the plate spinner. This amazing fellow had eight long sticks at the end of each stick was a plate that he kept spinning. As one would come close to stopping he ran to twirl it again, then raced to the next one that was slowing down. As each plate looked like it was going to fall the crowd panicked and screamed and pointed to warn him. Somehow, he managed to keep all eight spinning for as long as he wanted while the crowd gasped and never stopped shrieking as one was about to fall, then cheer as he managed to spin it until another began to stop. Now his father is a wine spinner. It helps to have two other people assist with the spinning. He managed to keep them all spinning asleep.

"We've got to hurry, they'll be coming around again pretty soon. I don't want to give them too much ichacha."

Li Wing said, "I'm going as fast as I can. If there is an actual metal lock we are looking for, it would be easy to find. Let's see if we can keep tapping along this wall until we can find some subtle sound difference leading to an opening that works as the entrance to the cabinet. Be still because the differences in sound will be extremely subtle. Once we find it, we'll have to experiment with different levels of pressure to open it."

As Li Wing kept tapping, he thought he detected a slight difference in sound. "Come here. Listen, do you hear it?" He began pushing at each edge until a door opened a little. We smiled as we pulled out a set of plans that contained the hidden rooms and passageways and we began poring over them. We spread out the plans until we found what we were looking for.

The hidden passageways were like a series of spider webs with the densest networks connected to the Chancellor's living quarters and workspaces. I said, "Let's start with the Jade Room. I think it's the Chancellor's favorite space in the castle. It's the room where all my troubles began."

"If you were in the Jade Room you'd be surprised at how small it is, yet look here at the plans. The room has three hidden corridors. Two that lead to other rooms within the castle and one long one here that seems to lead all the way out of the castle."

"Where does it end up?"

"Just outside the castle at the northeast end. There's a note here saying there's a small gardener's shack with a trap door. It's where the Chancellor would be able to make his escape. The escape route itself is almost half a li long leaving him at the edge of a forest."

"That's brilliant. Do you think this was the Chancellor's idea?"

"No. Ri Loo told me the credit goes to his Viceroy. Apparently, he's a sneaky bastard who no one likes … except for the Chancellor, and I don't think he really likes him much either. But when it comes to deceit and treachery, few can match him." I had to take several deep breaths to calm myself. It was the Viceroy who had me drugged and beaten.

We looked at all the other hidden rooms and escape routes. On the walk back to our rooms the smile never left our faces. "Tomorrow we'll have to take a walk and locate that gardener's shack."

Three days after Soo Lin began working with Lee Shin the General was so pleased he insisted every soldier be placed on the new diet. "It'll take several days to gather the additional herbs for so many men. Your long term goal should be to grow them here and become self-sufficient."

"That's a wonderful idea, but how soon can we have a trial day to assess the effects of the diet on *all* my men at once?"

"Before that I have another requirement. Please get me a list of all your soldiers organized by their function. How many are archers, how many in pike brigades, sword fighters … that sort of thing?"

"Why the Hell do you need all that information? That's going to be a pain in the ass to collect. Is it that important?"

Soo Lin made a show of his frustration by turning away from the general and expelling a large breath through his mouth. Then he turned back around, took another deep breath and spoke in a slow, deliberate tone as if he was talking to a child, a not very bright one.

"The more I know about what they do, the more I can customize their diets. There are herbs that promote better long-range vision. That helps archers, but wouldn't be useful for the men in pike brigades … now would it? On the other hand, pike brigades handling those heavy weapons need more strength. There are different herbs for that. Sword fighters don't need strength as much as they need fast twitching muscle actions. Different herbs again."

"That's brilliant. I'm sorry. Know that I never doubted you. I just wanted to understand in the event that I'm asked questions about these diets. I'll make sure you have your list before the day's over. I hope you don't think I ever doubted you sir. I can't believe the change in my men already. I'm so proud to be working with you. It's too bad I'm already a general because the Chancellor can't promote me any higher. You two have done me a substantial service, one that I promise never to forget."

They all agreed that Friday was the day to try the diet out on the entire army.

The Viceroy was lounging on the Chancellor's chair in the Jade Room. As soon as he heard footsteps, he jumped off and stood as the Chancellor entered. "Your Excellency, I have some interesting news for you. The attempt on your life is being planned for Friday. Lo Wan's sister-in-law and father have been working in our kitchens with our General. It's kind of funny that they're actually doing wonderful things for your army while they've been ingratiating themselves here. They've been putting herbs into the men's meals to make them more productive."

"Interesting idea. How's it working out?"

The General says he's amazed. He's been trying it out on different samples of his army and comparing it to men who remain on their normal diets. He's seen a pronounced difference. The best part is the herbs are very inexpensive and soon we'll be able to grow them here on our own grounds. We'll be saving money on feeding our men while we're making them more efficient."

"Fine, now let's get back to that other thing you mentioned, Oh yes, the attempt on my life. I consider that to be a bit more pressing than my soldiers' diets. How do you know it'll be this Friday?"

"The General is planning to feed his entire command this new diet and knew you'd want to attend their demonstration to observe its effects. It'll be on the large drill field."

"Meanwhile, Lo Wan's wife has been working in the Silk Room under an assumed name. I asked the Chief Tailor to have her create a new embroidered robe for you to mark the occasion. She'll present it to you personally to begin the festivities."

"My dear Viceroy. You are a malicious bastard, and that's why I want you managing my affairs. So that takes care of the father and the two girls. What about Lo Wan and his brother?"

"I was saving the best for last. My spies have discovered that the brother has been working for Ri Loo."

"Who's he and why should I care?"

"He's the master builder who was in charge of renovating this castle. My spies had to persuade him to cooperate with us. He was finally convinced to tell us that Lo Wan's brother volunteered to work with him. He swears he did not give away any information about the castle's structure. As an aside, your worship, Ri Loo's a good man who had to be beaten severely to cooperate with us, and I recommend not killing him. He had no idea of Lo Wan's subterfuge and didn't cooperate in any way. He's highly skilled and we'll need his talents again in the future when we have to renovate again."

"Yes, fine. We won't kill him, but what did you find out?"

"We don't have any idea what they found out, but it's safe to assume they learned about the passageway from the Jade Room to the Gardener's shack. That's the best way to sneak into the castle. I'm planning a warm welcome for them there."

"I want to be involved with planning that warm welcome myself. It'll make my game of Go more interesting."

"Of course your Worship."

Chapter 11

Soo Lin looked over the list the General gave him. "That's a lot of soldiers we're going to feed. My assistants and I will have to work every day to gather enough herbs to feed this many men."

"Good…good. On Friday I'll…I mean we'll give the Chancellor an eye opening demonstration. I've already told the Viceroy about you and Lee Shin. He and the Chancellor are both anxious to meet you. We'll all share in this triumph."

The Chancellor sent for the Viceroy. He was sitting on his chair in the Jade Room. "On Friday afternoon the General has promised me a startling event. He'll show me how enervated our army will be by this new diet. It'll be a fine performance. You said Lo Wan's wife has created a new robe for me. Make sure to have her place it on me herself as the first part of the day's festivities."

"My dear Viceroy, I'd like to share my plans for Friday afternoon with you. Only you and my closest bodyguards will know the plan in advance. I don't even want the General to know. When he finds out that he was harboring two of the conspirators he'll come forward and volunteer to commit suicide. I will show my compassion by forgiving him, which will bind him to me forever."

"Before the healer and his brother reveal themselves, we will have subdued the other three members of his family. As soon as the brothers reveal themselves, you'll let out a signal to have every soldier on the field form a tight circle around them and subdue them. Seeing such numbers, and their family in captivity, they'll have no alternative but to submit and kneel. Then the fun begins. We'll bring the Healer and his wife to my chambers. We'll tie him down so he can watch me ravage his wife. When I'm finished we'll call my elite guards in one-by-one to do the same. He'll witness this as well. You can have a turn if you'd like. If she manages to survive all of the rapings we'll call for my Punisher. He's an expert at administering a slow, painful death. He delights in the opportunity to ply his craft and particularly enjoys putting on a show for me. I want to savor every minute of horror reflected across Lo Wan's face as he witnesses it all. I want to relish every squirm, every beg, every cry and every instance of rage he emits."

"Then we'll repeat the same procedure with his brother tied down watching the same thing happen to his wife. Of course Lo Wan will see this as well. I understand she's quite a beauty so I'm looking forward to being the first one with her too. Then for the finale, we'll have the healer watch his brother die slowly at my order to the Punisher. But I won't kill his father. Rather, I'll place him in one of our dungeons as a way to warn the Healer about what would happen if he makes another foolish attempt on my life. I think of this as a small insurance policy."

Now here's the part that exhibits my flair for creativity. After he's been totally broken, I will painstakingly explain what we'll do next. First we'll drug him again, then beat him again and place him on a ship bound for America to begin the whole cycle again.

The Viceroy applauds. "My Lord Chancellor, when you said you were turning this into a game of Go, I knew you were planning something brilliant, but this is the stuff of legends. Every twist and turn of this plan radiates your genius."

That night at the boarding house we are making our final plans. "Lo Wan and I have found the gardener's shed containing the hidden passageway that'll take us to the Chancellor's Jade Room. We'll have to disguise ourselves. Mei Sam, do you think you can get us two army uniforms?"

"That shouldn't be a problem."

"You two will already be on the field with the General awaiting the Chancellor. Mei Sam, we'll have to find some way to get you over to the training field to participate in the event."

"The Chief Tailor ordered me to create a new robe for the Chancellor to mark this occasion and he wants me to present it to the Chancellor personally."

"The army that'll be present will barely be able to move based on what father and Lee Shin plan to feed them, but the Chancellor will arrive with his own bodyguards. I don't think we should try to make any more plans than what we already have because we want to be free to improvise. Things rarely go according to plans."

———————————

Lee Shin and Soo Lin arrive at the kitchen early and begin stirring the herbs into the huge mounds of food that they'll give to the soldiers that morning. The General arrives a short time later. "I'm so excited I could barely sleep. I want to eat the morning meal with my men. I want to experience everything that happens to them."

"We'd be flattered to have you as a fully participating member. The Head Cook also asks to join you at the table. We couldn't be happier."

Lee Shin works hard directing the cooking staff. She wants to insure that the food isn't just palatable. It has to be delicious. And it is. The men eat with gusto. They laugh about how stuffed they all feel. The General has them line up and marches them out onto the field with their weapons in hand. It will take about half an hour for the herbs to begin kicking in.

The Chancellor waits to make his entrance surrounded by his ten armed bodyguards. These are his most elite fighters. He is led to an ornate chair in the center of the field. "This will be a very special day for me. I'm so glad you're all here to share it. I've ordered a special robe for this occasion. Please bring it forward." The Chancellor shoots a smirk at the Viceroy. He has plans for Mei Sam.

Lo Wan and Li Wing arrived at the gardener's shed. Neither brother can see the five men concealed in the shrubbery. They are ordered to let the brothers enter the tunnel before following them in to ensnare them. They are the most skilled members of the Chancellor's elite Spear Corps. When they first got to the site, their leader gave them an inspirational talk.

"The Chancellor is giving us the honor of capturing the man he's been hunting for over a year. He selected us because of our martial prowess. He considers us his most elite fighters. Our job is to subdue the man and his brother. The Chancellor insists we bring them to him alive, but the condition we deliver them in depends on how much of a fight they put up." The leader smiles and put his hands on the shoulders of two of his men. "The Viceroy pulled me aside and told me he knows Mu Chow and Foo Sam here prefer the physical company of boys to girls. He said that you two may have your way with both brothers as long as you do it 'quickly' and 'roughly.' Those were his exact words. He said the idea of delivering them in that condition pleased him."

"This is a great honor the Chancellor is bestowing on us. Conceal yourselves well. Remember how Sun Tzu stressed the element of surprise." The five men tapped their spearheads together, grunted and hid.

Lo Wan and Li Wing arrive with lanterns and plenty of oil. They decide not to enter the tunnel together. I enter first. Li Wing will wait a few minutes. If anything happens to me, Li Wing will have the element of surprise with anyone attacking me. It seems like a rational plan.

The spear corps couldn't believe their luck at seeing the brothers separate with just one left outside for them to attack. To have a bit of fun, the leader sends out his two best spearmen to face him. One man steps in front of Li Wing while the other moves behind him. As soon as Li Wing sees them he runs to the side of one man to force them to meet him one behind the other. He pulls out his small dagger and uses it to parry the spearmen's attacks.

Lee Shin and Soo Lin follow the soldiers who march out onto the field. The General leads his men into a formation facing the Chancellor. He has rehearsed his introductions. The Head Cook is also with them. Like the General, he has also eaten with the men that morning. Both men are nervous about appearing before the Chancellor.

The General claps Soo Lin on the back and whispers, "I've been dreaming about this day. It'll change all of our lives forever. Thank you again for everything you've done for us."

Both spearmen laugh at Li Wing's tiny weapon and begin lunging at him with their long spears. One yells to the other, "Move over and give me some room so we can fight him together." Li Wing continues to circle. He is able to cut one of the spearmen's arms deeply. This brings out the other three spearmen.

Because the fight is at the edge of a forest, and they all have long spears, Li Wing makes a dash for the trees. He is able to use them as an ally so he can't easily be surrounded. One of the Chancellor's men circles back and throws his spear catching the side of Li Wing's leg wounding him. Fortunately it cuts him, but the spear doesn't embed itself in his leg. Although he is hobbled a bit, he can still move and his adrenaline enables him to stay in constant motion.

As another spearman gets close, Li Wing cuts the man's arm, but the well-trained spearmen know how to work together and are soon able to surround Li Wing with four spears a foot away from his neck. Li Wing drops his dagger in submission. The leader asks Mu Chow and Foo Sam to throw Li Wing down on the ground and tells them to have their way with him. Li Wing is struggling, but has three large, well-trained men holding him down as one of the soldiers begins pulling on his tunic. The two men are playing a finger choosing game to see who will get the honor of ravaging Li Wing first. One of the other men yells out, "Make him squeal like a little girl." Another man yelled out, "… or a little boy." Everybody laughs. Li Wing struggles but the weight and skill of the large men holding him down and the spears at his throat keep him in place.

Foo Sam, who has won the prize of sodomizing Li Wing first, gets down on his knees behind Li Wing and begins arranging his uniform to claim his prize.

———————

Soo Lin whispers, "It's going to be at least fifteen minutes until the herbs begin to take effect. Their archers could cut us down before we have a chance to do anything. Let's hope the boys get here in time. All we can do is keep smiling. Nobody seems to have a clue about us.'

———————

After a few minutes, when I don't hear my brother following me, I run back out of the tunnel. I hear the yelling and laughter before I see what's happening. As soon as I get out of the tunnel I pick up a few heavy stones. As I run closer, I throw a stone hitting one of the spearmen in the head knocking him out. One of the other spearman sees me and approaches as I toss a stone in the air above the spearman's head so that it will drop on his head. As soon as the spearman looks up, the other stone in my hand finds its mark and hits him in the forehead knocking him out.

That leaves just the two spearmen who are holding Li Wing down. I picked up two spears and run to help my brother. When the spearmen turns to look at me, Li Wing throws the men holding him off and I toss my brother a spear.

Now each of us is facing a lone spearman, with a similar weapon. I face a man who clearly had a Chi block at the Three Heater meridian. He works hard to cover up his Yang tendencies by emphasizing the Fire sign traits of intensity and bravery, but it's clearly an act.

I smile at the man in front of me. "Does having years of training with a spear give you an advantage or does my lack of training give me an advantage?"

"Idiot! Of course I have the advantage with so many years of training."

"Maybe, but you move in conventional ways. With your years of training you do those stylized movements quite well, that's obvious. On the other hand, I will use the spear in unorthodox ways you aren't used to. You may not know how to defend against my moves."

"Piss on your moves. Shut up and fight me."

"Maybe talking while I fight you is one of the unusual strategies you're not used to."

I feint with the spear tip then twist the spear around and bash the man's hand with the stick end causing the man to howl in pain. Now he can only wield his spear with one hand.

"Still want to piss on my moves? Did you know the hand is the most sensitive part of your anatomy? It has more nerve endings than any other part of the body. That's why you're feeling so much pain there … you foolish 'piss mover.'"

The man lets out a scream and charges me holding his spear in his good hand. He expects me to move out of the way or retreat, but I just stand there. As the man thrusts his spear using his good hand it's easy for me to knock it aside and bring the other end of my spear around to hit him on the side of his head knocking him out.

Although Li Wing's leg is bleeding profusely, he has his man pinned against a tree with the butt end of his spear pushing into the man's throat. The man has dropped his spear and is making a gurgling sound as I come over and hit him on the head with my spear. I rip part of a uniform from one of the spearmen on the ground and use it to bandage Li Wing's leg. I run back to the gardener's shack and bring back some rope. "Look brother, this was meant to bind us. We have to remember to thank them for being so thoughtful. Let's tie these fellows up and gag them. They'll come in handy in making our entrance onto the field."

We stop the bleeding on the man who Li Wing cut with his dagger, then tie their hands, gag them then loosely tie their feet so they can walk, but not run and force them to walk into the tunnel.

I warn them to make as little noise as possible to avoid a terrible amount of pain. I hear a faint noise up ahead. The sound of suppressed heavy breathing from more than one man. I look down and find a few stones and roll them ahead and two guards reveal themselves blocking my path. Each is carrying a long dagger. The walkway is narrow so one is partially blocking the other.

Since I am also wearing a soldier's uniform, I attempt to bluff my way through, "Do you have authorization to be in this tunnel? This is an official inspection."

Both guards laugh at my attempt. "Good try Lo Wan. We know who you are and why you're here. Hello Li Wing. Come back with us quietly and you may both live long enough to get to see sunlight again. Resist and you won't be able to see what the Chancellor intends to do with those pretty wives of yours." Both men are laughing and making obscene noises and gestures. That diminishes the element of surprise.

"Do you know that the Chancellor tried to kill my wife three times? Is this the kind of man you want to give your allegiance to?"

They both laugh. "If the Chancellor asked me to kill your wife, I wouldn't give it a second thought. But I would beg him to let me rape her first." The other man nods in agreement. He points his dagger at me, "Let's get moving."

"I want to thank you both for revealing your character so honestly. It makes my next actions easier on my conscience."

The first man jabbed his dagger at me, but didn't notice that I still carried one of the stones in my hand. I threw it as hard as I could catching him in the face with it. He howls as he falls. The second man charges me with his dagger and finds himself staring at that dagger that was just in his own hand a moment ago. He is focusing on trying to stand because of his now shattered knee. I bend down and pick up both daggers, then tie up both men and gag one of them.

We bring up the spearmen who we'd tied up. I approach the man who was regaining consciousness. "I have a proposition for you. If you answer a few questions, we'll let you live. If we have to torture you to get the information we want, you'll experience more pain than you ever imagined possible and then you'll tell us what we want to know. But then we'll leave you to rot in this tunnel. In all that time you'll be begging us to kill you mercifully."

"I'll count slowly to five. If you haven't agreed, you'll have no more choice in the matter."

"One, two, th ... "

The man said, "What do you want to know?"

"How many more men are waiting for us in this tunnel?"

"There are three more waiting just before you reach the Jade Room. They're three of the Chancellor's best fighters."

"If you're lying and we have to come back here to find you, do you understand what'll happen to you?"

"I swear on the lives of my parents and grandparents, what I've told you is the truth."

"Please remove your uniform."

"Why"

"Because you're the same size as my brother and he'll be wearing it for a while. I'll borrow another one from one of your comrades tied up behind us. You can wear our uniforms. Now please sit down here."

I bind the other two men and gag them. Two of the men are unable to walk so we leave them tied up on the ground. We get the other five to stand. "We're all going to march forward together as if nothing's wrong. We'll place your spears under your arms so it looks like you're carrying them. When we get to the three soldiers in front of the Jade Room, we'll tell them we refused to surrender and you lost one of your men. You were forced to maim us because we put up such a fierce fight. You need their help to carry us to the Chancellor. Do you all understand? If you do, nod your heads."

The men all nodded. "Because you're all soldiers, I'm sure you have two thoughts running through your heads. You'd like to be heroes and, that if you cooperate with us; the Chancellor would do something terrible to you. That gives you all a tremendous incentive to be uncooperative."

"As seasoned soldiers, you've all experienced pain in battle. As healers, we've dedicated our lives to helping relieve people's pain, but we know how to cause it in ways you can't imagine. Take a good look at your fallen comrade here. His knee is shattered so he can't walk with us. I thank you for volunteering for this demonstration. He's gagged so you won't be able to hear him scream, but you all know what pain *looks* like. Li Wing, please administer a pain level of nine to this unfortunate man for a period of three seconds."

Li Wing places his knuckle into the man's spine and twists it. For three seconds the man twitches, shudders and screams into his gag...he begins crying from the moment the pain begins. After three seconds, Li Wing stops the pain. The man is left quivering and sobbing. Li Wing removes his gag. "Have you ever felt pain like that before?" The man continues shaking and whimpering. "Please answer the question, unless you'd like some more."

"No … no more please. I've never felt anything like that before. Please, no more … I'm begging you. I'll do anything … just no more."

"That was pain level nine. That's not on a ten-point scale. It's a twenty-point scale. I'm sorry we had to do that to you, but someone needed to be our model. Keep in mind what you were planning to do to us."

"For anyone not cooperating in even the smallest way, expect at least a fifteen point pain for much longer. Nod your heads if you truly understand me."

They all nodded looking at their comrade who was still trembling and weeping.

"Hopefully, when we reach the guards near the Jade Room, we can surprise them. We prefer to overtake them rather than kill them. As an extra incentive, if you value your comrades' lives, you'll cooperate for their sake."

Mei Sam is escorted up to the Chancellor with the ornate robe she created draped across both arms. "I'm proud to be given the honor of helping you on with the robe I created for you, your excellence."

"You may do that and more."

She stands behind the Chancellor and helps him remove his outer robe, and then she helps him on with his new one. He turns and bows to her in thanks, then grabs her. He has two of his bodyguards come forward. Each grabs one of her arms.

"This is the young woman I've been trying to kill for almost a year and a half and she just walked right here into my arms. Now I wonder where her husband is?"

He looks at Mei Sam and laughs, "Did you really think you could hide here in *my* castle. I have spies everywhere. I knew where you, your father-in-law and sister-in-law were from the moment you took your first step onto my castle grounds. It's ironic that while the three of you were here in my castle plotting against me, you were all serving me quite usefully. I now possess this beautiful new robe. That pleases me greatly and for that I thank you. Your father-in-law and sister-in-law have made my army more efficient and at the same time they'll save me money on my food costs. The three of you have been quite useful to me. It's too bad I'm going to have to thank you all in such a painful way. Well, this act of our little opera is drawing to a close, and the curtain is coming down."

Four guards had walked over. Two grabbed Soo Lin's arms and the other two held Lee Shin's. "I won't do anything to you until your husbands reveal themselves. But if they don't hurry, I might amuse my men with some interesting physical exercises with you two lovely girls."

He begins fondling Mei Sam's breast and then tears her silk gown down the center and sticks his hand inside. He laughs and calls for his Viceroy. "I prefer the left one, which do you prefer?"

The Viceroy places his hand inside her gown, fondles each of her breasts and says, "I agree with you my lord. Definitely the left one. You have excellent taste. Perhaps we may be more objective if we obtain more opinions."

The Chancellor laughs. Hearing this, the rest of his bodyguards also begin laughing.

Li Wing and I push the guards ahead of us. When we get within sight of the Jade Room I muffle my voice and speak quickly, "They hurt one of our men. We had to injure both brothers severely to subdue them. Then we trussed them up. We need your help to get them to the Chancellor … hurry."

As the three guards begin running forward, Li Wing delivers a sidekick to the first guard and he falls to the ground trying to breathe. The other two guards draw back and pull out their large daggers. I use one of the long spears to keep him at bay by thrusting at him with the blunt end. He swings his blade and I step back and at the end of his stroke, I hit his hand and he lets out a howl. He switches the dagger to his other hand, swings it and I hit his other hand. His dagger is now on the ground and he is howling in pain.

I turn toward the third guard. "I hit him in the hand each time. If you come forward to fight, it will go badly for you. Li Wing grabs one of the long spears. "Brother, let's have a contest. Try to break his left hand before I break his right." Li Wing nods.

"Before we start, I'd like to speak to this guard who is about to be hurt more than he can remember ever being hurt before. The hand is the most sensitive part of your body. If I hand you a fine porcelain bowl and say, 'Notice how smooth it is,' you wouldn't rub your penis against it, you'd use your hand. Since your hand is the most sensitive part of your body, it's got the most pain cells so one or both of us is going to hurt you a lot before you can move your dagger anywhere near us. Are you sure it's what you want to do, or would you rather just lay it down?"

The guard charged me and Li Wing smashed his hand. Instead of switching his dagger to the other hand, he just drops it.

Li Wing and I tie the hands of the three guards. All eight of the guards have their hands bound tightly with weapons tied to their bodies giving the illusion that they are carrying them. I explain the virtues of cooperation to all of them. I ask one of the other captured soldiers to describe the pain we had inflicted on their comrade. The three new guards agree to cooperate based on what they hear from their fellow guards and the pain in their hands.

We move the eight captured soldiers through the castle pushing the men toward the field.

Li Wing and I stand in the center of the guards looking as if we have been captured. The Chancellor claps his hands and yells, "At last. Bring them to me."

We join our family, the Chancellor and his bodyguards.

In the middle of all these distractions, Soo Lin sheds his captors and moves in a blur. "Chancellor, I think you may want to wait before you make any rash decisions." He is walking with a man whose arm he holds in a lock while his other hand holds a dagger to his throat. "Your Viceroy may have some advice he'd like to share. Perhaps we can work out some sort of a trade."

The Chancellor says, "Bravo Soo Lin. It looks like you've won. Bring my Viceroy to me. I'd appreciate being able to confer with him."

Holding on to the Viceroy, Soo Lin walks over to the Chancellor. The Chancellor whispers something into the Viceroy's ear and before anyone realizes what was happening, he pulls out his own dagger and stabs the Viceroy through the heart.

He leans over to Soo Lin and softly says, "You're a very skillful negotiator. I always detested that man."

The Chancellor grabs Mei Sam and backs away as he yells, "Archers, shoot them all."

That's when the Chancellor discovers why this day will be so special. He knows he has his bodyguards surrounding him and all his soldiers on the grounds ready to obey and protect him. He just doesn't know what condition every soldier except his personal guards is in.

The archers have trouble coordinating movements like pulling arrows from their quivers and nocking them. When a few are able to coordinate firing an arrow, three of the Chancellor's bodyguards fall dead without ever knowing they are targets. In the confusion, Soo Lin breaks the knee of one of the bodyguards holding him and dislocates the arm of the other. He goes to help Lee Shin who has already poked the eyes of one of the men who is trying to hold her. He knocks the other unconscious. That leaves three bodyguards still standing. The Chancellor is screaming. "Don't just stand there, kill them."

One of the bodyguards draws his sword and faces Li Wing. He employs a wide swing as Li Wing ducks and somersaults past him and grabs one of the spears from the Chancellor's tied up guards now resting on the ground. Li Wing thrusts his spear at the guard slowly making it easy to avoid, The guard takes the opportunity to close. He doesn't realize that Li Wing used his thrust as a diversion. He uses the other end of the spear to knock the unsuspecting swordsman unconscious.

The Chancellor points to Lee Shin and screams for the guard next to him to grab her. She waits as he moves then exposes one of her breasts as she says, "Is this what you want?" The man stops and stares as she closes in and kicks him in the groin. Then as he bends over she uses her blade hand to hit him on the back of the neck knocking him out. That leaves only one guard.

Four members of the family surround him. The Chancellor is screaming, "What are you waiting for? Kill them all."

In the middle of all the chaos, I hold up one hand and address the guard. "Relax for a moment. I have a question for you. You've seen what just happened here. Do you believe you have a chance of killing all four of us?"

"It's my duty to try."

"If you haven't noticed before, you must understand by now that your Chancellor is a deranged, crazy man. The question is, would you prefer to live through this day or die for this crazy, vengeful maniac right here and now?"

The man looks at the Chancellor who is screaming at him like a madman, and then he looks down to see his prostate comrades and takes a deep breath. In a very soft voice he says, "I would prefer to ... run."

"You're making an excellent choice. If you drop your weapon and begin running without looking back, I don't think we'll bother to chase you ... if you begin right now. If you hesitate, we might change our minds."

The guard throws down his sword and begins running as fast as he's able with the Chancellor's curses in his ears.

Now we all turn toward Mei Sam who is still being held by the Chancellor. The Chancellor is beginning to understand how this puny healer he's been chasing for over a year destroyed so many of the best fighting men.

He screams at the hundreds of soldiers on the grounds to rush over and save him. "If you're still outside here tomorrow morning when they wake up, they may follow your orders, but now they're preparing to have some wonderful dreams thanks to the herbs we fed them. The Chancellor laughs and says, "I've still got her so just move back ... all of you ... or else."

Lo Wan smiles and nods his head saying the word 'instep'. Mei Sam smiles back, nods and stomps her heel on the Chancellor's instep with all her strength. He releases her as he begins screaming and hopping in pain. That's when she employs her front kick to his groin displaying the excellent form she's practiced so rigorously. Li Wing and I grab the Chancellor by the arms and we all run back to the Jade Room dragging the Chancellor. No one is following. By the time we get there, the Chancellor is starting to come around. I lock the door from the inside and grab the large carved ivory tusk and begin smashing the jade walls with it. It appears to be an act of both rage and revenge. With each swing I watch the Chancellor react in horror as his jewel of a room is being destroyed.

There is more than rage and revenge on my mind as I'm smashing the jade walls. "Take as much jade with you as you can carry to commemorate this day. These jade pieces will be worth a fortune and will help finance the next chapters of our lives. Stuff your pockets, carry large chunks in your arms." Li Wing exposes the hidden door. He locks it from the outside and the group hurries through the long hallway and out through the tunnel that leads to the gardener's shack weighted down by the huge amount jade they're carrying. As they come across the two tied up guards, they knock them unconscious again. They drag the Chancellor deep into the woods.

When they are many miles away and certain they haven't been followed, they bind the Chancellor and finally sit down to relax. The Chancellor never stops cursing and threatening them.

"Chancellor, a short while ago, you were sarcastically praising my negotiating skills. It does seem as though the tables have turned a bit. Do you think you're elevating your negotiating position by your cursing in an attempt to frighten us? I would suggest that you take stock of your current situation while we formulate our plans for you."

I stand in front of the Chancellor. "The first question *we* have to answer is should you live or die? If we decide to kill you, then we have to decide whether we should be merciful and do it quickly, or draw it out since you made Mei Sam and me suffer for a year and a half, and if your plan had succeeded, I shudder to think of what a cruel mind like yours would have conjured up; especially if evaluating my wife's breast was a recent representative sample."

"On the other hand, if we decide to let you live, it won't be in the same state in which you woke up this morning. You won't have learned a lesson that way. You would continue to pursue us … so I don't think that would be a fruitful alternative. Chancellor sir, what do you think we should do with you?" I bowed deeply to the Chancellor.

"You're all peasants. I shouldn't even waste my time talking to you. Here's what I have to say. It's an ancient Persian curse on you all, *I spit on the place where you part your hair!* When my men get here, it's you who'll all pray for a quick death."

"You're making our decision easier with each word. Let's try this a different way. You made three attempts on Mei Sam's life and then, on top of that, you personally humiliated her today. Would you like to take this opportunity to apologize to her?"

"I hope she comes back in her next life as a dung beetle."

"I don't believe you understand the reality of your position. I think we should help you reappraise your situation. To begin, I'm going to tie you to that tree."

I tied him so that his back was against the tree. "Now I'm going to remove your pants and leave you wearing just your loin cloth. Now wait here for a moment, won't you. I'm going to bring you back a surprise."

The other four laugh at the Chancellor trying to hide his partial nakedness. They enjoy the little dance he's doing. Mei Sam walks up and spanks him a few times. Lee Shin looks down at his groin and asks Mei Sam if she prefers the left one or the right one. Everybody is laughing when I return. Everyone is staring to see what I'm holding in my hand.

"I noticed a small beehive back there and have brought back some honey. Mei Sam, dip this stick in the honey and place it all over his exposed skin, and make sure to place some by the parts he used to enjoy using."

Using a stick, Mei Sam applied the honey. I continued talking to the Chancellor. "There are many different types of insects in this forest that love honey. Also, there are many animals in the forest that do as well. First, the insects will find you and they'll all take very small bites of the feast your body will offer them. I'm not going to ask you to apologize to Mei Sam again, but I'm curious to see how long it takes for the idea to spark inside of you. We have nothing but time to enjoy hearing you repent for your sins."

Soon the Chancellor begins to scream.

"Oh, those are just the ants. They always arrive first. You'll barely feel them. They take such little bites. Wait till the spiders and beetles get here. And who knows how long it will take by the time the squirrels and rabbits have their fill of you and leave you to the wolves and bears for the finale."

"I'm sorry. I'm sorry for everything. I just lost my head because my daughter died. I know you tried to save her. Please forgive me. Give me another chance." Tears were flowing down his face and his entire body is shaking.

After fifteen minutes, I untied the shaking Chancellor from the tree and he falls to the ground. He tries to remove some of the honey and insects, but he can't get much of it off. The operation is particularly difficult because his feet and hands are still bound so he has considerable difficulty trying to brush off some of his small assailants. He tries rolling on the ground. He is not a good dancer.

"Thank you for that heart felt apology. There are people I've met who, given a similar apology, might have made me believe them, but ... the way you killed your Viceroy put a bit of doubt in my mind about your sincerity. You didn't hesitate for a moment. And he was so loyal to you. I think we would be doing the world a big favor if we disposed of you. So, the next question is fast or slow. What should we do with him?"

Mei Sam walks up to the Chancellor. I'd like to cast the initial vote. "The first three men you sent suggested that they tie me down so Lo Wan could watch them rape me until their copulation killed me. I guess that doesn't make me feel very lenient. Especially when they said they believed you would give them a bonus for their creativity." She turns back to everyone and says, "I think he should be put back up on the tree." She picked up the stick with the honey and added more both outside and inside his loincloth. Everyone applauded.

Soo Lin said, "I always taught my sons that they were put here to eliminate suffering and save lives not take them. I taught them that the highest mission in life is to be a healer. But, seeing how many lives you've taken, how many people you've tortured ... You even co-opted a healer into becoming a killer. I think ridding the planet of you will save many lives ... so, if we're voting, I vote with Mei Sam. With that, Soo Ling picked up the honey stick and added more honey to show his vote. He did it by placing additional honey into the chancellor's ears. This made the chancellor scream.

"Father, I have been consumed with trying to convert bad people and place them on a higher spiritual path. Do you believe that's possible?"

"Occasionally, when an evil person goes through an experience leading to him hitting absolute rock bottom, and then *he* decides he has to change, it may be possible, but it's enormously rare."

Soo Lin takes a long breath, and then lets it out even more slowly. "What I have learned is that there are people who are intrinsically bad. They do not have a conscience, and feel no empathy. They do not want to change. You told me that Chan Lee showed you some research about such people. I have read some of the same information and agree that they are incapable of changing. And if you believe they are changing, you are probably being taken in by one of their manipulations."

"The man you see before you is a case study in brain pathology. Li Wing, what do you think?"

"While my knowledge about this terrible man is all second-hand until today, everything I've heard about him is despicable. Lo Wan battled his daughter's infirmities for three days with no sleep. He did everything he could to try to save her. His reward was to be sent to a new country where everyone would hate him, where he couldn't speak the language, find himself in debt and all during that time, to wait for him to find people to love so they would be killed with him watching. This man has nothing I can find remotely redeemable. Father, can I borrow the honey stick to cast my vote?" After adding honey on his lower abdomen he created a trail downward and into his loincloth. The Chancellor squirmed and screamed.

"Lee Shin, what do you think?"

"He tried to kill my sister with her husband watching for the crime of trying to save his daughter. Let's put him back on the tree and mix the honey with some of his blood and see what that attracts." She held out her hand. "Li Wing, the Voting Stick please." She added gobs of honey to his thighs leading to his loin cloth and laughed at his attempts to drag himself away from her."

As the five family members sat around the fire deciding what to do next, the Chancellor saw his opportunity to escape by trying to crawl away on his belly propelling himself though only able to use his knees. He believes it is working even though I was pointing at him and we were all stifling our laughter. We silently get up and follow at a slight distance. The Chancellor can only see what is in front of him because his arms are still tied behind his back and his ankles are also tied. He awkwardly moves on his knees.

After managing to move a short distance in this manner, he finds himself looking into the eyes of a wild boar. He begins shrieking for help.

I got down on one knee and look him in the eye. "Are you asking for our help?"

"Yes, yes … I'll give you anything you want. Just don't let that thing tear me apart and eat me. Anything you want!"

I walked up behind him and snap his neck, killing him instantly. "He finally kept his word. He said he would give us anything we wanted … and he did." We leave him there and start our trip home.

When we get back to the house, I ask everyone to sit down at the table to decide what to do next. "When I came back I had two main concerns. One was about the Chancellor, but our future was my other worry. I hoped you would let me handle this alone, but I made a contingency plan knowing you probably wouldn't."

"It won't be safe for any of you to remain in China. I used a little of the money we earned mining to buy us all passage on a ship to San Francisco. As soon as I got here, I sent a telegram ordering an additional ticket for my new sister-in-law." He smiles and bows toward Lee Shin.

"I have an influential friend who is forging some papers giving us new names and identities so we'll be safe when we board. While I lived in San Francisco I worked with two exceptional healers. They said they'd welcome all of us to work with them. They're two of the finest men you'll ever meet.

Mei Sam and I are going back to America. The three of you can stay here and always be looking over your shoulder worrying that someone will come to arrest you, or come to America where we can be together and work with wonderful people and all begin a new Chapter of our lives. Mei Sam and I have quite a bit of money put away and we now have a fortune in jade to supplement it. So, your choice is: over-the-shoulder paranoia or Mei Sam and I can begin teaching you English tonight.

The End

Acknowledgements

There are four friends who are pros and went way beyond the call of friendship in giving me their editorial expertise in shaping this book: Robert Carroll, Jeffrey Davis, Rick Schultz and Everett Murdock. I wish I had the boundless energy it would take to thank you all appropriately.

Special thanks for my long time friend and collaborator Betsy Rodden for creating such an inspiring cover illustration.

I would also like to thank all of the friends who read the manuscript and gave thoughtful comments. If there ever was a test of friendship … you all passed with flying colors.

Most of all, I would like to thank my wife Cheryll for remaining at my side and supporting me through the emotional turbulence it took to get through from the initial conception to the final period.

www.ingramcontent.com/pod-product-compliance
Lightning Source LLC
Chambersburg PA
CBHW030115260626
47156CB00008B/2668